Living in the Pink

A NOVEL

Living in the Pink

A NOVEL

SHARON TUBBS

MOODY PUBLISHERS
CHICAGO

Edited by Francesca Gray
Interior Design: Ragont Design
Cover Design and Logo: Sonja Moffett
Cover Image: iStockPhoto modified by Sonja Moffett

Library of Congress Cataloging-in-Publication Data

Tubbs, Sharon.
Living in the pink / Sharon Tubbs.
p. cm.
ISBN 978-0-8024-1650-6
I. Title.
PS3620.U25L58 2011
813'.6—dc22

2010047186

1 3 5 7 9 10 8 6 4 2

Printed in the United States of America

This is why I speak to them in parables: "Though seeing, they do not see; though hearing, they do not hear or understand."

—Matthew 13:13 NIV

CONTENTS

INTRODUCING . . .

LET ME INTRODUCE myself to you: I'm Laura Pinkston, aka Sister Pinky.

It is my spiritual duty to warn you that, should you choose to keep turning pages, you will enter into The Pink, or rather the lives of about a dozen women who in some way or other have elected to live there. I know you're wondering what "living in the pink" actually means. It's simply this: Are your sins red like scarlet, or are you seeking God so that He can make them white as snow? Or are you satisfied *living in the pink*? Now, I've only got a few moments to spare before starting my next assignment for the Lord, so just suffice it to say that this pink place is nowhere you should be—at least not if you hope to reach your full potential in Christ.

You'll learn a lot more after a while, perhaps more than you wanted to know, because I'm certain that the women in these stories aren't unique. Not at all. They're just like you, going through the same things you've been facing and standing at the same crossroads where you've gotten stuck. As for me, I've been there, too, which is one reason I believe God taps me to talk to them, to tell them what I know because of what I've been through.

Now, it is not my practice to tell other people's business, so please understand that this little collection of stories was not my idea. See, I know people are thinking, *There she goes again, constantly lurking around the church. You never know when she's coming but she seems to know everything about everybody.* Regardless of how it came to be, it is what it is, and as long as it's the truth I won't complain. God will make some good out of it. He'll make it personal for you. That's why those questions at the end of each story are important. Meditate on them. Discuss them with a group or with your girlfriends.

I'm not foolish enough to think that you all will agree with the outcome of everybody's story. Truth be told, neither do I. Wouldn't it be nice if the lives of people around us turned out just how we thought they should? And if, in the end, everyone made the right choices, so we could feel a warm tingle in our hearts and believe that all is right with this world?

If that were the case, though, we would never be living in the pink, now would we? You'll see what I mean.

—Sister Pinky

REVELATION

THE CHOIR'S soft melody filled the sanctuary and set the atmosphere for worship. All over the church, heads bowed, eyes closed. Bodies swayed side-to-side in time with the music. Laura Pinkston stood in the balcony, watchful and careful not to be lulled into the moment. God had given her an assignment that required she stay alert and ready to intervene in somebody's life at precisely the right moment.

Better known as Miss Pinky to children and Sister Pinky to anybody grown enough to pay rent, she had counseled, steered, and supported more women than the human mind could tally. But no matter how many the Lord led her to, there would always be someone new, or someone old with a new situation. You'd expect as much in a world this big where everybody is connected in one way or another, even if you have to go all the way back to the garden.

On this particular Sunday, however, Sister Pinky needed to go no farther than the seat to her left. There sat Camille Peters with her eyes shut tight as if in some sort of meditation. In truth, her thoughts had drifted away from worship to the salacious details of the prior evening. Her lips curved into a smile, the kind of grin that comes after a woman has indulged in rich chocolate cake or a full-body massage or, in Camille's case, a man like Blackwell Spencer.

She had started on the road to such gratification a few months before when Camille's friends talked her into a girls' night out at Club Monet: "Get a life," Trisha had said. "You're too young to sit at home every weekend."

Less than twenty-four hours later, Camille donned black slacks, a fitted periwinkle blouse, and black shoe boots with a four-inch heel, enough to put her well above five foot ten. She had gone to the beauty shop that morning, perhaps too much effort for a dive where wide-hipped women roll themselves against men in spandex muscle shirts.

After a group dance with the girls and an hour with her back literally against the wall, Camille turned to leave when she saw him approaching. "Him" being the guy she had observed for weeks on the sly at Believers Ministries International Church. That she had noticed him at all among more than five thousand members said a lot. There, ushers guided latecomers to tiers in the balcony, and the person sitting beside you on any given Sunday could be a complete stranger. Even so, he must have noticed Camille, too.

"Don't you go to Believers Ministries?"

Being coy, she replied, "Is that where I know you from?"

The two introduced themselves and he pointed to a table nearby where they could sit down. They screamed to hear each other above the din of dance music, and she managed to find out that he was thirty-three and an accountant. Blackwell learned that at age thirty-five, Camille aspired to become a fashion designer in New York someday. In the meantime, she worked as a buyer for a boutique here in Tampa, her hometown.

He called the next day, and in the weeks that followed he took her to fine restaurants, the movies, to stage plays at the performing arts center. They didn't kiss for almost a month—Camille wanting to present herself as a real lady.

The pace gradually sped up. They sat together one Sunday at church, considered to be the public seal of a serious relationship. And last night, they climbed to even higher ground. Camille grilled some steaks, made mashed potatoes and her specially seasoned green beans with homemade bacon bits. After dinner, they created their own dance floor and slow-rocked to a CD of Luther Vandross's greatest hits. Midway through one of Luther's low notes, passion lured them first to the couch, then to bed.

"Oh, Lord," Camille now said aloud.

"It's all right, baby. You want a tissue?"

Finally, she opened her eyes. The choir was singing a different song now: "Order my steps in Your Word, dear Lo-OORD . . . " And the woman next to her held out Kleenex.

"Do you want a tissue?" the woman repeated, her eyes fixed on Camille's. "I have more in my purse. You sounded like the Spirit had grabbed hold to you."

"No thank you," Camille said, looking for a way to disguise her true thoughts. "God is good, isn't He?"

The woman nodded. "All the time," she said, "all the time."

Sister Pinky put the tissues back into her purse and settled in her seat to hear the day's sermon. Camille didn't know Pinky, but Pinky knew her. She noticed when Camille first joined the church and observed how Miss Peters sashayed through the doors with her matching shoes and purse, looking straight ahead. She would find her seat, at which time she surveyed the sanctuary to see who came to church and what they were wearing. Pinky observed it all, including the day Camille and Blackwell sat side-by-side.

"Jesus, help 'em," Pinky had whispered.

Camille plus Blackwell equaled a dangerous combination, at least righteously speaking. They both hovered around the same spiritual level, the one where you can make it to the church singles meeting to mingle and eat finger sandwiches, but not to the prayer group on Wednesday nights. They were "living in the pink," as Pinky liked to say. And though the phrase she coined sounded like her nickname, it wasn't about her.

People who live in the pink are stuck between what the Bible calls a scarlet stain of sin and striving to become pure or "white as snow." They say they believe in God, but only enough to call themselves "spiritual" without having to make significant changes in their lives. Don't be fooled, Pinky would say, they might go to church and say eloquent prayers or sport a Jesus bumper sticker—all while nursing sins that they're unwilling or afraid to let go. They want to believe in God, just not *too* much.

Something about Camille's divalike stride and the way Blackwell nuzzled against her clued Pinky to their pinkish state. And this morning Camille obviously had her mind on something other than the Lord. The look on her face betrayed too much natural satisfaction to be holy. Pinky asked if she needed tissue just to bring her back to reality. "God sure is good," Pinky mumbled to herself.

On a regular Sunday, Pinky would sit on the east side, third row from the front. She occasionally wore a broad-brim hat over her short gray-tinged hair and carried a hanky to wipe sweat droplets from her caramel face during praise and worship time. She didn't let people walk by without giving them a hug and a "How you doing today?" She was known for knowing God's Word, like last year when she spoke at the annual Women's Day breakfast. Her message, titled "Tell the Devil to Go to Hell," came straight from the book of Revelation. And every woman, from the twenty-somethings to the saints in high hats, stood to her feet by the end. "That woman sure did preach," a few said afterward, confirming the obvious to no one in particular.

Some kept their distance, especially when they wanted to talk about the bishop's wife, or the worship leader, or Sister Gaines's drug addict son. "I don't listen to mess," Pinky told the last woman who tried to engage her in he-said she-said. She propped reading glasses so low on her nose that people wondered whether she really needed them at all—she didn't when it came to spotting the Devil's wrong, that's for sure. Most often, her glare settled on the women at Believers Ministries or one of its branch churches. Her influence over the years had transcended the church property and even Tampa, Florida, where Pinky had moved with her daughters after living the pink life herself.

These days, she would get to know single mothers and find out whether they struggled to pay their bills. If so, she'd help them get assistance through the church benevolence fund. She refereed catfights between so-called sisters in Christ and watched for those who were overly ambitious, weary, or lonely. She mentored mothers in raising their children to revere God and encouraged women to own up to their mistakes because no earthly consequence was worth eternity in hell. She helped others wise up, especially when it came to men. Pinky knew who was dating whom and who *wanted* to date whom.

Which is the very reason she sat in the balcony today.

At the end of service, Pinky faced Camille. "I've noticed you here for some time now," she told her.

"Really?" Camille said, beginning to recognize the woman's face. "I arrived a little late to the Women's Day breakfast but remember hearing part of your 'Tell the Devil to Go to Hell' message. I bought the CD."

"Everybody remembers that one, but I wish I had titled it differently. People got so wrapped up in the 'hell,' they forgot the glory."

Pinky's first instinct urged her to schedule what she called a "sister intervention" where she and Camille would meet over lunch or dinner, the idea being to talk on a personal level. But just as she opened her mouth to invite Camille over, Pinky's inner voice whispered: "Wrong time." If she knew anything, she knew she'd better wait on God's cue, so she started talking about the church's singles ministry instead. She introduced Camille to a few members who had gathered after service.

Once the sanctuary cleared, Pinky spread her arms for a hug. Camille felt a strange sincerity in the lengthy embrace, like the love she felt when she visited family back home in Ohio. Pinky finally released her, and then wrapped both of her hands around one of Camille's for what Pinky called a love-shake.

"We'll talk again soon," she told Camille. "And I mean that. Once I've spotted you, I won't let you go unless the Lord says so."

Camille watched Pinky walk away. Something about that woman made her feel secure, even if only for the moment. Like a loving mother with wisdom seeping through her pores, one who meant it when she said she would not let Camille go.

A typical Saturday and Camille twisted in the salon chair at Gladys's House of Style where she had a standing appointment. Gladys shaped many a hairdo for the metro area's local news anchors and football players' wives, yet she knew how to customize Camille's short cut. Her strong hands massaged mousse into Camille's freshly washed hair, then smoothed it flat and shaped it for Camille's turn under the dryer.

On a typical visit, she and Gladys would gab away, but Camille's mind was divided this morning as she held a cell phone to her ear. "What did you say?" she asked her mother. How rude to talk on the phone while in Gladys's chair, but her mother had called for the third time that morning. "Mama, is something wrong?"

"Wrong? Not in my house. I've been trying to get in touch with you to find out what's going on at yours. After all, you never gave me the details of your sexy date with Blackwell last weekend."

The older Brenda Peters got, the more she lived vicariously through Camille. They talked several times a week, Brenda often calling for fashion tips or to get the scoop on Camille's friends. In Brenda's mind, intimate details with men weren't off limits, either, although Camille cut her mother short when Brenda offered a little too much information about a night with her significant other.

In Ohio, Brenda served as treasurer of the usher board for Little Rock Church in Mansfield. The head deacon was “Uncle Fred,” as Camille called her mother’s longtime boyfriend. They both taught Camille Bible stories and made her say grace before meals. Her father had left before Camille could jump rope but came through town once in a while to leave her a twenty-dollar bill to buy herself a pretty dress. One time she bought enough fabric and accessories to create her first “designer” skirt.

Camille kept the cell pressed to her ear while under the hair dryer and, as expected, Brenda veered into her usual rant about Uncle Fred. Rather than pay attention, Camille tuned it all out and triggered memories of her childhood. She remembered going off to bed while Uncle Fred watched TV in the living room then waking up to find him sipping coffee at the kitchen table. She couldn’t remember when she realized he must’ve been sleeping in her mother’s room, but whenever it hit her, she certainly didn’t see anything wrong with a man and woman doing what came naturally.

As long as she’d been in church, of course, Camille heard preachers and leaders talk about sex and sin. Yet they seemed to pay it little attention in their own lives. Her mother and Uncle Fred weren’t the only leaders at Little Rock to share a bed. The pastor himself had business to tend to, like the baby he fathered with the head of the church nursery, a woman who strutted her swollen belly around the sanctuary without shame. He admitted his transgressions from the pulpit one Sunday, his wife standing staunchly at his side. Two weeks later he was preaching about God’s mercy, the mistress had joined a church across town, and the members were angry—not with the pastor, but at a newspaper reporter who’d stumbled upon the mistress’s claim for child support at the courthouse and wrote a story about it.

Camille heard it all while sitting cross-legged in front of the TV or standing by the kitchen table as Brenda talked to visitors and to friends by phone. She couldn't have been more than eight or nine when she asked her mother what "sex" meant. Brenda told her it was something that two adults can agree to do together when they love each other.

"Like you and Uncle Fred?"

"Yes, sweetheart, like me and Fred."

All these years later, Fred still brought his overnight bag to Brenda's house on Fridays, and Camille had once questioned why they never married.

"We thought about it," Brenda said, "but we've gotten old and set in our ways now. Why bother? Getting married and moving in together would only complicate matters when things are as good as they're gonna get already."

But that's a long way from exciting, which may be the reason Brenda couldn't stop dipping into Camille's business a thousand miles away.

"Did you play that Luther CD like I told you?" Camille heard her mother asking with playful wickedness in her voice.

"Yes, Mama, I played the CD, but I'll have to call you back later," Camille said, ending the call.

For one, she couldn't get into specifics in the middle of the beauty shop. Secondly, something about telling the details of love-making to the woman you call "Mama" just didn't feel right. She would keep dodging her mother's calls for another week or so, hoping that would give Brenda enough time to forget and stop asking about that special night.

Camille went to the singles ministry bowling event, mostly out of obligation. Pinky had taken the time to introduce her to the organizers, Damian and Jacinta, so she didn't want to seem ungrateful. When she arrived, most of the faces were people she had noticed in church, often praying openly or standing with their arms raised high during worship, as if surrendering to God above.

It didn't matter who watched or what anyone else around them did. They were true worshipers whose praise came from the inside, and Camille observed their sincerity from her perch in the balcony, hoping to someday reach that level in her spiritual journey.

Any single person at the church could attend the singles outing, but no more than twenty showed up. Didn't take long to figure out why. Group regulars were serious believers, who would rate perhaps as high as a cream or even off-white on a Pinkymeter. Damian kicked off the gathering by forming a circle of prayer, right there in the middle of the bowling alley with other bowlers standing back in reverence. Later the group sat around eating pizza and hotdogs when, out of the clear blue heavens, Damian and Jacinta started talking about their recent engagement and how they wouldn't make love until their wedding night.

"I respect this woman too much to put her in a position that would jeopardize her relationship with God," he said.

Jacinta leaned her head against his shoulder. "I'm so blessed to be with him," she told the group. "You know your man's love is real when he's willing, not only to protect you from harm, but to guard your relationship with Christ."

Camille tried to disguise the resounding "puh-lease!" she felt in her heart by maintaining a neutral facial expression. She questioned what compelled them to announce their sex life, or lack thereof, to a roomful of people. But since they brought it up, she asked the one question she couldn't resist.

"I'm curious, are you both virgins?"

Damian shook his head vigorously. Jacinta laughed. "No, not at all, although we wish we were," she said. "Our past is just that, the past. We've been born again and we want to live as Jesus said so that our new life together glorifies Him."

Uh huh. The vow to celibacy didn't make much sense to Camille, especially since their sheets were already dirty. But one thing stuck with her after the evening ended—the part when Jacinta talked about Damian guarding her spiritually. The words sounded corny at first, but then Damian put his arm around Jacinta and softly kissed her forehead. Camille sensed in their relationship the same kind of genuineness she had perceived between the others she saw in the group.

Camille tilted her head and looked into Blackwell's eyes. "What would you say if I wanted to be celibate from now on?"

"What?"

"You heard me, Black. What if I didn't want us to sleep together anymore?"

Blackwell unhooked the arm that had held Camille close to him and scooted away to get a full view of her face.

"You can't be serious. We've already slept together countless times."

"I know, but—"

"Are you trying to tell me something?" Blackwell said.

"Yes, I am trying to tell you something but as usual these days, you're not listening. I'm trying to tell you that I'm reclaiming my virginity."

Blackwell laughed. Obviously Camille had been spending too much time with those religious overkills at church. "I don't know what your new bowling friends told you, but I'm sorry, that's one thing you can't get back."

Camille went to her weekly beauty shop appointment that next morning, then stopped by Nordstrom's. She moved from rack to rack, browsing the size 8 pantsuits just to get her mind off of the discussion with Blackwell the night before. The more he laughed, the angrier she became. Be your own woman, he told her. Stop listening to those people in the singles ministry. They're probably lying anyway, just like all the other church leaders who pretended to be so righteous.

He totally dismissed Damian and Jacinta's story, which unnerved Camille for reasons she couldn't totally explain. All she knew for sure was that she was getting more involved in church while he drifted away. He rarely attended services these days and changed the subject whenever she tried to discuss a recent sermon or Bible verse she'd read. He turned down her invitation to the singles event and future meetings. The group just didn't fit his style.

How, Camille wondered, would she motivate him to take her and his relationship with God seriously?

Hours passed before she checked the time on her cell phone and realized she had less than thirty minutes to get to Pinky's house. A few days earlier, Pinky had called and invited her to a barbecue. She had been keeping watch over Camille's involvement with the singles group. Now, the time was right to step in.

Camille used her GPS system to find Pinky's two-story house on the east side of town and pulled into the driveway where she met Brother Willie. From what Camille could tell, he seemed a good match for his wife. She remembered him standing at the main door during church services, shaking hands and ushering people to the sanctuary. Unlike Pinky, he was quiet and had a stately air about him. He offered a simple nod in place of saying hello, like a man who relied on his actions to speak for him. After Camille stepped out of her car, he introduced himself then stepped aside and opened the front door for her.

Prints of serene landscapes on the walls accented the blue-gray couch with huge pillows. Crocheted doilies covered a cherrywood bookshelf and coffee table. Old-school gospel wafted from a CD system on a shelf beneath a flat-screen TV that seemed slightly out of place in the otherwise simple and homey surroundings. The music created a soft undertone for conversation.

Pinky handed Camille a plate piled with tossed salad, potato salad, baked beans, and pork ribs slathered in a sweet, tangy barbecue sauce. "I hope you ain't trying to keep that skinny figure because we like to eat around here."

"Thank you, ma'am," Camille answered, looking around the room. She expected to see more people from the church, talking and laughing. Yet the only guests appeared to be a few older men who stayed outdoors with Willie. They sat out on the backyard deck telling stories and laughing. Not a single other woman had shown up.

"Is anyone else coming?"

"No, no one else," Pinky answered. "I invited you over, just to chat."

Camille wondered what they would chat about. "This certainly is a nice home you have," she said as a conversation starter.

But Pinky, who had no heart for small talk, steered the conversation to a personal discussion, asking about Camille's job and her parents, then about how and when she became a Christian.

Camille seemed unsure about the answer to Pinky's last question. "I guess I've been a Christian most of my life. My mother raised me in the church, and I remember being baptized when I was a little girl."

Pinky didn't say much in response, and Camille grew curious about Pinky's background. "You seem so happy and confident. How did you get involved in church?"

"Now there's a story," Pinky said with a light slap to her thigh. "You see Willie out there? We're old, but we've only been married five years. He's my first husband, but not my first man, if you know what I mean. I have two grown daughters.

"I was something else when I was your age. Thought I was Miss It. I would go shopping and get me a new outfit and go to church thinking I looked good. Don't get me wrong, there's nothing bad about being put together. It's just that, in my case, I thought the outside mattered more than my inside. I showed up every Sunday, but I hadn't made a commitment to God."

"Really?" Camille said, thinking about the ensemble she'd bought for church.

Pinky nodded. "I didn't realize it but I was insecure. I thought my hair and clothes were what mattered most. I hardly ever made time to pray, unless something went wrong at work or with my family.

"And you're going to think this is crazy," Sister Pinky went on, "but sometimes I visited a different church just to check out the men."

"What?" Camille said, trying to sound surprised, although she had done the same thing in the past.

"That's how I met my daughters' father. He was playing church just like me. Nice-looking man with a good job. After six months, we got an apartment together to save money. We always said we'd get married when we got our finances together. We went to church, side-by-side, like we had said wedding vows. A few years passed before we realized we didn't love each other anymore. He moved out and started mailing his child support.

"After that, all I wanted was another man. I found another, and another. I made sure anybody I dated went to church, though. I wanted a real Christian man, someone who believed in God, so we could have a nice churchgoing family."

"I know exactly what you mean," Camille said, thinking about her disappointment in Blackwell's behavior when it came to church.

"You know what an old wise woman told me one day?" Pinky said. "She looked me in my eyes, like I'm looking at you now, and she said: 'Baby, you can't lead a man to God, while you're sinning and sleeping with him at the same time. If you want a Christian man, first of all you've got to be a true Christian woman.'"

"Oh." Camille felt uneasy.

"That was a long time ago," Pinky continued. "Eventually, I stopped trying to find a man and started talking to God. As I prayed and meditated on His words in the Bible, I found peace and I dedicated my life to Him," she said, looking up, as if the Lord, Himself, rested on her ceiling. "Eventually," she said, "Willie found me."

Camille glanced upward and saw the time on Pinky's wall clock. It was nearly seven, and she and Blackwell had made plans to spend the evening together. She quickly said her good-byes and rushed to her car. She called Blackwell who luckily was also running late.

Perfect, Camille thought, as she started her car. She forced the conversation with Pinky to the back of her mind and turned on the radio, not wanting to think about God or celibacy or right or wrong.

"Did you bring clothes for church?" Camille asked Blackwell the next morning.

"Nah, I've got some work to do," he told her. "Call me when you get home."

Not the response she'd hoped for.

In many ways, she had the ingredients of success: a handsome boyfriend, her own fledgling career, and a sense of style. With her hair in place and new white linen pantsuit, she looked impeccable. Yet, as she walked out the door that morning, somehow she felt undone.

Sister Pinky's wisdom churned in her mind: "If you want a Christian man, you've got to be a Christian woman." Camille put a copy of Pinky's message from Women's Day into the CD player and truly listened for the first time.

"God is not pleased with lukewarm Christians who sin on Saturday and act saved on Sunday. Be either hot or cold, says the Lord," Pinky said. "He's waiting on you to let Him fill the emptiness in your life. 'I stand at the door and knock,' He says in the book of Revelation. The Devil is a hypocrite. Don't let him keep you from being the woman God wants you to be, from having all the blessings stored up for you in heaven. Commit your life to Christ and tell the Devil to go to hell!"

Camille walked into the sanctuary, spotted an empty seat next to Sister Pinky and made her way there. The saints were singing and clapping, but Camille couldn't stop thinking. She felt something, a presence much stronger than she had ever known, rapping on her heart. Should she let it in? In the midst of the music, she lifted her arms high, surrendering herself to God. Her life would have to change, this much she knew.

She tried to wipe away the tears before anyone else could see, but felt a hand softly resting on her back. It was Sister Pinky's. "Would you like a tissue, baby?"

THINK ABOUT IT

1. How is Camille living in the pink?
2. During most of the story, how does she view her Christian walk? How might her upbringing have shaped her view?
3. What are your thoughts on intimacy and dating? What strategies can Christian men and women use while dating to get to know each other without compromising their values?
4. What was it about the "true worshipers" she saw at church and Damian and Jacinta that drew Camille's attention, and why?
5. How does Sister Pinky relate to Camille? What's the difference between biblical counsel and just meddling in other people's business?
6. Discuss Titus 2:3–5a (NIV), below, with your group. How does the passage relate to Sister Pinky and her relationship with Camille? Do you think that these teachings would be useful in today's culture? Why or why not?

Likewise, teach the older women to be reverent in the way they live, not to be slanderers or addicted to much wine, but to teach what is good. Then they can train the younger women to love their husbands and children, to be self-controlled and pure.

7. Isaiah 1:18 (NIV) says: *Though your sins are like scarlet, they shall be as white as snow; though they are red as crimson, they shall be like wool.* What do you think of Sister Pinky's "living in the pink" philosophy? If you had to put your relationship with God on her color spectrum—from white to crimson—what shade would it be?

MAMA'S HEART

CORRINE SCURRIED to the kitchen to find her purse on top of the table where she'd left it. Her fingers fumbled past the clutter to the tattered billfold inside. She had just cashed her Social Security check, thank God, so she had the two hundred dollars in cash they wanted. Not the time to think about the electric bill or groceries or even the Lord's tithes. When you've got two thugs standing at your front door, one of them with a .38-caliber gun to your son's back, you can't do nothing but what they tell you to.

She handed over the money without a word. What could she say? Melvin had run up a debt and somebody had to pay it, they'd told her. The short one with the gun stood stout and bowlegged, looking at her with an expression so dead Corrine wondered whether he was, too—if he was dead, that is, at least inside. Probably around sixteen years old, seventeen at the most. Nothing about Corrine seemed to shake him, and she figured he must never have known a mother's love.

The tall skinny one snatched the stack of twenty dollar bills and counted aloud: "Twenty, forty, sixty, eighty . . ." When he finished, he tilted his head and twisted his lips into a sadistic grin. "Thank you, ma'am," he said, before giving Melvin a slight shove forward. The short one withdrew the gun and backed away.

Melvin stumbled into the living room wearing the same funky clothes he'd left in three days before. Corrine slammed the door and locked the deadbolt behind him, then hooked the chain and peeked out the curtain to make sure those boys had driven away. Melvin said nothing and headed straight to his room. It was the same room where he'd grown up, where he once played with toy cars and finished his schoolwork by lamplight.

She watched him closely, couldn't stop looking at him, the little of him that there was left. His sunken jowls. The ashy tint to his amber-colored skin. His eyes, bulging yet tired and red. The only thing she could think to do was call out to him. "Melvin," she said softly, her voice cracking. He lifted his head slightly, but quickly turned away again, then entered his room and shut the door. Corrine slumped onto the couch and bent over, burying her face in her lap to muffle a wailing cry. She didn't want Melvin to hear her pain.

When a child is young, he sits on his mother's lap. But when he grows older, he sits on her heart. At least that's what the old folks used to say, and Sister Pinky knew the saying well. She thought about it standing over the stove, stirring a pot of chili. They were her mother's words, from way back when they'd sit out on the porch and watch the sun rest over the country fields in backwoods Florida. Pinky didn't fully understand it till she had two growing daughters of her own. Just like any mother, she shared in her children's anxiety. No matter how grown they got, when they hurt, she hurt, too.

That's why she could relate to Sister Corrine Gaines. She envisioned her friend's face round from years of good cooking and typically framed by a short-styled black wig to hide all that gray hair underneath. The kind of woman who kissed people on the cheek when she hugged them and made extra sweet potato pies just to give away.

But that son of hers had been sitting on Corrine's heart for years. With every disappointment, her shoulders slumped a little more. She didn't walk as spry as she used to. And people seldom heard that high-pitched laugh of hers nowadays. Most anybody who lived on Tampa's east side knew Melvin Gaines lived for his next high, a "crackhead" is what the young folks called him.

Pinky couldn't be a hundred percent sure, but the man she saw yesterday slouched on the sidewalk outside a drug house on Nebraska Avenue sure did look like Melvin. She'd been on her way to the neighborhood fruit and vegetable stand early that morning when she saw him. Then, later that night, Corrine didn't show up for the women's Bible study meeting. Pinky got up this morning and cut up some fresh tomatoes and peppers, as well as some meat she got from the market. Corrine loved her chili recipe, and Pinky intended to use it as an excuse to invite herself over. She wanted to see if her friend needed support.

In the beginning of Melvin's addiction, Corrine had asked the bishop to say a special prayer for Melvin on Sundays. But the situation only got worse over the years. Money disappeared from her purse so often she started taking it to bed with her and locking her door. Melvin went in and out of rehab centers, quick fixes that only drained Corrine who took out bank loans and a second mortgage to pay for the treatments. Jobs he got through temporary staffing agencies lasted only until his next three-day drug binge. He'd moved out once, having maintained a gig at a call center and saved enough money for his own apartment. It lasted four months before he was "back out there," Corrine admitted to the women's group at church.

Two months ago now, he reemerged. Corrine hadn't seen him in so long she didn't even know if he were alive. She grabbed him and held him tight that day, then ushered him to the bathroom for a hot shower. She went to his old room and found some clean jeans and a T-shirt in the dresser drawer. They fit baggy on his frame, all skin and bones from days without an appetite for anything but drugs. Then she fed him good: pot roast and potatoes and carrots, collard greens and corn bread.

When he asked about moving back in, she couldn't say no. Pinky remembered her coming to the women's meeting that same night, asking the ladies to pray for her son. Maybe, Corrine had said, this was it. Maybe the drugs had taken him down as low as he could go and it was time to rise up, to be the man she always knew he could be. When the meeting ended, Pinky led the group in a special prayer for Melvin.

"Lord, give him strength to resist the Devil," Pinky had said to a steady chorus of "yes, Lords."

"Draw him into Your everlasting arms," she continued, "so that he knows there is no greater high than the love of Jesus."

Corrine's older son and daughter had moved away with families of their own, one in Atlanta, the other way up in New York City. Nobody but Corrine and Melvin now stayed in that little yellow house—where the Gaines family had lived as long as anybody could remember. Just a ten-minute drive from Pinky's place. Pinky put the pot of chili in a big thermal bag that she used for such food drops and secured it on the floor of her car.

Melvin had been in his room since the events of the day before. Corrine couldn't sleep at all and heard his door creak open for the first time last night. She held her breath, hoping he wouldn't walk out the front door and into the streets to find more drugs. Instead, she heard him go into the bathroom for a while, then back to his room. Between him inside the house and the drug dealers outside, she couldn't find any peace.

Still, she got up that morning and made scrambled eggs, grits, and bacon, and knocked on his door. "Melvin, come on out, son. You need to eat something."

No response. She opened the door slowly to find him in a hard sleep, snoring, his mouth hanging open. He probably hadn't slept for days. She went back to the kitchen and fixed her breakfast, then sat down to watch her favorite courtroom dramas to get her mind off of her own. It didn't work. Between Judge Judy's rants, Corrine tried to figure out how her son's life had come to this. Her thoughts landed where they usually did: Melvin's father. They'd been married long enough to have three kids and a mountain of debt before his drinking consumed the marriage and their bank account. She filed for bankruptcy, then divorce.

She kicked Alfred Gaines Sr. out of their house and neither she nor the kids saw him much after that. Melvin, being the youngest, didn't remember much about those years. He just knew that he had a father one day, and the next he didn't. If her ex-husband had gone to Melvin's Pee Wee League football games or took him out fishing or hunting once in a while, Corrine reasoned that Melvin would have turned out differently.

Too late for that now. The man died of a heart attack, alone in a low-rent apartment about four blocks from the family's house. She called the kids into the living room to tell them. Al Jr., seventeen at the time, showed no emotion. He had watched his mother struggle to pay bills over the years before getting a job at the grocery store to help out. By then he considered himself the man of the house. At fifteen, Veronica thought of herself as a daddy's girl, at least on the few occasions Daddy came around. To the funeral, she wore a new black dress that Al Jr. bought out of his paycheck from bagging groceries. Sitting beside her, ten-year-old Melvin hadn't stopped crying since he saw his father's sculpted face lying in an open casket. His hope of ever having a relationship with the man who gave him life would be buried that day, six feet under.

Corrine remembered comforting her children the best she knew how, wrapping her arms tight around them and telling funny stories of when she and Alfred first met. Melvin, however, remained inconsolable, longing for something that Corrine could neither identify, nor fulfill. His personality differed from Al Jr., strong-willed and always the leader of the pack. Melvin behaved more like Corrine, herself, sensitive and docile. Thinking back now, she figured she should have protected him more. Prostitutes and johns littered the surrounding streets, alongside abandoned duplexes and a rundown convenience store where grown men whiled away their days drinking, cussing, and playing dominoes. She warned Melvin against hanging with the bad people, but maybe it wasn't enough.

Back then, she worried most about Al Jr. who had a mean streak fit for application into a street gang. Instead, praise God, his determination propelled him to the military where he grew into a fine, disciplined man, Corrine thought, staring at the wall portrait of her oldest in a crisp army uniform. As for Veronica, she went on to community college to become a licensed practical nurse. These days Corrine prayed that Veronica and her live-in boyfriend would get married so their two children could grow up in a household that honored God.

As for Melvin, Corrine had never worried too much about him, and she figured that might have been her biggest mistake of all. He was a "Yes, Ma'am-No, Ma'am" type of child who got decent grades in school—As, Bs, and an occasional C. Corrine stood back and gave him a little room in high school to experiment with parties and girlfriends. She noticed his grades dropped a bit at the community college in town but convinced herself that he was just getting a handle on his manhood. Then, that summer between his first and second year, money went missing and he started staying out all night, paying her warnings little mind. Before she realized it, the streets had swallowed him up. Now, eight years later, Corrine sat absentmindedly watching TV, while her adult son slept in his childhood bedroom with nowhere else to go. The sound of a car outdoors jolted her thoughts. In the last twenty-four hours, she'd grown jittery whenever an engine came close to the driveway. Would those boys come back to rob the place, knowing she couldn't defend herself and that Melvin might do anything for a rock of cocaine or one of those little pills the addicts were popping these days? She couldn't call the police, though. They might take Melvin away, too, considering he had done as much dirt as the dealers. She pulled back a corner of the curtain to peek outside just as Sister Pinky walked up the driveway, carrying a Crock-Pot.

"Hey, Corrine!" Pinky's voice bellowed, as she stepped through the doorway. The fall breeze followed her, and Corrine hurriedly shut the door, not wanting to turn on the heat and run up another bill she couldn't pay. "You were on my mind so I thought I'd bring you some of my homemade three-meat chili."

Corrine smelled the chili powder, onions, garlic, fresh tomatoes, and kidney beans, mixed with beef, Italian sausage, and bits of baby shrimp. "Girl, you know I just love your chili."

"Yes, I do know, and it's been cooking all morning just for you, so you're in for a treat, if I do say so myself."

"You shouldn't have gone through all this trouble, Pinky, getting up cooking and then carrying your Crock-Pot all the way over here," Corrine said, wrinkling her brow. "What's gotten into you?"

"No trouble at all. You know how I like to cook. Besides, it gave me a reason to come over here and see my friend," Pinky said, "especially since we missed you last night at Bible study and nobody had heard from you."

Corrine paused. With all that happened with Melvin, she'd forgotten about her women's group meeting on Tuesday nights. She looked over at the refrigerator and, there, sitting on top was the plastic container with the pound cake she made two days earlier for the ladies to snack on.

She looked back at Pinky. "My goodness, I'm so sorry. It totally slipped my mind, and last night was my turn to bring dessert. I don't even know what to say."

"It's all right, Corrine. Don't you worry. The last thing our old hips needed was a piece of pound cake," Pinky said to ease Corrine's guilt. "We were concerned about you, though. I tried calling after the meeting, but nobody answered."

Corrine vaguely recalled hearing the phone ring, but she'd made no move to get it. She didn't even want to talk to God, let alone a human being who could do nothing to solve her problems. Pinky sensed Corrine's discomfort and helped herself to a seat at the small round kitchen table. "What's wrong, Corrine? What's happened?"

Corrine knew she couldn't fake it now. Her transparent facial expressions gave her away every time. A part of her searched for a release to her frustration anyway. Perhaps Pinky would understand. She struggled for the words.

"Well, I . . ."

"Is it Melvin?"

Corrine closed her eyes and nodded. "Yes, it's my son."

For the next hour, she recapped her latest nightmare, confessing her greatest fear: That Melvin would die from the drugs or a gunshot before the Lord could save him. When she finished, Pinky rested her hand on top of Corrine's and sat in silence, waiting on the Holy Spirit to supply her with words to say. She didn't want to belittle Corrine's pain by tossing around a few trite Bible verses, as if simply saying "the battle is the Lord's" would suddenly make everything right.

"Corrine, I can't sit here and tell you that I know what you're going through, and I pray to God that I never do," Pinky said, deciding to speak simply what was on her heart. "But one thing I can relate to, the love you feel for your son. It's a mother's love, the kind that would do any and everything it takes to save her child."

It was Corrine's turn to sit and listen now. Pinky saw despair in her weary eyes.

"Our love for our children is so strong that sometimes we don't realize that it isn't perfect," Pinky said, carefully choosing her words. “We don’t understand that no matter how much we care for our kids, our love can’t fix everything. Sometimes it’s just not enough.

“When it comes down to it, Corrine, you can’t force a grown man or woman to live how you want, even if they did come from your own womb. God gave them the right to choose the outcome of their own lives. And sooner or later, they’ve got to face the consequences of those choices.”

Corrine interrupted. “Drugs mess up a person’s brain, Pinky. These drug addicts, they can’t even think for themselves, they can’t make good decisions.”

“But you can’t fix the problem. You can’t make that boy get off drugs and think straight.”

Corrine opened her mouth to speak, but Pinky kept right on talking.

“This is too big for you, Corrine. Your love is everlasting and it flows from down deep within your soul, but not even that can rescue a child when the Devil’s got him strong-armed in the pit. Only the love of Jesus can bring him back, but you’ve got to move out of the way first. Sometimes we believers say our faith is in God, but we really don’t trust Him to handle our problems at all, so we keep trying to solve everything. Corrine, you have to let that boy go. If you don’t, the Devil will wear you out and take you down right along with Melvin.”

“But Melvin, he’s not even saved!” Corrine said, her pressure rising. “I didn’t start him out in the church when he was young. He don’t know God, he—”

“This is not your fault,” Pinky said, cutting her off. “You weren’t the perfect Christian mother, none of us were. But you have planted the seeds of righteousness in this house. Melvin is almost thirty years old. He knows enough to call on the name of the Lord. This is between him and God now.”

“So you’re telling me to kick my own son out on the streets like a dog, like a homeless man?”

"No, that's not what I'm saying—"

"You sound like Al Jr.," Corrine said, paying no attention to Pinky's response. She'd already called her oldest son in New York for help with the bills this month. She didn't tell him about Melvin and the dealers, but he figured that his younger brother was behind her shortfall. He agreed to wire money, but warned her to "stop taking care of a sorry, grown man."

Corrine became angry, remembering the negative things Al Jr. had said about Melvin and now Pinky's harsh advice. "Neither you nor Al Jr. was here when my baby came off the streets, looking like skin and bones from hunger and begging me to let him in. You're telling me to turn my back on him, but I don't serve a God who would do that. My God helps those who need Him most."

"Yes, so let God help him—not you. If you had what it takes, why is Melvin still in your bedroom addicted to drugs?"

The kitchen fell silent. Corrine didn't have an answer, and Pinky felt ashamed for letting what was supposed to be gentle counsel spiral into an argument. She had allowed her words to turn sharp.

She broke the silence. "I'm sorry. I shouldn't have said that." Pinky grasped Corrine's hand. "And I'm not trying to convince you to kick Melvin out right away. I don't know if that's the answer. All I want you to see is that you've got to give this burden over to God."

Pinky rose from the table to leave, and Corrine followed her to the front door. They broke the tension with a long embrace.

"You know you can call me anytime you need me, don't you?"

"I know," Corrine said nodding. "And I will."

Melvin remained holed up in his room for two days, coming out only for restroom breaks and to make a plate to eat. Finally, he stayed out long enough to actually talk with his mother. He told her how ashamed and sorry he was for all that had happened.

“Mama, I want to stop. I do. It’s just that sometimes the pull is so strong that I can’t.”

Corrine heard helplessness in his voice, as he explained what happened the other day. He’d gone to the day labor office to get a few hours of hard manual work on a construction site. The job paid a lot more than most, ten dollars an hour, and the foreman handed him a hundred dollars in cash at the end of a long day, more money than he’d felt between his fingers in months. Tired and sweaty, he saw nothing wrong with stopping by the convenience store to pick up a cold beer and to hang outside with some guys playing Tonk. That’s when one of his old dealers saw him and asked if he “needed anything.”

Melvin wanted to stop the story there, but Corrine wanted details. This culture of drugs and dealing and hustling transformed how she saw the world, and she wanted to know the reality for all those young boys she saw on the streets with sagging pants and hats turned sideways and no hope for the future.

With a little money in his pocket, Melvin told her, temptation overpowered him. One hit to the pipe turned into three days of getting high, sometimes bumming a smoke off of someone else at an abandoned house where druggies hang out. At some point, he couldn’t remember when, he swiped a bag of rocks from one of the street hustlers who stopped by the house, the short mean-looking guy who threatened to kill him. To save his life, Melvin told them he knew where they could get the money.

“I—I’m sorry, Mama,” he said, so choked with tears that the words caught in his throat.

Corrine used a spare rag to wipe the drivel from his mouth and the snot from his nose. What surprised her most was that she didn’t start crying herself. She supposed she had done all the crying she could do, leaving only sadness now like a weight crushing her spirit.

“I know what I need to do,” Melvin said, regaining his composure. “I’m gonna go to that men’s meeting at the church this afternoon 'cause I can't do this on my own. I need help, Mama, I need help."

Melvin had never suggested going to church before. The few times he'd been there over the years occurred at Corrine's nagging. She figured this must be a sign from the Lord, letting her know that Melvin would soon be delivered.

"Baby, that's wonderful!" she said, so energized she sprang from her seat. "God can snatch that taste for drugs right out of your mouth and leave you thirsting for Him and Him alone."

She went to the bedroom and got her purse and car keys off the dresser. The Brothers Keepers meeting would start soon and she didn't want him to be late for his first visit, nor did she want to give him time to change his mind. Within minutes, Melvin sat silently in the passenger seat, and Corrine mumbled, "Thank You, Jesus," all the way to Believers Ministries.

Pinky's husband, Brother Willie, led the group, so Corrine knew her son would be in good hands. She had already called to give him a heads-up, so Willie would be prepared to talk to Melvin on a deeper level. She dropped him off in the parking lot then headed to the grocery store to get fixings for a big Sunday dinner with homemade dressing and turkey legs and all the side dishes. Al Jr. had sent her a little extra for spending money, so she might even scrounge up enough for homemade banana pudding, Melvin's favorite.

It took her three trips back and forth to the car to carry in all those groceries. By the third go-round, she heard the phone ringing inside and almost tripped trying to get to it before it stopped. It was Pinky.

"Corrine, I thought you said you were bringing Melvin up here for the meeting?"

"I did bring him. I dropped him off almost an hour and a half ago."

"You did?" Pinky said, sounding confused. "Well, I just stopped by so I could give him a hug, but he's not here. Willie saw me waiting and excused himself from the group for a moment to tell me that Melvin never showed up. The meeting's almost over."

Corrine fell silent, so stunned she dropped the grocery bag full of cornmeal and fresh bananas on the floor.

"Corrine?"

"I'm still here."

"I'm sorry, Corrine, but I even asked a few of the other people at the church in case he got lost looking for the meeting room, but nobody's seen Melvin."

"I see," Corrine said, before another long pause. Then, "Would you do me a favor and ask Brother Willie if he could stop by my house after the meeting today? I'm going to need his help."

Three thirty in the morning. That's when Corrine heard the sound she knew would come at some point, Melvin's key turning in the lock—or rather, attempting to turn the lock.

At Corrine's request, Willie had come over and sized up the locks on her doors, then got a locksmith friend of his to help change them all that same evening. Willie insisted on paying for the locks himself, and the friend did the job at no cost.

Corrine couldn't sleep that night. She made herself a cup of hot tea and sat in her recliner rocking chair with a Bible in her lap. She wasn't giving up on her son, she told herself, just letting him go for now, so the Lord could deal with him. She read the Scriptures all night to gain strength until she dozed off. The key rattled her awake. When she heard it, she kept sitting there, rocking, looking straight ahead, like a woman mesmerized. She didn't even move when Melvin started banging on the door. He had to see the light shining in the living room and he kept banging and banging.

Like a robot, she grabbed the cordless phone on the end table and pushed the button that speed-dialed Pinky. She'd told Corrine to call when Melvin came knocking, no matter the time. Pinky was already awake and seated in her living room recliner to avoid disturbing Willie. Soon as the phone rang, she put on her reading glasses and took out a sheet of Scriptures. She picked up the handset and heard Melvin's screams in the background muffled by Corrine's heavy breathing.

"Don't you open that door," Pinky said. "You can do this. The Bible says we can do all things through Christ who strengthens us."

Corrine just kept sitting and listening, and Pinky talked calm and low. After a few minutes, Corrine looked down at the cover of her Bible and familiar verses came to mind. She opened her mouth and started reciting Scriptures for herself.

"Cast all your cares on Him because He cares for you," she whispered.

"Mmmhmm," Pinky encouraged on the other end. "That's right."

Melvin couldn't hear her, but figured she was there. He called out angrily: "Mama, come open this door! Maaaa-ma!"

Corrine kept reciting. "Be still, and know that I am God."

"Mama, please! I can explain," he said, his screams yielding to sobs. "Just give me another chance, Mama, just one more chance."

"God has not given me the spirit of fear, but of power, love, and a sound mind."

Outside, a neighbor yelled for Melvin to shut up because the whole block could hear him. He walked around to the living room window and tapped on the glass. There, he saw his mother's silhouette against the light and tapped again. Corrine's fingers gripped the armrests tight. She dropped the phone and at some point Pinky hung up, knowing the end would rest on Corrine's faith alone. Corrine listened to Melvin's pleas, soft and begging now.

"I ain't got nowhere else to go, Mama. Please."

Was she doing the right thing? How would she ever forgive herself if something happened to her son out there on the streets?

"Trust in the Lord with all your heart," she whispered, "and lean not on your own understanding."

Finally, Corrine heard her baby boy's footsteps running then fading away.

Melvin's chest heaved. He didn't know where to go. His mother had rejected him, turned her back on him. All his life, she was the one person he could count on, the one he knew loved him no matter what.

He turned down an alley and stumbled to the ground. Gathering himself, he sat up and rested his back against the side of an abandoned building. Voices in his head told him he was worthless, so bad that his own mother didn't want him. "Kill yourself," the voices said. No more lying and stealing. No more guilt or pain. He wished he'd had a gun or, better yet, so much crack to smoke that he would bust his heart wide-open. He caught his breath and scoured the dark alleyway for anything that could do the job, even a broken shard of glass. There was nothing but a few cardboard boxes, some rotten food, and what looked like a raccoon a few yards away. His pulse settled, exposing the night's chill, and he pulled his frail knees to his chest to keep warm.

That's when a stream of moonlight caught his attention, and Melvin looked upward. Instinctively, he opened his mouth and spoke words he never had before.

"If You're really there, God," he said, his eyes fixed on a heaven far away, "please, help me."

THINK ABOUT IT

1. Corrine, a Christian woman who loved her son, prayed constantly for his deliverance from drug addiction. Yet, how did her actions reveal that she was living in the pink in at least one area of her life? Why do you think God had not yet answered her prayer?

2. In the end, did she do the right thing by locking Melvin out of her home, not knowing where he would spend the night or how he would get by? Discuss why or why not.
3. Melvin's drug addiction was taking a toll on his mother, not only by depleting her finances and dampening her spirit, but also putting her in dangerous situations. How can we avoid letting our loved ones' problems and hardships steal our joy?
4. Think of a time when you had to let go of someone you loved, at least for a season. How did it feel? How did you cope?
5. Is "letting go" of someone you love the same as "giving up" on that person? What's the difference?
6. If you are a mother, what is it that you fear most with regard to your children's future? What has kept you up at night? Now, especially if your children are older, ask yourself if you have control over the outcome.
7. Drug addiction has become widespread, forcing families of all races and social classes to deal with its torment. Yet there are many testimonies of those who recovered from what seemed to be a point of no return. Are you tempted to give up on someone you love? Don't. Instead, find and write down five Scriptures or passages that you can use in prayer for that person's deliverance. The story of the prodigal son (Luke 15:11–32) is a good place to start.

LITTLE FOX

BISHOP EVERETT never saw anything divide his congregation so decisively in the last twenty years. He had watched God expand his influence from a Bible study in his living room to Believers Ministries International and, now, a network of branch congregations: Believers Community, Believers Tabernacle, and Believers Promised Land. He groomed his assistants to take over the sister churches, sending them out to spread God's Word in communities throughout the metropolitan area. With each church plant, some of his members left to be part of the new work, but the Lord always sent more in.

That wasn't to say that Believers Ministries never had trouble. Once, a newspaper reporter did an exposé on church collections and made it seem like Bishop swindled people out of their money because he preached about the tithe. The saints knew better than the media, though. A prophet named Malachi, not Everett, had already outlined the plan for supporting the church thousands of years ago.

Then came the time when one of the assistant ministers and his wife almost split. Rumors of cheating, mismanaged money, and meddling in-laws filled the vestibule every Sunday. But the Lord—and a good Christian marriage counselor—worked that out.

And then there was the food incident. The culinary ministry served a buffet for the summer picnic, including a big tray of macaroni salad. It tasted so good that dozens of people asked for seconds. Too bad every one of them fell sick by sunset. Mayonnaise must've been spoiled was the best anybody could figure. To this day, nobody knows whose kitchen that salad came from, except the one who made it and the three other ladies on the cooking team. They all stood on the pulpit the next Sunday and apologized. No use in pointing fingers at one person, they'd said.

Still, none of those experiences compared to what Bishop faced now.

He reached for another sip of his grape juice then took the handkerchief from his pocket to wipe his brow. Before tonight's church meeting, he had discussed his plan with his wife, Sister Madeline Everett, Assistant Pastor Meacham, and Sister Pinky, who oversaw many of the women's ministry activities. This, he assured them, would encourage more togetherness in the church. After listening to the details, both his wife and Pinky had their doubts. They advised him to approach the concept slowly at the church meeting, lest he rile every woman in the place. He'd brushed their warnings aside, however, reasoning they were overly cautious.

The evening began with an update on the status of the church plants, each of which submitted financially stable records and boasted of growing memberships. The oldest, Believers Community, was preparing to build a bigger sanctuary to accommodate its bulging attendance.

With everyone in high spirits, Bishop segued into a brief discourse about the church's role as a "family."

"The church—and when I say church I don't mean these four walls, I mean the Spirit who lives inside of us, that drives us to do right, to love our neighbors just like we love God—the church, I say, is a family," Bishop said, just short of preaching rhythm.

"Amens" filled the sanctuary, and he sensed he was on the right track.

Until, that is, he revealed the actual plan, at which point the "amens" turned into "uh, whats?"

Most of the disgruntled were women. The men, like Bishop, looked around with wide eyes and wrinkled brows.

"Did we hear you right?" Sister Moore, the children's Sunday school teacher, blurted out before Deacon Moore could hush her.

Sister Sho'nuff (nicknamed such for exclaiming, "Sho'nuff, Preacher," during sermons) stood to her feet, holding a textbook-sized Bible straight in the air like a dagger. "No disrespect, Bishop Everett, but I need you to show me in this book where it says God wants us to focus on this!"

"Me, too," Sister Towery exclaimed, still wearing her green doctor's assistant scrubs.

Pinky and Madeline gave Bishop "I told you so" glances then lowered their gazes.

He braced himself and stood firm.

"Ladies, I'm sure if you calm down, you'll see the value in what we're trying to do here. Things have become too cliquish in the house of God. This little experiment will encourage everyone to meet new people. I think you'll enjoy it."

"So you're saying this is how it's going to be?" Sister Towery asked defiantly.

Bishop maintained his calm. "I'm afraid so."

Then he reiterated the new rule: "Effective immediately, the common practice of saving seats during church services will end.

"That means the empty seat next to you belongs, not to your best friend who hasn't arrived yet, but to the first person who wants to sit there. Please do not place your Bibles, purses, or journals on empty seats to discourage others from sitting down.

"In addition, I am asking all of you who sit in the same seat every week to sit somewhere else, so you'll meet new people. This is mandatory for church leaders, unless you are a minister who sits on the pulpit. I've heard too many members say they can't get to know the leaders because they all sit together in the front of the church."

He paused in a room so silent you could hear a prayer cloth drop. Cold expressions stared back at him.

"Again," Bishop resumed, "I'm surprised by your reaction. I thought this would be a fun and interesting exercise for us all. I'm disappointed that some of you aren't interested in stepping outside of your comfort zones.

"And to my dear sisters who asked for a Scripture to support this mandate, I thank you for the request," he said, nodding curtly in the direction of Sister Towery and Sho'nuff. "We always want to be led by the Word of God. There's a verse you may recall in the book of Acts that says God is not a respecter of persons. He doesn't esteem one person more highly than the other. And since we are God's seed, we should behave likewise. We should be willing to sit beside whomever, not clamoring to get with Sister or Brother So-and-So each week."

With that, Bishop picked up his attaché case. "That's all, church," he said. "You are dismissed."

Sister Towery hurried through the parking lot with Sho'nuff on her heels. They couldn't speak their minds in the church because Bishop had too many "go-tell-its" who reported back to him every time they heard someone whisper his name. This new directive would affect their Sunday ritual of holding a place for each other in the front. Sometimes Sister Towery ran late because of thick traffic or because she had to pick up her grandkids, but she knew her seat would be safe with Sho'nuff. Every now and then, Sister Sho'nuff mingled too long in the lobby, but if Towery was on time, she needn't worry.

After the meeting, they slid into their cars and simultaneously picked up their cell phones to discuss the matter on the way home.

"Can you believe this?"

"No, it's ridiculous," Sho'nuff answered. "If Bishop thinks he's fooling somebody as to what this is really about, he is out of his mind. I've been going to church all my life, so I *know* church. I know church folks. I know pastors. I know how they think, and he ain't fooling nobody."

"He said he wants us to get to know new people. You think there's more to it?"

"Of course, there is. No seat saving? Please! Does that sound like something a bishop would come up with to you? At every church in the whole United States of America, the saints are saving seats for their friends, and somehow people are still getting saved, still being filled with the Holy Ghost. He's trying to make saving a seat into some kind of a big sin and ain't nothing sinful about it. Jesus, Himself, probably saved seats for Peter, James, *and* John."

"So what do you think is behind it, Sho?"

"It's about what every single crazy thing at Believers Ministries is always about: Pinky and her silly ways of trying to get us all to be her little clones."

"Huh?"

"Okay, let me just break it down for you. Remember that Sunday last month when Pinky came to church and the ushers had already sat a new member in her spot—you know, that chair in the third row near the aisle? Pinky and her husband had to sit someplace else."

"Can't say that I paid any attention to that."

"Don't you get it? This whole idea is Pinky's. The 'Queen Bee' had to switch seats, so now she wants everybody else to do the same."

"Sho'nuff, I think you have lost your mind," Sister Towery said, laughing. "What Bishop asked us to do won't change a thing. When his little experiment is all over, people will go back to sitting with their friends, but I don't think Pinky would be that petty."

"I'm telling you, it's not Bishop," Sho'nuff said. "I bet that after she lost her own seat, she convinced Bishop that people who save seats are 'living in the pink.' If I hear her say that stupid phrase one more time, I just might lose my mind.

"Living in the pink, living in the pink . . ." Sho'nuff continued, speaking in a mocking squeaky voice. "No doubt, Pinky just wants that woman who took over her old seat to have to get up and move so Pinky can get it back again."

"Oh, come on."

"Be naïve if you want to, but I don't think anybody at Believers Ministries knows better than me the conniving side of Miss Laura Pinkston. One day you'll understand, but for now just trust me when I say she ain't the righteous woman of wisdom she wants everybody to see."

Sister Sho'nuff talked to herself the rest of the way home after having to cut short the call with Sister Towery whose granddaughter had beeped in on the other line.

"I can't believe people still fall for her mess, watching her sit up there in front of the church with her Bible open and her highlighter sticking out of her purse at the ready—just as phony as a three-dollar bill. She might fool the rest of 'em, but not me. No . . . not me."

Most in the congregation had long forgotten the drama years earlier in which Pinky and Sho'nuff played starring roles. As church mess goes, this one endured for a relative moment before being eclipsed by another ordeal. It still lingered in Sister Sho'nuff's heart, however. Each time she tried to move on, Pinky did something to get on her nerves, something sneaky like this seat-saving foolishness, or something just as underhanded as what she did seven years ago.

Back then, Sho'nuff's spirit was still tender from the death of her husband of forty-three years, and she liked to go to his favorite

Parker's Restaurant, the one on Walters Avenue, for senior citizen Mondays and to feel a little closer to him. One afternoon, her eye caught sight of a gentleman sitting alone, focused on a plate of fried catfish and what looked like a thin pamphlet off to the side of his plate. The full head of hair with gray flecks at his temples clued that he might be slightly less seasoned than her, but once a man or a woman reached fifty-five a decade or two in age difference didn't amount to much. Must've been the Lord compelling her to approach and, the closer she got, the better she could tell that the pamphlet was actually a Sunday school booklet. He was handsome in an older pudgy sort of way. After she introduced herself, he graciously invited her to sit down. They talked the whole evening long, that being the first real conversation Sister Sho'nuff had with a man since Cletus went on to be with the Lord.

The gentleman introduced himself as Willie Pinkston, a widower who at the time was attending a small church in the next county where he had grown up. Well, Sister Sho'nuff felt it only right to invite him to Believers Ministries, seeing that the church stood just a few blocks from where the man said he lived and that the bishop could teach and preach just about as good as any old-school preacher Sho'nuff had ever heard. He accepted her invitation, and the very next Sunday Sister Sho'nuff had Sister Towery save her seat while she chatted with him awhile in the vestibule before service started.

She had no intention of sitting with Willie, at least not yet. It wouldn't be proper for two old folks to nestle thigh-to-thigh in the sanctuary unless one of them wore a wedding ring. But she popped up from her seat as soon as the benediction ended, hoping to catch him before he left. She walked briskly, physically dodging a few groups of people so her wide-brimmed hat wouldn't scrape someone's head. After a while, she caught up to Willie all right, smack in the middle of the lobby. Too bad he wasn't alone. There he stood giggling and hee-hawing with Sister Pinky.

Now, "friends" had never been quite the word to describe the relationship between Pinky and Sho'nuff. They hadn't really clicked, although both did serve as elders for the women's ministry, which held regular meetings and organized the annual prayer breakfast, a movie night, and a few potlucks. At their very next meeting, which happened to be the Tuesday after the Sunday that Willie visited the church, Sister Sho'nuff made a point of sitting next to Pinky and bringing up his name.

"I saw you talking to my friend Willie after church Sunday."

Pinky turned her head about thirty degrees in Sho'nuff's direction then answered evenly. "He's a friend of yours? Oh, I didn't realize that."

"He probably figured you saw me getting him settled before service just like everyone else did and thought you already knew that I was the one who invited him here."

"Well, he seemed to have a good time, so I can only assume that he appreciates you for telling him about our church."

Pinky shifted in her seat to face Madeline who, by now, stood at the front of the group to start the women's ministry meeting. The tension in Sister Sho'nuff's questioning had not escaped Pinky who wanted no part in any immature love triangle. She decided to be as brief, yet cordial, as possible.

In the weeks that followed, Willie joined Believers Ministries, having enjoyed an easy camaraderie with Bishop and other male leaders. Sister Sho'nuff studied his routine of lingering in the rear west corner of the sanctuary before services where he talked with a few brothers he'd gotten to know and started positioning herself there, too. Always polite, Willie would shake her hand and smile.

"How are you this morning, sister?"

"I'm blessed and highly favored," she'd answer with her signature enthusiasm.

That was the extent of their relationship. No questions about her family or other interests. No inquiries as to her plans after service that day. Sister Sho'nuff, however, noticed Willie having lengthier conversations with Pinky after church. Occasionally,

Sister Madeline and Bishop joined the frivolity, and Sho'nuff could have sworn she overheard them talk of getting together for dinner some place about a month or so after Willie joined. All speculation ended the morning Sister Sho'nuff noticed Sister Pinky saving, not one seat, but two in her usual third row. Just as the praise team sounded their first selection, Willie strode down the center aisle until he reached Pinky's side.

It was Sister Towery who called Sister Ferris who tapped on the shoulder of Sister Daniels to spread the word that Pinky had stolen another woman's man like a heathen in heat. Several called Sister Sho'nuff for details, which she provided, including how God had brought her and Willie together at Parker's that day, how she'd invited him to church, and how a certain shine in his eyes assured her of his interest. Until, of course, Pinky launched a manhunt to make him her own, even going so far as to get Bishop and his wife in on it. Not that Pinky's tactics should have surprised anyone, Sister Sho'nuff would say, pointing out that Pinky, as old as she was, had never been married and used to shack up with the father of her two grown daughters.

Of course, smears of this nature worked themselves around to Pinky's ears. She wanted to defend her character, to tell people that Willie never intended to date Sister Sho'nuff. She wanted to call Sho'nuff and tell her where to go and how to get there. But every time she picked up the phone, her spirit forced her to put it back down. Scriptures would come to mind like, *The battle is the Lord's*. Pinky knew she had to trust Him to win this fight. As much as she wanted to have her say, doing so would only prolong the matter. Her words would be twisted and used to damage the example God wanted her to set with other women in the church. She offered a brief explanation only to those who asked her directly, careful to avoid bad-talking Sister Sho-nuff. She did her best to smile and offer a brief "Hello" to Sister Sho'nuff when they passed in the church walkways.

Willie took a similar tack, especially after Bishop announced his engagement to Pinky. The couple held a private reception, but invited the entire church to the wedding ceremony. Sister Sho'nuff did attend, strutting through the sanctuary with her shoulders back and head held high, stopping briefly for chats with other members before the formalities began. She wanted to make the point that Pinky may have stolen her man, but she couldn't take away Sister Sho'nuff's joy—not back then, and certainly not now.

"Don't even say it," Bishop told Madeline after the church meeting. Not that his words were necessary. She had been right in cautioning him to move slowly with his plan, but he knew she wasn't the type to boast about it. They fastened their seat belts in silence. He started the car and drove out of the parking lot with the weight of a congregation on his mind.

"Why are Christians so tied to things in the house of God, rather than the purpose of the house? Are we in this thing to please God, to please man, or to please ourselves?"

Technically it was a question, but Madeline knew better. He didn't want her to respond. He just wanted her presence there so he wouldn't feel strange talking to himself.

"We have such good things going on in our church. Our choir is on a higher level of worship these days with Dina, our new worship leader. Attendance is steadily rising. Members are being healed. People are weathering the recession and still able to pay their bills. God is good, I tell you.

"Despite all that, I can't believe grown folks would make such a fuss about switching seats." Bishop glanced at his wife while waiting at a red light. "I know, I know. You and Pinky tried to tell me, but I didn't listen. I guess I should've been more sensitive to the potential backlash and eased in the new approach. Once I introduced it, though, I couldn't back down after some of the leaders defied me in front of everyone. They were way out of order, and I couldn't give in."

Madeline's cell phone rang, and she answered it.

"Yes, Pinky, he's talking about it now," she said, then paused to listen. "I was just thinking the same thing. I'll take the leaders and staff with last names from A to M and you take the rest. What was that Scripture again? Okay, I'll tell him."

"What are you and Pinky cooking up now?" Bishop asked, keeping his eyes on the road.

"We're going to call the women leaders in the church and talk to them about the new mandate. We'll explain to them that this is not only a good idea but a God idea. The fact that so many people got angry is proof that it's needed. We need to shake up the church, and something as simple as changing seats will get things started."

"Amen!" Bishop said with a chuckle. "You and Sister Pinky should've handled the whole thing huh?"

"I just remembered that Sister Sho'nuff's last name is Cornelious and I have to call her, which is best since everybody knows she can't stand Pinky. She's probably finding a way to blame Pinky for everything that went on tonight, and this would only cause more dissension. When the Lord conceived her in His mind, it must have taken awhile because that woman is a piece of work."

Bishop stopped the car in their driveway and turned off the ignition. He closed his eyes and shook his head. "I'll have to pray hard tonight to keep loving her."

Madeline smiled, then handed her husband the note she'd just written down. "By the way, Pinky suggested you look at that verse in the Song of Solomon when you have time."

Madeline opened her Bible, knowing she'd have to be prepared before dialing Sho'nuff's number. She had prayed before making each of the phone calls to church leaders about not saving seats, and most received what she had to say. Sister Moore even apologized for her outburst and said she not only planned to sit elsewhere on Sunday, but she would make a special effort to greet new faces and encourage them to come to Sunday school.

"This was not just about seats, it's about obedience and breaking out of our comfort zones," Madeline said during each call. "If we're not willing to sit beside our brothers and sisters *inside* the church, how can we reach out to people *outside* the church and win souls for Christ?"

Nearly everyone had agreed and committed to the new cause, but Madeline saved Sister Sho'nuff for last.

She had been a member of the church more than two decades, before Glenn Everett took over the pastorate and renamed it Believers Ministries. A stickler for tradition, she raised a big fuss when Sister Pinky suggested ladies wear whatever they wanted to the annual Women's Day breakfast, instead of deeming white the official color. She always wore suits and matching hats with plenty of glitter and sometimes a feather or two. Months, perhaps even years, would pass before new members found out Sho'nuff's real name: Lois. The nickname had become her trademark, mostly at her own promotion. She liked introducing herself to newcomers: "Just call me Sister Sho'nuff," she'd say, and then repeat it when people looked confused. "If you keep coming to church," she told them, "you'll understand why."

And, sure enough, Sho'nuff would yell out her refrain at least twice during the sermon, no matter who preached that day. "Sho'nuff, Preacher!" she'd say as the speaker made a critical point in the message. At times, she took a matching scarf from her purse and waved it, adding emphasis to her exclamations.

Some enjoyed her lively presence, especially visiting ministers who welcomed the encouragement. Others tried hard to excuse the theatrics, reminding themselves of Cletus's death and that Sho'nuff had been sickly often since he passed away. Her daughter lived in New York and rarely visited. In the years since the gossip died about Willie, Madeline and Pinky had actually joined together to pray for Sho'nuff, asking God to bless her and to bring the companionship that her heart desired. With someone in her life, they figured, Sister Sho'nuff might be less troublesome and not try to attract so much attention. So far, their prayers hadn't worked.

"I was waiting on your call," Sho'nuff said. "Sister Towery called awhile ago and told me that you and Sister Pinky divided a list of church leaders. I'm not surprised that Pinky got Towery to agree with this new rule of yours—she's a slick one. I can tell you right now, though, it won't be so easy to convince me."

"I'm not trying to convince you," Madeline said, "that's the Holy Spirit's job. I've called to give you a better understanding of why my husband asked us to change seats. And to answer any questions you might have."

Madeline went straight into the talk she had given the other women then waited for a response.

"You say this would be good for the church," Sister Sho'nuff said, "but are you sure this idea didn't come from a certain person who has a certain agenda and wants to control the church?"

Madeline had a feeling that Sho'nuff was referring to Pinky, but refused to entertain the subject. "This was Bishop's idea and it came straight from God. The Lord wants to change some things and some people in our church. When we all come together on small things inside the church, we can really do powerful work in the community around us."

"Well, that *sounds* good," Sister Sho'nuff said.

Madeline could tell that the wall around Sho'nuff required a force stronger than Madeline to be torn down. "That's all I wanted to talk with you about," Madeline said, ending the conversation. "Will I see you on Sunday?"

"I've been a member of that church for twenty-nine years, before it was even called Believers Ministries, before it was a thought in your or Bishop Everett's mind, and I sure don't plan to leave now. Will you see me Sunday? If the good Lord sees fit to let me see the sun shine that day, then yes you will. Absolutely."

Bishop Everett's eyes swept over the congregation, a broad smile on his face. The atmosphere had transformed from a few nights before. The same people who rejected him now approached him before Sunday service, some with spoken apologies, others with hugs of support. A few giggled as they looked for new seats and relinquished the spots they had deemed to be their own thrones. Leaders introduced themselves to people they recognized as fellow members but hadn't bothered to get to know.

Bishop explained the purpose to the general congregation, many of whom hadn't attended the meeting. "Can we all agree to try this out and see what the Lord wants to happen here?"

Heads nodded in agreement.

"I believe this very small step is just a foretaste of how God will move us from our comfort zones in the year to come, of how He will break down invisible barriers that we create between ourselves and our Christian brothers and sisters, no matter their past or their race or how much money they have in their pockets. But we have a role," he continued. "Some things we have to change, despite a religious system that doesn't always like change."

Then, just as he opened his Bible to delve deeper into the Word, Bishop's gaze landed on the middle section, fourth row, seat closest to the center aisle. There sat Sister Sho'nuff, in the same spot that had been hers since anyone could remember. She grinned as their eyes met, and he offered a courtesy smile back before quickly returning his focus to the message. He asked the congregation to stand and read along with him from the Song of Solomon 2:15: "Take us the foxes," they read, "the little foxes, that spoil the vines."

THINK ABOUT IT

1. Sister Sho'nuff had been a prominent member of the church for decades, yet how does her behavior suggest she was still living in the pink?
2. Think of a time when you were forced to make a change in your routine. How did you respond? Looking back, what emotions—fear, desperation, excitement, etc.—were at the root of your reaction?
3. What are some benefits of maintaining church or family traditions? What are some of the disadvantages? How do you decide whether to hold on to a tradition or long-held belief or to introduce something new?
4. Is there a difference between a clique and a small circle of women who happen to be good friends and like to go places together, sit beside one another, and so forth? Why or why not?
5. Acts 10:34–35 (NIV) reads, *I now realize how true it is that God does not show favoritism but accepts men from every nation who fear him and do what is right.* What changes would occur at your church, home, or workplace if more people abided by this principle? What would happen if the no-saved-seat rule were instituted at your church, workplace, or family reunion?
6. Notice how Pinky responded to Sister Sho'nuff's gossip surrounding Pinky's relationship with Willie—she remained mostly silent. How do you tend to handle it when people talk about you? Do your actions tend to quell or prolong the problem?
7. What little foxes, or seemingly small issues, are eating away at the root of spiritual growth in your life?

ON TOP OF THE WORLD

CHANDRA LOOKED AROUND the crowded coffee shop to make sure no one in earshot listened to the conversation she was being drawn into. She hated talking about this, especially in public places, and frankly thought the stranger sitting across from her was rude for asking about something as personal as her religious beliefs.

"If you died today," he asked, "are you sure you would live eternally in heaven?"

"If I died today, I wouldn't care where I lived because I'd be dead," she answered with attitude.

None of his business anyway, whoever he was. He had walked over to her table and introduced himself as "Marcus," saying he just wanted to talk. Chandra saw no harm in it, not at first. With a tall slim build, light brown eyes, and a strong jawbone, he didn't look bad. He even seemed a little familiar. Chandra must've seen him in her favorite café at some point since moving from her hometown Tampa to Philadelphia fifteen years ago. She hadn't pegged him for an evangelist, especially not at Sacred Pot. Here the cove in back with a sofa and high-back chairs usually drew eclectics who drank espressos or chai tea with soy milk and who read books about ethnic cleansing in the Sudan, about finding their core energy, about the government's secret plan to keep the impoverished poor and to make the wealthy richer.

Somehow this Holy Roller had found the place and targeted Chandra to practice his technique in leading unbelievers to the Christian faith. She wondered what he would say if he found out she already knew the Bible verses he mentioned. Back in the day, she had memorized the same lines, hoping to force her beliefs on everybody else. Most times she failed, and the person walked away unchanged. She would feel good, though, like she had planted a seed of the Lord's truth, which is probably what this guy in front of her thought, too. In a way, she pitied him. What a poor, misguided man.

Chandra grew up around tent revivals that consumed her entire neighborhood, or that tried to anyway. During revival week, the women dressed up in skirts that hung to their ankles and walked the streets inviting sinners to meet the "Light of the World." If that didn't bring them in, the music would. The fast-paced rhythm and choir voices singing, "Jesus! Jesus! Jesus!" lifted high above the tent and seeped through the open windows and cracked door frames of houses nearby.

When she got old enough, Chandra went out fishing for converts, too. In the neighborhood, at the park, in the corner store. She talked about God so much at school that the boys called her "Chastity Chandra" behind her back. She never paid them any mind, though, fearing the wrath of her righteous Savior far more than the taunts of teenage heathens doomed to hell. The Bible clearly states that if you deny Jesus Christ on earth, He'll deny you in heaven—the very reason that Chandra proclaimed His glorious name from the rooftops rather than fall to the temptations of this world, be they the girl cliques in high school or the lanky boys on the basketball team. Their giggles and snickers only nudged her closer to the Word of God. Encouraging herself to stay on the narrow path, she mumbled Bible verses while passing circles of classmates in the hallway between classes: *Blessed is the man that walketh not in the counsel of the ungodly, nor standeth in the way of sinners, nor sitteth in the seat of the scornful.*

That was a long time ago. Back when her grandmother, rest her soul, was her filter to the world, when the height of disobedience equaled failing to clean up the kitchen or to do laundry. That was before she went off to college and saw God through more intellectual lenses. Before "religion" became a bad word and she began to describe herself as, not a Christian, but a "spiritual person."

Now, her inner light guided her. It set her on a moral path of dos and don'ts without the cloak of religiosity. It offered the freedom to do what felt good without the guilt of commandments. Like, just the night before meeting Marcus, when that light led her to a party in Philly's Center City area. A time to unwind, Chandra chilled with some friends passing a blunt and took a couple tokes. Between the wine and the weed, she dozed off on the couch, where she woke up that next morning. She looked herself over in the mirror and knew she needed one thing: a good cup of coffee.

Never mind that she looked a hot mess. No makeup. Her afro matted on one side of her head. The same clothes she wore the day before, only scented with smoke and stained with spilled gin and pineapple juice. Kebuti, a big man of well over six feet and nearly three hundred pounds, would understand. He wore shoulder-length dreadlocks pulled back in a ponytail. Ever since he opened Sacred Pot, Chandra had come in at least every other day, or night. He had even seen her in a tuxedo ball gown on the way to a swank Christmas party. His special brew had nursed her recovery from plenty a hangover, so when she arrived looking like she did, he simply started the machine for a double espresso.

"Excuse me, Miss," Marcus had said. "I was just sitting and

reading my paper when I noticed you walk in. Do you mind if I take a seat and share something with you? I promise I won't take up too much of your time."

How Chandra wished now that she had said no. Instead, she motioned for him to sit down and the evangelism began. He even took out a hand-sized Bible and turned to John 3:16. "For God so loved the world," he'd said.

"I know," Chandra told him, before smartly finishing the verse. ". . . that He gave His only begotten Son."

"Girl, listen to this: I'm sitting in Sacred Pot this morning, looking tore up from last night, right? And from out of nowhere this man comes up to me like I'm homeless or something and starts telling me, as he put it, 'about the love of Jesus.'"

Chandra said all this in the direction of her speakerphone, while looking in the mirror to apply a fresh coat of no-smudge lipstick, before taking a sip from her glass of white wine.

"You're kidding?" her friend Tenisha said on the other end. "You must've been a mess!"

"I was," she said with a chuckle, "but he still had no right to approach me like that. I listened to what he had to say and at the end of the conversation I quoted some Scriptures so he would know that I already know the Christian evangelism game. Then I told him I have a master's degree in business administration and my own PR consulting firm. I'm the face of some of the most respected names in Philly's social circles. Obviously, I don't need to be 'saved.'"

"Bravo, Chandra! These Christians always talk about God's love, yet they're the most judgmental people I ever met. I believe in karma and having good morals. But that's not enough for them. If you don't believe like they believe, then you need to be 'saved.' Saved from what? The successful life I'm already living?"

"Thank you!" Chandra said. "I used to be one of them, but if

I have anything to be thankful for, it's that I got out of that foolishness."

"Amen! Amen!"

They both laughed.

"Tenisha, you are too funny."

Changing the subject, Chandra asked if Tenisha would attend tonight's gathering at Blue Xavier, the premier jazz restaurant and club downtown. The event would launch a new business endeavor created by one of Chandra's clients and promised to be a swank affair.

"Not to mention that I made sure some extra fine and eligible men will be in attendance," Chandra said, hoping to lure her friend with man-bait.

"What are you doing scouting eligible men when you already have one?"

"Who? Kendrick? Girl, you know good and well he's just a quick fix when I need a tune-up—a friend with benefits, as they say. I'm still very much in the market for fineness."

Still, Tenisha declined, saying she had to finish up some work for the community forum radio program she hosted on Sunday mornings.

"Have a good time, and please be careful out there."

From the back of the police cruiser, Tenisha's last words echoed in Chandra's head like the scratched 45s she used to play on her grandmother's stereo: *Be careful out there. Be careful out there.*

She remembered how the time had raced by earlier that night and how she rushed to the garage of her condo complex. As emcee and event organizer, she could not be late, so Chandra slid into the driver's seat, started up her Avalon, and reached full speed on the highway. Just a few miles before her downtown exit, she changed lanes to pass a creeping SUV and make up some time. She didn't see the Elantra just ahead of her, though, not until her car scraped its rear, the force sending her into a tailspin and the Elantra crashing into a guardrail.

She got out with a small bruise on the head, likely from hitting the steering wheel, and ran over to the other car where two adults in front lay unconscious. The driver sprawled over the wheel, his chest pressing on the horn, which blared and added more chaos to the scene. In back, a baby strapped into his seat screamed and looked straight into Chandra's face as if pleading for rescue.

Paramedics seemed to arrive in seconds and shooed her away, followed by police officers who blocked off the road and beckoned her to the side. One driver, the one in the SUV that Chandra had tried to pass, stopped on the shoulder to give his version of the accident. Hysterical, Chandra tried to explain what happened, that the Elantra appeared from out of nowhere. One officer interrupted her halfway through her story.

"Ma'am, have you been drinking?"

Chandra recalled the glass of wine she sipped with dinner, then the others to relax while getting ready that evening. Was it two or three glasses, or maybe four?

"Drinking?" she said to the officer. "I'm not drunk, if that's what you're asking."

Two field tests said otherwise, and police escorted Chandra to the backseat of one of their cruisers. She asked that they retrieve her purse from the front seat of her car. The officer who did returned with a small plastic baggie of marijuana that he'd found on the passenger side floorboard. Probably fell out of the glove compartment on impact, he said, theorizing why it was lying in plain sight. Chandra remembered stuffing it there after the party the night before. Officers talked among themselves in the front seat and took notes for their report, while Chandra sat behind the Plexiglas intended to shield them from violent criminals.

"I should not be here," she thought as her lips began to tremble. "I should not be here."

News of Chandra Stedman's arrest circulated quickly through the city, even before her court appearance in front of a judge the next morning. Hundreds had expected her at the jazz club and when she never showed, her client and others who'd helped with the event went down their cell phone contact lists trying to find her. Chandra called Tenisha, who put up the bail money. By the time she got out, the story had played on the morning news flashing a haggard-looking jail mug. The driver of the Elantra reportedly lay in a hospital bed in critical condition. His wife was treated for a concussion and released.

Chandra didn't talk much in the car on the way home, and Tenisha decided it best to let her sit in silence. She really didn't know what to say anyway. Chandra took out her BlackBerry and noticed thirty-two missed calls and who knows how many text messages. Immediately, it rang again. She saw the number of a former client who was also an attorney and decided to answer the call.

"What are you hearing?" she asked.

"You know how people are," he told her. "They're saying all kinds of lies, stuff not even worth repeating. Those of us who know you know the truth. And I'm hoping I can get you out of this. So don't worry, okay?"

Chandra said okay, but more to ease her friend's mind than anything else. How could she not worry at the lowest point of her life? Drunk driving—which a blood alcohol test confirmed—drug possession, and a critical accident that she caused. The charges could send her to jail.

Tenisha sensed the depression, heard it in her friend's long sigh after ending the call with the lawyer.

"Chandra, you know that whatever happens, I've got your back," she said, keeping one hand on the wheel and extending the other to rest on her friend's shoulder. "I'll do all I can to help you."

"I appreciate that, but with all the trouble I've caused, it'll take a lot more than somebody having my back."

Chandra closed her eyes and tilted her head back onto the headrest. In her mind, she saw the accident victim and his wife lying in the front seat of their car. She thought about the baby in back. "Please," she said aloud, as if to no one in particular, "let that man survive."

Ever since he saw the news reports, Kebuti expected Chandra to stop by the café sooner or later, Sacred Pot being like her second home. She arrived three days after the arrest, comfortable in a pair of jeans and fitted V-neck T-shirt with fashionable flip-flops, a headband pulling back her Afro, light makeup and dangling hoop earrings. Kebuti wondered if she'd dressed down to avoid attracting attention but decided not to ask. He didn't want to burden her further with questions about what happened or what would happen as the case progressed, although he and half of the city's movers and shakers wondered as much. Instead, he fixed her a special chai tea with a twist, a secret ingredient. Chandra sat down in the cove and thumbed through a magazine, steering clear of the local newspapers.

For the past three days, she lay in bed crying, occasionally picking up the phone. She turned on her computer and logged into her Facebook account, only to find that people she had called friends revealed their true thoughts online. Some speculated that her PR firm was a front for rampant drug activity. Others said she'd been an alcoholic for years. Even her friend-boyfriend Kendrick claimed in a Facebook post to have begged Chandra to stop drinking. He had left several messages since the accident but Chandra hadn't returned his calls. Good thing she hadn't put much trust in him to begin with.

The only people she talked to were her lawyer, Tenisha, and the client whose launch party at Xavier Blue she'd ruined. Chandra promised a full refund and to bear any expenses that couldn't be recouped by rescheduling the event. He agreed, but decided to hire another firm to take it from here. He couldn't allow the controversy surrounding her name to overshadow his project. "I hope you understand," he told her. Chandra couldn't blame him, bracing for more clients to pull their business.

Good thing her grandmother hadn't lived to see or hear this. If she had, Mama Stedman would likely be on her knees right now in a closet, praying that God would "bring her back home"—the same prayer she had prayed when Chandra abandoned the faith in college. No telling what her father might be doing or where he was. Chandra had met him only once. He stopped by her grandmother's house during a short stint out of prison.

Something about a crisis makes you analyze every domino that led up to it. For three days, Chandra thought about what might have happened if her mother hadn't died after contracting AIDS. Where would she be if, at age four, she hadn't been turned over to Mama Stedman and her strict religious lifestyle? What if she hadn't seen her college classmates drinking, sniffing cocaine, and smoking weed for the first time at that house party a dozen years ago? What if she hadn't tried it herself? At home in bed, she never came up with the answers, only the questions.

Now at Sacred Pot, she didn't want to think about her past or anything else for that matter. Her critical thinking took a vacation, as she sipped her chai tea and flipped through magazine pictures. Marcus, however, had been coming in and out of the café hoping to see her since news broke of the accident and arrest. He walked slowly to her seat, careful not to startle Chandra from her focus on a magazine article.

"Excuse me, Miss Stedman. I don't know if you remember me from a few days ago, but we talked for a short time at one of the tables up front."

He extended his hand for a shake, but Chandra left it lingering. "Please, I'm really not in the mood to get saved today."

"Ha, that's funny," he said, "but I actually wanted to come

clean with you. The other day, after I realized you didn't recognize me, I should have told you that we've met before, years ago. We actually went to school together. Wilson High? Tampa, Florida?"

Stunned, Chandra scanned his body for a hint of recognition.

"Top Hat, is that you?"

"It sure is," he said, smiling. "Only now that I'm a grown man without my signature high-top fade, people call me by my real name: Marcus Windham."

He extended his arm again. "Will you shake my hand now?"

They shook hands, and Chandra invited him to have a seat in the chair next to hers.

They talked for a few minutes about how each wound up in Philly. Chandra had gotten a scholarship to Temple University. She felt pulled to get from under her grandmother's wing and see more of the world. Mama Stedman cried the day she stuffed her belongings into two mismatched suitcases, one with duct tape holding it together, and headed toward the bus station. She saw her granddaughter off.

"Don't you get out there and forget everything I taught you," she'd said just before Chandra's bus pulled into the station. "Don't you forget the God you serve."

And, in Chandra's view, she hadn't forgotten Him—or, rather, it. She just saw Him differently, after watching the other students get dressed up for parties and acting giddy after swigs of alcohol. They didn't fear doing or being whatever made them happy. How could she release her own free spirit?

An experiment: Persuaded by one of the roommates in her suite, Chandra bought a skirt that stopped midthigh, a big no-no in Mama Stedman's house where dresses, skirts, and shorts had to fall below the knee for modesty's sake. What would happen? Would men whistling or ogling as she walked by sully her reputation? Or worse, would some maniac see the skirt as an invitation to take advantage of her? That's the kind of thing Mama Stedman would say.

By the end of the day, nothing had happened at all. In fact, Chandra's skirt attracted so little attention that she took offense that no one noticed except her suitemates. There came no punishment either. No lightning. No rebuke from the heavens telling everyone that Chastity Chandra was a harlot. Even the good Lord seemed to go about His business as if it were a regular day.

"I started to see that most of what I talked about back home had nothing to do with the higher being whose energy stimulates this universe," she told Marcus, grateful now for any discussion that wasn't about the accident, even one about religion.

In a religious studies class, Chandra explained, she learned about different faiths and how they contradicted themselves, especially Christianity. "When it comes to the events of Jesus' life, the biblical Gospels all tell different versions, so how can any of it be right?"

Gradually, Chandra's perspective of right and wrong, of holy and unrighteousness, evolved. Nothing about life seemed black or white, only gray—not red or white, just pink.

"Now, I'm sorry, but I have to laugh when I see people like you, absolute heathens in high school, behaving like you're devout believers today," Chandra told Marcus. "Like you're so religious, you want to save me."

Marcus responded by telling Chandra the spiritual journey that led him and his wife to Philly where he worked as a school principal. After Wilson High, he got a basketball scholarship to the University of Florida where one night he got drunk at a fraternity party and headed to a coffee shop near campus for a cup of coffee.

"Which is one reason I could relate to your, shall we say, hangover the other morning," he told Chandra with a chuckle.

"But getting back to my story, a girl named Denise stood in line behind me and invited me to a church service. She attended a smaller college, also in Tallahassee, and said the Holy Spirit prompted her to tell me about a revival at her church. To tell you the truth, I didn't care about the revival; didn't care about the Lord.

I was young. I could already do whatever I wanted and felt like the world was mine, like I could be whoever I wanted to be. Only thing I cared about was getting to know Denise. She was fine, and I couldn't let a hangover make me pass that up," Marcus said, eliciting a laugh from Chandra.

Nothing happened at first, but so enchanted with Denise, Marcus went back to the revival again and again, clapping along with the choir music, pretending to listen to the preacher's dramatic speech. Then, on the third night, the atmosphere felt different, even though the music and the people were the same.

"I heard the pastor say that we can only find true peace when we each realize God's purpose for us because our lives are not our own," Marcus said and looked away from Chandra, as if in a calm daze. "Then that pastor recited a Bible verse: *The earth is the Lord's and the fullness thereof, the world and they that dwell therein.* And that touched me deeply, because I had heard it only once before."

Marcus looked back at Chandra. "Do you remember when?"

"When you heard that verse?" she asked, confused. "No, I have no idea."

"I heard it fifteen years ago, in the hallway at Wilson High. You see, there was this girl I used to tease a lot because she lived with her grandmother and wore long skirts, and ponytails, and no makeup, and who always talked about God. On this particular day, my boys and I were psyching ourselves up for the state finals that night, feeling confident because everybody favored the Wilson Wildcats to win. We were slapping each other's hands and, as team captain, I said something like, 'This is our game. This is our world!' to pump everybody up even more.

"That's when we saw that girl walking toward us, and we paused to look at her, probably hoping we'd come up with a new joke to crack about her. When she got closer, she smiled and wished us well in our game. Then she quoted Psalm 24:1 because she had heard what I said and she wanted to tell me that this universe belongs to God. ‘One day soon,’ she told me, ‘you’ll realize that.’”

Marcus observed the surprise in Chandra’s eyes and continued with his story.

“Well, we all laughed as she walked away holding her books tight against her chest. But that night, we lost in the biggest upset of the team’s history. As the buzzer sounded to end the game, I remembered what that girl had said, just like I remembered it a few years later in college. Only the second time, I listened.”

After hearing his story, Chandra vaguely remembered the scene he described. Top Hat and his crew had teased her so many times she couldn’t remember them specifically. She didn’t know how to respond, so Marcus took her silence as an invitation to keep talking.

“Chandra, when I saw you the other day, I saw the man that I used to be. I’m not talking about your achievements in life or your intellect. Anyone can see that you are a smart lady with a lot going for yourself. I’m talking about what I saw coming out of you from the inside. It was the same drive toward success mixed with this attitude that the ‘world is mine.’

“Then I heard about the accident later that night. I came back to this shop hoping to run into you. I wanted to tell you that God is still here for you.”

Chandra closed her eyes and covered her face with both hands. Marcus sensed the turmoil churning inside of her and anticipated the debate in her head.

“Don’t allow all these New Age ideas or intellectual arguments about the Bible to pull you away from your Savior. I guarantee you that for every point a scholar made to debunk the Scriptures, I can direct you to another scholar, equally smart, whose work will show you that the Word of God is true.”

From behind the counter, Kebuti saw Chandra slump and strode over to ask whether Marcus had upset her. Chandra assured him she would be okay and that Marcus should stay.

"Actually," she told Kebuti, "I need this."

Her words encouraged Marcus. Until now, he doubted that he would get through to her. He watched as Kebuti hesitantly walked away, then reached over and wrapped his hand around Chandra's.

"Why would God help me now?" she said, releasing sobs of regret. "I was so stupid to drink before I got in that car! What was I thinking?"

"That doesn't matter now. What matters is where you go from here. There will be consequences, but if you ask Jesus for forgiveness, He'll have mercy on you. His strength will help you through this."

Chandra put her head down. Above her sniffles, Marcus heard her whisper, "Oh Lord, please, please forgive me."

She was about to say something else when her BlackBerry signaled a new text message from her lawyer. She held it up and read the message aloud. "Good news! There's been a turnaround for the man in the car accident. Out of critical condition and doing well today! Doctors expect a full recovery."

Chandra looked at Marcus, almost in disbelief as the meaning of the text message sank in.

"Hallelujah," Marcus said quietly. "God is truly awesome."

THINK ABOUT IT

1. Chandra had grown up in the faith, but as an adult preferred to declare belief in a higher power. How might someone with those views be seen as living in the pink?
2. What is your view of God? Is He the God of the Bible whose Son, Jesus, died so that you could have eternal life, or is His identity vague, just a "higher being," for instance? Has your sense of who God is changed your life? Or has your life simply changed your view of God? Discuss the difference with others in your group.

3. In this story, Chandra had come from a very strict religious upbringing. What are the pros and cons to this method of child rearing? Why do you think Chandra rebelled and turned from God after high school?
4. Chandra thought that her efforts of evangelism were unfruitful, only to find out that her words had touched Marcus in a special way. Think of an experience where someone's simple words or action positively affected your life for years to come.
5. Proverbs 22:6 (NIV) reads: *Train a child in the way he should go, and when he is old he will not turn from it.* What does this verse mean to you? Why do you think so many children go their own way and refuse to follow their parents' faith?
6. Talk about a time or situation in your life where you lost sight of God's purpose for you and, instead, were only concerned with your idea of success or pleasure. What were the consequences?
7. Are you a "secret agent" Christian who believes that your faith is a private matter that should not be discussed openly with others? Meditate on Matthew 10:33 (NIV): *But whoever disowns me before men, I will disown him before my Father in heaven.*

HOMECOMING

JOY HAD GAINED seventy-five pounds since the divorce. Seventy. Five. Pounds.

It crept up on her, the way weight tends to do when you're a connoisseur of stretchy knit fabrics with elastic waistbands. The magnitude of going from a medium to an extra-large hadn't hit her till recently, and this wasn't exactly the best time to arrive at such a revelation.

She hadn't returned to Believers Ministries, or the state of Florida for that matter, since she and Brent parted ways. At that church's altar they vowed to stay together until death, through sickness and in health. They promised to give themselves only to one another, an oath that seemed like a given at the time. But the strength of their love weakened with the pull of another woman, and the marriage lasted just shy of two years, not even as long as the courtship before it.

Joy had grown suspicious well before the moment of reckoning. Who wouldn't? The man had started taking his cell phone into the bathroom with him, then reappearing with a work emergency that required leaving the house for hours. The Bible says what's done in the dark will one day come to light—or something like that—and it's especially true if you get in your car and secretly trail your man across town, like Joy did.

She didn't like to reflect on that time in her life. It was easier to think about Entenmann's doughnuts and pepperoni and mushroom pizzas with marinara dipping sauce for the crust, about pints of chocolate ice cream with bananas and hot caramel on top, or plates of linguine and bread sticks, fried chicken, macaroni and cheese, green beans, and corn bread.

Now the days of shopping the racks for a size 12 evolved to scouring the limited plus-size section for a size 22, which is why she started avoiding the malls in Charlotte, North Carolina, altogether. QVC and Home Shopping Network were a blessing with their mail-order fashions—the dark-colored jogging suits and non-wrinkle polyester blend stretchable slacks.

With all that said, though, Joy could not miss the wedding.

Her cousin Rebekah was getting married, and the girl had gotten saved, too, a miracle in itself. She even planned the ceremony inside the Tampa church where she grew up and where her mother had been a fixture before she died.

Joy and Rebekah hadn't seen each other in a while, although they behaved more like sisters than cousins back in the day. Their bond loosened in high school when Rebekah chose the more alternative crowd and Joy took the church route, staying involved in the teen ministry and keeping up her grades in school. The phone call that came several months back about Rebekah's fiancé and plans for a Christian wedding with all the fixings completely surprised Joy. Then, after an hour of recounting how she fell in love, Rebekah asked the question Joy had hoped she wouldn't: "Would you be my maid of honor?"

No way could Joy say no. This was, after all, her first cousin on her mother's side, the daughter of Joy's favorite aunt Lizelle, who'd been resting in peace for three years by now.

"I would be honored," Joy had said, despite feeling anything but.

Five years earlier, those words would have been true. Today, being in that wedding meant overcoming emotions that Joy had tried to elude. She would have to go back to the place where her marriage fell apart and face all those people who knew the embarrassing details. They would take one look at the sacks of fat hanging from what used to be triceps and gasp. And she wouldn't blame them either.

Joy stared out of the plane window, as the pilot announced their descent to Tampa International Airport. She put the last of a family-size pack of cherry Twizzlers in her mouth. "Why, Lord?" she mumbled. "Why me?"

Long before the plane landed, the dress had already given away Joy's secret. She'd told Rebekah the strapless bronze number for the bridesmaids wouldn't work for her, which Rebekah relayed to Pinky's daughter Brianna who coordinated the wedding. They searched the wedding catalogues for something comparable with sleeves, figuring that the maid of honor could wear a slightly different dress. But every time they phoned Joy and asked her to try on alternatives at various chain boutiques, they got a message days later that those dresses hadn't looked good on her either.

Finally, they decided to have her dress made. Everybody knew that Madeline Everett could work a sewing machine as good as any high-priced designer, and they weren't just saying that because she was the bishop's wife. As a tribute to Rebekah's late mother, Madeline had insisted on doing the job for free. Madeline, in fact, got so excited that she scoured the fabric stores for special material even before finalizing the details with Joy.

Then Joy called with her measurements.

"That can't be right! Did you go to a professional seamstress like I told you? Baby, with that many inches you'd be double the

Joy I remember. I'd have to go out and get more material." On and on she went, laughing at her own jokes, until she realized Joy hadn't said a word.

"You still there?"

"Yes, ma'am."

"Did you hear what I said? You should go to another—"

"Sister Everett, the measurements are correct. I . . . I've put on a lot of weight since I moved away."

"Oh?"

"I should have said something earlier. I'm trying to lose a few pounds before the wedding, but I haven't lost as much as I had hoped. I'll be happy to pay you for any extra material you need."

"Girl, don't be silly! I was just flapping my gums. I didn't mean a word of it," Madeline said, realizing she had hurt Joy's feelings. "Please forgive me. I know how those pounds can sneak up on you. Looking at me today, you probably wouldn't believe that I was a size 6 when Glenn and I got married, so don't you even think about that another minute 'cause you are going to look so beautiful in this dress that Rebekah might get jealous."

Joy managed a brief courtesy laugh before saying good-bye and hanging up the phone.

Madeline later told Pinky about the conversation, only verifying what Pinky had already figured out with each rejected gown along the way. After what Joy had been through with that ex-husband of hers, who could blame her for eating to numb the pain? Food was as good a vice as shopping or overwork or lazily watching TV.

Pinky remembered how happy Joy and Brent seemed at first. They would come to church hand in hand. He wrapped his arm around her shoulders during the sermon. She rested her palm on his thigh. It didn't take much for Pinky to notice his roving eye, though. Joy would have her eyes closed, her hands clapping or exalted in worship as the choir sang. Brent would have his eyes open and focused like lasers on the buttocks of the nearest woman in a fitted dress, jiggling to the music.

At some point, a pretty young thing who fancied expensive two-piece suits and several shades of gold-toned high-heeled sandals started attending Believers Ministries. Pinky watched as Brent's eyes stopped on her, in particular, Sunday after Sunday. After service, while Joy fellowshipped with friends, he would go to that girl and ask if she felt comfortable at the church or if she had any questions, like he had formed his own little welcoming committee. They'd be smiling at each other when Pinky just happened to walk by and interrupt. Then one Sunday he didn't look at her at all, didn't even turn his head her way. They didn't wave or stop to chat after church. And that's when Pinky knew they had something going. It was like her elders used to say: "As long as a dog is sniffing tail, he's just trying to get what he wants. But when he stops sniffing, he already done had the real thing."

Pinky was still figuring out what to do when Lizelle called a few days later, explaining that Joy had followed Brent to some woman's place. He'd told her he had to leave work and go straight to the airport for a business trip, but he drove instead to a little town house. He carried an overnight bag to the door then took a key out of his own pocket to let himself in. Joy watched in disbelief for a moment, then marched to that door and banged on it nonstop, screaming Brent's name so loudly that the neighbors opened their curtains to watch the drama unfold. Not a sound came from inside. "I know you're not pretending like no one's home when I just saw your no-good tail walk in there!"

When Joy started tapping on windows, someone called the police. They escorted her to a cruiser, giving her time to calm down, and persuaded her to go home. Alone that night, she called Brent's cell phone and left the longest message she could before his service cut her off. She listed everything she had done to support him while he went to school for his master's degree in business administration. After this, she could never trust him again.

He came home three days later. His story: He stopped at the town house to pick up a coworker for the business trip, he said, and they hurriedly left out the back door. When Joy knocked, they must've already been gone. His coworker's girlfriend thought she was a crazy woman and called the police. The business seminar took place in the mountains of New Mexico, and he had no idea that his cell phone wouldn't get reception there. He and his coworker couldn't make calls or even get their messages until they arrived back in Tampa.

"You've been gone for three days and that's the best lie you could come up with?" Joy had asked.

"That's the truth, and if you can't trust me," he'd told her, "I guess we don't have much of a marriage anyway."

"Well, your truth doesn't match what I found out at the property appraiser's office," Joy replied, relishing the dumbfounded look on his face. "The town house at 108 Summer Harbour Circle is owned by one Miss Maxine Short, that little high-yellow trollop you've been grinning at after church."

Willie, standing at the doors to the church, saw Joy first that Sunday. She got out of her car wearing loose-fitting sweatpants, a gray T-shirt, and gym shoes like she planned to hit the gym any minute. Believers Ministries had no formal dress code and people were encouraged to "come as you are." Even so, the getup didn't fit Joy's typical conservative style, especially not for a Sunday service.

"Everything all right?" he'd asked as Joy whisked by, stirring the air enough to cause a slight breeze in her wake.

"No," she said, not bothering to look him in the eye, "but it will be."

Having gotten the word from Lizelle the day before, Pinky figured some mess would follow when Joy busted through the sanctuary's double doors. She cut short her conversation with another member and tried to make her way to the other side of the church without drawing too much attention. Good thing Maxine hadn't arrived yet because Pinky's slow gait lagged way behind Joy, who had already made it to the area where her husband's mistress usually sat. By then, the entire church was already standing and singing along to the praise music and most didn't even turn to notice the determined look on Joy's face. Only a few less caught up with the spirit of things gave pause.

"What in the world?" someone mumbled.

Not that it mattered much to Joy what any of them thought at this point. When you've lost everything, or at least feel like you have, a few startled expressions and a little gossip don't mean a thing. More importantly, the heifer was nowhere to be found. Joy stalked down the center aisle of the church heading back toward the lobby when Pinky positioned herself at the door, arms crossed, like a Rock of Gibraltar.

"Where you think you going?"

"Pinky, with all due respect, I don't have time for hugs and Bible verses and stories about red, white, and pink. Besides I know that you already know what's going on, so ain't no sense in acting like you don't. All I want right now is to set a few things straight."

Joy hadn't stifled her volume, so just about everyone on the back two rows of the church turned and observed the commotion. To avoid interrupting service any further, Pinky stepped aside and followed Joy out the door, only to come face-to-face with Maxine who had just arrived.

"Just the 'lady' I was looking for," Joy announced sarcastically.

"Jooooy," Pinky said, in a tone that attempted to soothe and warn her all at the same time.

By now Lizelle had heard of the inevitable scuffle and maneuvered her wheelchair to the lobby. Willie and a couple other deacons stood at the ready to handle whatever went down. Each one of them might as well have been invisible to Joy who didn't even hear their pleas to end the standoff.

Startled at first, Maxine quickly straightened her back in preparation for a woman-to-woman bout. After Brent told her about Joy's research at the property appraiser's office, Maxine initially planned to leave the church, just as Brent had. Then she thought better of the decision. Why should she leave? That marriage deteriorated long before she came along, Maxine figured, so she hadn't done anything wrong. Joy managed to drive her husband away all by herself, constantly fussing about money and complaining that he needed to do more around the house. Brent also had told Maxine how Joy would come to bed wearing raggedy cotton pajama bottoms, an old T-shirt, and an Aunt Jemima-looking scarf tied around her hair to keep that flat, dull bob hairstyle in place. He'd told of her refusal to do all it took to please her man. From what Maxine could tell, Brent had no choice but to seek the affections of another woman who would love him right.

No, Maxine determined, she had nothing to be ashamed of and at the last minute that Sunday, she slipped on a teal dress with her sparkly gold peep-toe pumps and went to praise her Lord. Seeing the way Joy looked now gave Maxine all the more confidence in Brent's decision to seek satisfaction elsewhere. She mimicked Joy's hand-on-hip stance and gave her the once-over, beginning at the scuffed toe of her gym shoes and inching up till she stared directly into Joy's face.

"Oh, yes?" Maxine said, conveying the coolness of a true diva.

Just as Joy raised her right hand to slap the shimmery blush off Maxine's left cheek, she felt Pinky's grip around her wrist, then the gentle pull of Willie's hands on her shoulders, nudging her backward.

"Stop it! Stop it," Pinky said, muffling her anger to avoid disrupting churchgoers still worshiping on the other side of the door. "Since y'all obviously have no respect for yourselves, you can go ahead and fight or whatever you want to do, but you'll have to leave here. As long as I'm in this place, I won't let you disrespect God's house."

That's when Joy's chest started heaving like a track star after the fifty-yard dash. She bent over to catch her breath then started wailing. Not with tears in gentle streams like those spurned wives in the movies, but gushing from an inner reservoir where happy endings drown.

Pinky grabbed her around the waist and tried coaxing her to the door, but Joy fell as if the emotions had sapped the energy clean out of her. She curled up in the middle of the lobby floor and a handful of people from inside the sanctuary gathered to watch. Maxine stood back with her hand on her chest to distance herself from the scene, then gradually slipped out of the door. Willie finally got a hold of one of Joy's arms, while an assistant pastor grabbed the other. They pulled her to her feet and led her to the parking lot and sat her in Willie's car. Pinky grabbed her own purse and belongings to take Joy home. With her keys in the ignition, she turned to look at Joy sprawled across the backseat, her face in her hands, still sobbing like she'd never stop, and Pinky silently prayed that she would never again have to see a sight so pitiful.

Just days after the breakdown, Joy packed her things for a new start in North Carolina where she had family on her father's side. She refused to talk to anyone, including her aunt and Pinky who called and knocked on her door about every other day for a week.

Maxine became an outcast at Believers Ministries after word spread about the affair and the confrontation that followed. Lizelle, for one, relished the thought of Maxine's skin burning eternally in a fiery hell, but Pinky secretly looked up Maxine's number in the church directory after Joy left Tampa. She called, not to berate her, but to invite her to a singles ministry event at one of the branch churches. Maxine had sinned and caused a lot of pain, but Jesus could redeem even her. She talked with Maxine about her future, about being real with God—about leaving Brent.

In time, Maxine was singing high soprano in the choir at

Believers Community Church, just across town. She even wrote Joy a letter asking for forgiveness. It came back marked "return to sender," though. She understood—you sneak around sleeping with a woman's husband, you can't expect too much. Joy didn't return Pinky's calls either. The last time Pinky tried, Joy's cell number was no longer in service.

The divorce took just a few months. Joy and Brent didn't own a house and didn't have any children, so the deal amounted to him taking his stuff and Joy taking hers. Breaking the emotional ties, however, with Brent—and Maxine—would take much longer. Even five years later, Joy stepped into the airport terminal knowing that she hadn't healed totally.

She looked around for Pinky and Brianna, who actually recognized her first and hurried over. Other than the extra weight, she hadn't changed much. Still the same smooth walnut-colored skin, with eyes the shape and color of almonds.

"Joy, it's so good to see you!" Brianna yelled. Pinky said the same, before wrapping her in a tight hug, the kind that included rocking back and forth awhile.

Joy needed the instant acceptance to relieve her anxiety. Her lips curled into a smile as she walked through the airport and later observed the city landscape during the drive to Madeline's place. Construction barriers lined the sides of Interstate 275, the major highway through Tampa, and Joy commented on how different everything looked.

"A lot can change in five years, child," Pinky said.

Remembering the typical double meanings behind Pinky's words, Joy didn't know how to respond. "It's just a week before the big day," she said, trying to divert whatever deep conversation Pinky might have had in mind. "How's my Rebekah doing?"

"Wonderfully," Pinky said. "She is ready for marriage, and I am so glad. They used to be 'just friends,' you know, but I knew right away that he had a little something more in mind. He's a good man."

"Aren't they all," Joy said, "at least in the beginning?"

"Every now and then you'll find one who's good in the end, too," Pinky said. Then, "So when was the last time you heard from Brent?"

Brianna, still amazed by her mother's straightforwardness after all these years, looked sideways at Pinky, who kept her gaze on the road, glancing for just a moment into the rearview mirror to see Joy uncomfortably adjusting in the backseat.

"Sorry, darling, would you rather not talk about him? You know me. I just thought we might as well get that topic out of the way instead of tiptoeing around the man's name for the rest of your visit."

"No, no, it's fine," Joy said, trying to sound as mellow as possible. "I haven't heard from him since finalizing the divorce."

"Well, last I heard he was living in an apartment in Kissimmee, about two hours away from here. It just so happens that the church he goes to there is the same church where Sister Moore's ex-husband's cousin is a trustee. From what she says, Brent is engaged to the pastor's daughter."

"Oh, really?" Joy said, activating the high pitch in her voice so she could sound surprised yet unfazed, the truth being that she was neither.

Ever since the split, she periodically Googled Brent's name and recently came across an online engagement page for him and the new fiancée, which led her to the fiancée's Facebook page where Joy kept up on the latest news in their wedding plans, their friends, and their weekend jaunts. Not long ago, the happy couple spent a few days in the Florida Keys where Phoebe—that's the fiancée's name—went snorkeling for the first time. But Joy, who had looked at every picture posted on Facebook, remained unimpressed. Phoebe seemed way too thin for one thing. She got a point for her long, naturally wavy hair—or was that a weave?—but lost ground for that hook nose. The results were in and, bottom line, she did *not* look nearly as good as Joy used to, so amen and a Twinkie to that.

"May God help her," Joy responded to Pinky, "whoever she is."

With all the care that Madeline poured into making Joy's dress, it could've been for the bride. "I've got to make sure everything is perfect," she'd told Pinky. "Joy's had a rough time. I want her to feel special."

She'd bought the most beautiful taffeta material in a brushed bronze hue that perfectly matched the bridesmaids' gowns. Then she made a straight floor-length dress, with a mermaid bottom that flared at the knees. It was sleeveless, like the other dresses, but the material stretched to the edge of the shoulders to offer more support up top. Since Joy didn't feel comfortable with her upper arms exposed, Madeline made a short shawl-like jacket using complementary material sprinkled with tiny rhinestones. The jacket closed in front with a rhinestone and pearl broach that echoed the accents in Rebekah's wedding gown. The perfect bronze shoes, dotted with rhinestones, came from a small boutique. Nothing but the Lord's grace led the saleswoman to find the last pair of 8 ½s in stock.

Madeline and Rebekah waited eagerly for Joy's arrival. Madeline had already prepared her signature beef and vegetable pasta with country rolls and sweet iced tea for lunch. They were nailing down arrangements to pick up the two bridesmaids and the groomsmen at the airport when Pinky walked through the door first, then came Brianna. Then Joy.

Rebekah was so happy at the sight of her cousin. "I can't believe you're here!"

Joy couldn't contain herself either. They wrapped arms around each other.

"The last time I saw you, we were at Mama's funeral," Rebekah said, getting choked up at the thought.

"I know," Joy said. She stepped back, as if to survey the bride-to-be: "You look great."

"You, too."

Joy shook her head as she patted her hips. "The economy may be bad, but I haven't missed too many meals."

"Girl, please, you still look wonderful."

"That's what I say," Madeline chimed in. "Now, we've got to get down to business. Before we eat or do anything else, you've got to try on this dress," she said, proudly holding it up for all to see.

Joy gasped. "Oh my goodness, Sister Everett, that is beautiful!"

"Baby, I made every stitch with you in mind."

Joy took it to the bedroom, praying that she could fit it. Why had she eaten a whole bag of licorice on the plane? About ten minutes later, she walked into the living room and Sister Everett examined the fit, which was almost perfect, with just a slight bulge of material in the midsection. "No problem. I can take about a half inch off each side tonight," she said, sticking pins in the dress to mark the spot.

Joy pranced around like a top model as the others egged her on.

"Oooh, girl, you know you're looking good!"

"Watch out, Tyra Banks!"

Joy caught her reflection in the hallway mirror and decided she did look nice, indeed. "You know what they call this back in North Carolina?" she asked, running her hands along her silhouette. "Big Sexy!"

The women erupted with laughter.

The next week went by so fast that Joy couldn't remember it all. So many details for the wedding, so many old friends to talk to. She thought seeing everyone would be awkward, but the people she cared about most showed her love. She also had a chance to visit her mother, who had left Believers Ministries years ago and settled into one of the branch congregations. Seeing her mother's excitement made Joy realize how hurtful her absence had been. Before going to sleep one night, she thanked God for showing her how much she needed to reconnect with her family and friends back home.

She also thanked Him for not putting Maxine in her path all week. Mama had told her that Maxine attended another branch church now. Joy had received the letter from Maxine soon after the divorce, but wouldn't give her the satisfaction of opening it. Only lately had she been even slightly curious to know what it had said.

On the morning of the wedding, Joy put on her dress and noticed it was a bit loose. She'd been so busy that she wasn't eating nearly as much. For the first time in years, she hadn't thought about Brent in at least forty-eight hours. She hadn't even hoped that he would someday regret his choices and realize what a good woman he lost.

"Hello?" Brianna said, waving her hand in front of Joy's eyes. "I don't know what you are thinking about, but whatever it is, put it on the back burner, please. You need to be in position. You're up next."

Joy stood in the doorway that led to the sanctuary, as dozens filled pews on each side. A woman onstage crooned a love song, and Brianna stood to the side in the lobby area, where she gave the signal.

Slowly, confidently, Joy took her first step down the aisle for all to see.

THINK ABOUT IT

1. How is Joy living in the pink?
2. After five years, Joy is still healing from the pain of divorce and her husband's infidelity. Are you divorced? Did you endure the pain of an unfaithful husband? Share your experience in working through the ordeal.
3. A friend has just confided in you that her husband or significant other has been unfaithful. How might you respond to comfort her, rather than further anger or agitate her raw emotions?
4. Other than food, what vices do women use to overcome pain or disappointment? Do you have a vice? What is it?
5. Madeline Everett was ashamed of her hurtful response to Joy's measurements. In what ways have you contributed, intentionally or unintentionally, to society's tendency to mock or disregard full-figured women?
6. Many full-figured women are learning to embrace and love their curves. No matter our size, we are each valuable in God's eyes and made for a purpose. Share some uplifting Scriptures about the beauty that the Creator sees in us all. (For instance, *I praise you because I am fearfully and wonderfully made, your works are wonderful, I know that full well.*—Psalm 139:14 NIV)
7. What things have you done after a breakup to keep up with your ex, such as constantly Googling your ex, as Joy did? How does this behavior hinder the healing process?

MIRANDA'S BIRTHDAY PARTY

Dear Daddy,

I'm reely glad that you are my daddy. You are a good daddy and a lot of my frends don't have a daddy, espeshaly one as nice as you! I wish we could still go places together like we used to becuz I miss you. I hope you don't ever go away forever! And I want to invit you to my birthday party. I will finally be 8 years old! It will be a lot of fun, games and chocolat cupcakes.

I LUV YOU!
Your Pumpkin ☺

MIRANDA HOPED her father would like her letter. She had worked on it all afternoon, using pink construction paper and colored pencils to decorate the border with flowers, hearts, and smiley faces. She and her friend Krisha guessed that this would be the best way to get her father to pay attention. Give him an invitation like the grown-ups and people on TV do.

She had to do something. Daddy didn't stop by to see her like he used to, and on the few occasions that he did come over, he and Mommy would get into a fight. The last time had to be like two weeks ago. Miranda ran after him on the way out and asked if he would come over for her eighth birthday. He only said he would try, which didn't give her much hope.

They used to have so much fun together. He always called her "Pumpkin." He would pick her up and take her roller skating or swimming or just to his house to watch TV. She couldn't wait for his car to pull into the driveway in front of her grandmother's house where she and her mother live. She remembered the time he took her to the county fair, and they rode the big spider ride that spun around and around, and they shared an elephant ear and she got her own cup of cherry flavored ice. By the end of the night, the dye had turned her mouth as red as a clown's. When she saw herself in a mirror at one of the game booths, she cracked up laughing, and he did, too.

Things changed, beginning the night he came to pick her up with a new woman in the car. He might have gotten away with it, if Miranda hadn't looked out the window.

"Daddy, who is that in your car?"

Before he could answer, her mother pulled back the curtain to see for herself.

"Please tell me you did not bring one of your little playthings over to my house and think I would let you leave with my daughter!"

"She's my daughter, too!"

"You have lost your mind if you think my baby is leaving with that woman."

"She's leaving with me—her father. And you don't even know Tina."

"I don't want to know Tina or whoever she is. I don't need to know her. My daughter deserves better—"

"Oh, here comes the drama."

The scene went on like this long after Miranda's grandmother called her upstairs. At some point, her father looked around to give her a hug and noticed she was gone. He called her downstairs and promised to pick her up the next day. He showed up, alone this time. Later, he introduced her to Miss Tina, his fiancée. Miranda liked her. She combed Miranda's hair and played Go Fish. She smiled a lot and cooked really gooey macadamia nut cookies.

Then she found out that Miss Tina wanted to take her father away and that he was dumb enough to let her. Plus, he wasn't paying nearly what he should in child support. Not that he ever had, but his checks looked even smaller once Tina came along. No doubt, he spent his money getting her hair done instead of buying his daughter's school clothes. And it was a good thing he and Miranda's mother had never gotten married because he proved himself to be good for absolutely nothing. Miranda learned all of this, of course, by overhearing her mother tell the story to Grandma and Auntie and to her other friends over the phone for the next two days.

During Sunday school that next weekend, Miranda's teacher told the class that they should love everybody, just like Christ did, which Miranda repeated when her mother and grandmother came from the adult class to pick her up.

"That's right," her mother had said, holding Miranda's left hand.

"We should love *everybody* because that's what Jesus did," said her grandmother, holding the other.

But if that were true, Miranda wondered, why didn't they love Daddy or Miss Tina?

Miranda guessed that Daddy might not know she still loved him, even though Mommy didn't. Now, her only chance to get him back would be tonight. She overheard Mommy talking to him on the phone the other day, telling him he'd better drop off some money for Miranda's school uniforms. Tonight was that night. Miranda planned to walk with him out to his car and slip him the letter—without her mother seeing, so she wouldn't get in trouble.

"Miranda!" she heard Mommy calling as footsteps ascended the staircase. She scrambled to hide the letter under her pillow then to round up her colored pencils and stuff them into her crayon box. Just then the door opened.

"Miranda Reneese Collins, what in the world have you been doing in here with all this mess sprawled on my floor?"

"Sorry, Mommy. I was just coloring."

"Your father is here and he wants to see you before he leaves, so go on downstairs. You can finish cleaning up later."

Miranda hoped her mother would walk ahead so that she could retrieve the letter under her pillow, but she stood right there holding the door open, watching and waiting for Miranda to go.

"Come on, little girl. We don't have all night."

Slowly, Miranda walked out of the room, leaving her note behind.

Miranda and Krisha sat on the swings at Spring Lake Park, down the street from Krisha's house.

"You didn't even give it to him?"

"Nope. If I took it from under my pillow, Mommy woulda asked what it was and wouldn't let me give it to him anyway."

"What you gonna do now?"

"I don't know," Miranda said, shrugging. "My party is this weekend and I know Mommy won't invite him. She hates him, especially now since he's with Miss Tina and he doesn't give her any money to help pay for me.

"Mommy says I cost a lot because I keep growing all the time. She's gotta buy me new shoes and jeans again this year because my old ones don't fit no more."

Miranda thought about just calling her father and asking him to buy her the doll she'd wanted on TV. That seemed more possible than getting him to spend time with her at the party. Then she remembered what Grandma said one night after reading Miranda a series of fairy tales: "Baby, don't you waste your wishes on anything you can hold in your hands because that'll get old and fade away after a while. No, if you take the time to hope," she said, "might as well hope for something that'll last, something you can't hold nowhere but in your heart."

From what Miranda could see now, wishes of the heart never came true.

Krisha's mother, Rosalyn, sipped on a bottle of iced tea while keeping watch over the girls from a park pavilion. Beside her sat Sister Pinky, who'd recently gotten her first pedicure as a Mother's Day gift from her daughter at the Nail Boutique where Rosalyn works. Pinky had tried to get to know Rosalyn as she decorated her big toe with baby rhinestones. She needed more time, though, and when you're working with single moms, you have to be flexible. Pinky had put on her Capri pants with matching shirt and canvas sneakers to spend Saturday morning in the park with Rosalyn and her daughter.

She could really do without the puffs from Rosalyn's cigarette swirling in her face, though. But if Christ could suffer on the cross, Pinky figured she could endure a little secondhand smoke in the name of not offending a woman while trying to show her God's love. At least that was her original plan. Yet, ever since they arrived Pinky felt more drawn to Miranda, sitting there on the swing with her head in her hands. She and Krisha hadn't done a bit of swinging or sliding all morning, and it didn't take much smarts to see that she carried a weight too big for a little girl.

"What's going on with your daughter's friend?" she asked Rosalyn.

"I'm not sure," she answered, looking over in the girls' direction. "She's a friend of Krisha's from school, but I don't know her mother that well. I just pick her up and drop her off. From what Krisha tells me, there's some kind of drama involving the girl's father and his girlfriend."

"Hmmm."

"Come to think of it, I'm pretty sure her mother goes to one of the Believers Ministries branches. The one on the west side of town —Promised Land, I believe. Renee Collins is the name."

Pinky thought for a moment, but the name didn't sound familiar. "I might know her face if I see her," Pinky said.

"A few months ago, Krisha came home asking me if the reason her father left us was because he got a new girlfriend. I couldn't help but laugh," Rosalyn said, before pausing to take another puff. "I said, baby, that's the reason they all leave!"

On a typical day, Pinky would have addressed that comment in depth, beginning with something like, "Why in the world would you tell your eight-year-old daughter something like that?" But today she commented only briefly. "Something tells me your situation involved a lot more than another woman, and you might want to hold off on explaining that to your daughter until she's old enough to understand."

That quenched the laughter in Rosalyn's throat and started her to thinking a bit. Pinky, feeling called to another mission, gave her a gentle pat on the thigh before getting up from the bench and walking past the water fountains and across the soccer field to the playground area. The girls stopped talking and started staring when they saw her coming.

"Hello, little ladies. I just came to find out why y'all would rather sit here talking and looking sad instead of playing in this big, nice playground."

Krisha giggled nervously and looked over at Miranda bigeyed. Miranda looked away and held her head down to avoid Pinky's stare.

"Well, is anybody going to say anything or do I have to pull it out of you?"

"Um, Miranda's got a problem," Krisha said, unable to contain herself any longer.

Miranda darted her eyes at Krisha. "You got a big mouth!"

Then she looked at Pinky and shook her head quickly from side to side. "No I don't, Miss Pinky. I don't have no problems."

"That should be, 'I don't have *any* problems,' young lady, and from what I can see it looks like you do, or at least you think you do. Whatever it is, it's something you need to tell a grown-up."

"But she don't wanna get in trouble," Krisha said.

"She won't get in trouble," Pinky said. She looked at Miranda. "I promise."

The girls traded looks of uncertainty back and forth, and Pinky could see this would take some prodding. She decided to eliminate the worst possibility then work her way up from there.

"Is someone doing something bad to you, honey, something you don't like?"

"Noooo," Miranda said, shaking her head.

"Well, what is it?"

"It's about her father," Krisha blurted, then kept talking as if someone busted the piñata where she stored secrets and they all came tumbling out. "He don't wanna have nothing to do with her since he got his new girlfriend and he won't give her mother child support and Miranda's tryin' to get him to come to her birthday party, so she wrote him a letter but she couldn't give it to him 'cause him and her mother hate each other and she didn't want her mother to see, so she left it under the pillow."

Whatever that child said, Pinky could tell this situation wouldn't require getting the law—a relief. Not that she would have backed down even if it had. As much as she loved helping women, she had no problem turning one of them in to save a child. In Pinky's world, childish innocence always outweighed grown-up foolishness.

Miranda jumped from her swing and stood right in Krisha's face with her arms crossed. "You get on my nerves! I'm never telling you anything, ever again."

Pinky grabbed Miranda by the arm and gently nudged her back to her seat on the swing. "Now, you sit down and stop that. Seems to me like you need somebody to tell what's going on because you can't handle it on your own."

Miranda's eyes watered and, after a few sniffles, she told Pinky about all the things she used to do with her father and how she rarely saw him anymore. She talked about her parents' relationship and what she heard her mother say about her father and Miss Tina. Then she told her about the letter.

Pinky listened for a good while, glad that Rosalyn had run into someone she knew, likely another client, and stayed over by the benches in what seemed to be a deep conversation. In Miranda's story, Pinky heard the pain of a child caught in the middle of her parents' issues.

"I'm tryin' to see what I can do to make Daddy love me again, as much as he loves Miss Tina."

Pinky had no idea how much of what she heard about Miranda's father was true; after all this was an eight-year-old who got her information from her angry mother. The situation warranted a most careful approach, especially since Pinky didn't know any of the adults involved and she had no idea how they'd feel about her intrusion. She would have to pray for guidance on what to do. In the meantime, she couldn't let this little girl leave as sad as she looked now.

"Sweetheart, I don't know your father, but from what you've told me he does love you very much. That's why he used to take you to all those places like the skating rink and the pool. You're his little girl and he cares."

"But my mommy said—"

Pinky put a finger to her lips to hush Miranda. She didn't want to be put in the position of contradicting the girl's mother. "It's time to listen, okay. Just hear what Miss Pinky has to say.

"I want you to know that the love your father has for you is much different than what he feels for Miss Tina. Don't ever try to compete with her, with any other adult, or with any other child who may come along. If he's a good daddy, he'll have way more than enough love for you regardless of who else comes into his life.

"Now, I would really like to see this letter you wrote to him one day," Pinky said, trying to think of a way she could meet up with Miranda again to see it. No need. Miranda unzipped her shiny red hip purse and pulled out a folded piece of pink construction paper.

"Here it is. I been carrying it in my purse so my mommy wouldn't find it."

"Ooooo! I have an idea," Krisha announced, raising her hand as if in class. "Miss Pinky, why don't you give the letter to Miranda's father?"

Pinky reached out for the letter without answering Krisha. She read it in silence. Miranda's eyes got big and she smiled at Krisha, hopeful for the first time all day.

Pinky paced the floor of her spare bedroom, walking back and forth praying aloud. Sometimes she liked to move around when she prayed—seemed like she could rouse the Spirit a little better that way. And the Spirit definitely needed some rousing today. Miranda's little story touched Pinky deeply, primarily because her own daughters barely had a relationship with their father. He and Pinky had split years ago and he kept up with them at first, but in time all they got were support checks, birthday cards, and a visit when he could manage a stop through town on one of his truck-driving routes. He was a hardworking man who seemed to do what he could, but his relationship with the girls suffered more after Pinky had to move two hundred miles away from Jacksonville to Tampa.

In the end, their daughters missed out on the blessing of a father's presence—that much Pinky knew from growing up with her own father. Some women complain that there are no good men, but Pinky knew better. Earl Holt strengthened his son and pampered his girls. Pinky and her sister Courtney would sit on their father's lap as he read or recited stories to them. They didn't have much money growing up in the country just outside of Jacksonville, so a day of fun might be as simple as going to the field out behind the house and playing tag or hide-and-seek.

Most people assumed Pinky got her nickname because of her last name, Pinkston. But she was Pinky long before she married Willie. When she was a little thing, she had developed a special liking for the color pink. At one point—she had to be about three or four years old, according to her parents' version of the story—she would yell and scream whenever her mother tried to dress her in anything besides a little pink shirt and skirt that her grandmother had made with a patch of leftover material. From then on, her father called her "my little Pinky." The Lord just added a little humor to things by sending a man named Willie Pinkston her way.

"Guide me in a way that helps this little girl, and ease the pain that's in her heart," she prayed at home later that day. "Father, I ask that You satisfy the longing for her daddy's love. Move in a special way in the life of her parents. Reveal to them their daughter's pain so that they can get over themselves and be the mother and the father that she needs right now."

After prayer, Pinky sat on her bed reading Miranda's letter over and over again. She had mentioned only a little of what the girls told her to Rosalyn, just enough to find out where Miranda lived. At first, she didn't know what to do with the information. Then God gave her the answer she needed.

Miranda's mother strained to see who would emerge from the unfamiliar sedan that pulled up out front. Soon a woman, likely in her fifties or sixties, walked up the driveway. Renee opened the kitchen door before Pinky could get there to knock.

"May I help you, ma'am?"

"If your name is Renee Collins, you might be able to."

Renee nodded, and Pinky introduced herself as a friend of Krisha's mother. It took only a few seconds before they each recognized the other from Pinky's occasional visits to Believers Promised Land where her daughter Jasmine and son-in-law were members. Getting to the matter at hand, Pinky explained that she had met Miranda a few days earlier at the park.

"She hasn't gotten home from school yet," Renee said, offering Pinky a seat at the kitchen table.

"I figured as much. I'd rather have this conversation without her here."

Just then Renee's mother ambled down the stairs and Pinky asked her to join them. Miranda's grandmother, she thought, could figure into the girl's blessing as much as anyone else. She offered Pinky a glass of lemonade after acknowledging that she had noticed Pinky at church, as well.

Pinky thanked her and took a sip to clear her throat, before turning to Renee.

"Ms. Collins, I'm sure you already know this, but I first want to tell you how beautiful, sweet, and smart I found your daughter to be. I know that you are proud of her and that you can't help but love her a great deal."

"Of course, I do," Renee said, growing anxious. "But what is all this about?"

"It's about the look I saw on your daughter's face. She had a worrisome spirit around her, not what you want to see with a little girl on a playground. The good thing is, this is something that can be corrected, but I'll need your help."

Pinky unclasped her purse and pulled out the letter to Miranda's father. She showed it to the women at the table and asked them to take a look. She observed Renee who rolled her eyes as she read over her daughter's colorful writing. Grandma, on the other hand, sighed heavily and shook her head. She spoke first.

"I knew Pumpkin felt bad about all the mess going on between you and R.J.," she said to Renee.

"That's not my fault," Renee snapped back. "If her father was any kind of a man, he would come to see his daughter and pay his support and stop being so concerned about all his women."

"Sometimes I think you're more worried about his women than anyone else," Grandma said. "Whenever he does try to spend time with Miranda, you start arguing with the man about his fiancée."

"Excuse me? I could care less about who's in his bed, but I can't let him bring any old body around my daughter. And I'm not letting that tramp come near my baby."

"But you don't even know the woman."

"So this is my fault?"

"I'm not saying it's your fault that he's not doing everything he should be doing, especially when it comes to catching up on his payments. I'm saying that part of the reason he done stopped picking up Miranda is because you start fussing and acting a fool every time he does."

The conversation volleyed back and forth between mother and daughter, and Pinky wondered if the two women remembered that she was still there. Her presence had apparently given Grandma the spark she needed to say what was already on her mind. Not that Renee was willing to hear it.

"So you want me to just let him come over here and do what he wants to do when he's not giving me nearly the money he's supposed to? After all he's done to me?"

"Renee, that's between you and R.J. For one, you need to get over whatever happened during that mess of a relationship y'all had. And if you think he's lying about the cutbacks on his job, take him to court. But you've got to stop putting Miranda in the middle of this by bad-mouthing the man in front of her and everybody else. Don't you see? This is tearing up her relationship with him. You may not care about that, but you've got to think about what it's doing to your daughter. Every little girl wants to feel a father's love."

Almost everybody in her fourth grade class showed up to Miranda's birthday party. Her aunt and her cousins came, too. And when Daddy walked through the door, she ran over to him and hugged his waist.

"Daddy, you came!"

"Of course, I did, Pumpkin," he said. He picked her up and gave her a kiss on the cheek.

Grandma thanked God he came alone, giving Renee no excuse to go off on him. A few hours after Pinky's visit, Grandma put Miranda's letter in an envelope and mailed it to R.J. He got it the next day, and she answered the phone when he called the house for details. He would surprise Miranda by coming to the party, but wanted to make sure he and Renee could be civil. With Grandma standing nearby, Renee agreed not to talk about child support or anything from the past, if he agreed not to bring along Miss Tina.

They decided that he would buy Miranda the Rollerblading Barbie she had talked about for weeks. Her eyes bulged when she opened his gift and saw the doll. She led him around by the hand, introducing him to her classmates.

She had the most fun when he led all the kids to the backyard and directed a game of kick ball. He even played, too, on her team of course. He kicked the ball far and made it around all the bases before anyone could retrieve it and tag him out.

It turned out to be Miranda's best birthday ever.

As the kids jogged back inside to cut the cake, Krisha walked alongside Miranda. "So, I guess that lady in the park musta gave your dad that letter, huh?"

"I don't know for sure, but she musta done something!"

Grandma stood back, overjoyed while watching Miranda skip around, her round face beaming and ponytail bouncing. She had invited Pinky to the party, but she declined. Her work in the Collins home was done, she'd said. She trusted Grandma to take it from here. And Renee and Grandma decided it best not to mention Pinky's visit to Miranda, so she wouldn't think she had done anything wrong.

At the party, Grandma positioned the chocolate fudge cake

near the edge of the table, so Miranda could reach it.

"Now, baby, don't forget to make a wish," she told her.

Miranda closed her eyes tight and thought for a moment about what would be the best thing she could wish for, something better than her new Barbie or even the bike her mother had bought. Finally, she opened her eyes and saw Grandma looking back at her. She would wish for something she could hold in her heart forever. She parted her lips and blew.

THINK ABOUT IT

1. How was Miranda's mother living in the pink? How did that pink lifestyle affect Miranda?
2. Discuss other ways that children suffer when their parents can't get along.
3. Are you a single mother? If so, discuss your relationship, or lack thereof, with your child's father. If there is room for improvement, what are some steps that you can take toward that end?
4. If there is no father figure in your child's life, discuss ways that you might enlist male family members, role models at your church, or mentors from social service organizations to fill that void.
5. Think about your relationship with your father or your lack of relationship with him. In either circumstance, how did your father or his absence affect the woman you've become today?
6. Why do you think Grandma didn't step up sooner to intervene on Miranda's behalf? How do you respond when elders in your family offer advice in raising your children?
7. How far should you go in talking with your children about problems in your relationship with their father?

THE GIFT INSIDE

CAMILLE AND PINKY maneuvered around knees and purses to get to the empty seats at the other end of the row. "Excuse me," Camille said, apologizing for stepping on one woman's toe.

She had expected it to be crowded this morning, as was usually the case for the annual service held outdoors in Spring Lake Park, but this was a bit much. She arrived fifteen minutes early and still had trouble finding two chairs side-by-side. Since getting more involved in church, Camille had become Pinky's spiritual protégé, so to speak. They sat together, especially when Willie had to work parking lot duty, as was often the case. They would nudge elbows when the preacher said something profound, and Camille suspected there would be a good deal of nudging today.

This Sunday was different. Bishop Glenn Everett had known Pastor Todd Bailey since the two studied together in seminary, almost thirty years ago. Back then, they vowed that if ever they led churches, they would be as integrated as a Montgomery, Alabama, lunch counter in the sixties. It didn't quite happen that way, though. Just like the churches where they each grew up, the overwhelming majority of people in their congregations had the same color skin as the pastor—black for Everett's church, white for Bailey's.

Not long ago, Pastor Bailey approached the bishop with an idea. What would happen if they held a joint service where members of Believers Ministries and House of Faith worshiped together? When the bishop told his congregation, it didn't take much selling. Pinky and some other ladies in the women's ministry group had just discussed how old-fashioned it seemed to have segregated churches these days. Camille, for one, loved the idea.

House of Faith joined Believers Ministries for "Worship in the Park," which explained the crowd and the diversity this morning. People who were white, black, Hispanic, and even a few Asians sprinkled throughout the makeshift sanctuary setup in an open space a good distance away from the playground and basketball courts.

"You never know what God will do when we start opening up our churches and people of all races praise Him together," the bishop said. "Lives will be changed."

Neither Pinky nor Camille guessed how prophetic the bishop's words would be.

Camille kept turning around in her seat, hoping to spot Britain, one of her white friends from work. Britain grew up Catholic but hadn't stepped foot in a church in the last decade, so Camille figured she would feel comfortable in this untraditional park setting. She hadn't arrived by the start of service, however, and halfway through one choir song, Camille craned her neck to see if Britain were walking up the gravel path.

No Britain—although Camille did catch the stare of a man in the row of seats to her right. She could tell he'd been watching her for a while, and he didn't bother to turn away or try to play it off when she caught him. He apparently wanted her to see him looking.

Camille looked away, ending the stare-down, slightly giddy

from the obvious flirtation. It had been months since she broke up with Blackwell Spencer, and from what she heard he was already cozying up to the women of his choice at local nightclubs. Camille, meanwhile, still prayed for someone to glance her way. Typical. A man can leave a relationship, find another woman, go on a honeymoon, and have a baby while his ex is still rereading his love letters and Googling his name.

Was the stranger still looking? Camille wondered as much, while offering a cute, dainty clap to the up-tempo song. Good thing she'd worn one of her cute summer dresses that showed her feminine side. Most people dressed casually at Believers Ministries, but the park setting encouraged even more laid-back attire. Some strolled up in shorts, cut-off jeans, T-shirts, and flip-flops.

She tried to stay focused on the service. The joint choir with members from both churches sounded pretty good, especially since they had only practiced together for a month. Still, Camille couldn't wait for the singing to end so she could sit down and stop worrying about whether the man was checking her out from the backside.

Finally, Pastor Bailey approached the pulpit, signaling an end to the music and the beginning of his sermon. He would preach a shortened sermon first, then the bishop. Camille turned around again. She couldn't help herself. She looked first at the parking lot, as if still watching out for her guest. Then she made sure her eyes landed in the same spot as before, somewhere around four o'clock. Still staring. This time, Camille offered a courteous closed-lipped smile in return before shifting to hear Pastor Bailey.

"People try to separate us based on our skin color—even in churches," he said. "But the apostle Paul said there's no difference in a black Christian and a white Christian in God's eyes. We're all His children, and the sooner we all realize that, the better off this world will be."

"Amen!" Pinky said, nudging Camille with her elbow.

Camille turned and winked her eye at Pinky in a show of agreement, but her thoughts soon returned to the stranger. She had never seen him before, and it was obvious that he didn't go to Believers Ministries. He was white, tall with light brown hair—kinda cute, too.

"I don't know why you're acting so shocked," Trisha said between bites of a spinach and feta cheese omelet at Rise 'N' Shine, her favorite brunch spot to hang out with Camille after Sunday morning service. "We live in the twenty-first century and a lot of white men see the beauty in black women these days."

"I know that, Trish, but what I'm saying is that none of them ever took such an interest in me, so I never had to deal with it before."

"Well, you have to deal with it now, or you should anyway. Give the man a call, go out with him, have a good time for once."

Camille let the thought sink in, while cutting away at a banana nut pancake. She couldn't explain why she was making a big deal out of this. She didn't look twice at mixed-race couples she passed in the mall or on the street. Yet the thought of being in an interracial relationship herself felt unnerving.

After the closing prayer that morning, Camille had quickly hugged Pinky and excused herself to meet Trisha for brunch. She almost made it to the car when she saw the man standing with a big group from the House of Faith who were splitting into teams to play adult kick ball after church. Again, he looked straight at her, daring her to turn away.

"Hi," he said, reaching out for a handshake as she drew closer. "I hope you weren't upset by my staring during the service, but I couldn't help myself. You're a lovely woman, and I could tell by the way you worship that you have a relationship with the Lord."

Camille stood like a dazed teenager for a moment then managed just two short words: "Thank you."

Up close, she noticed his dark eyes and strong chin. He had to be a good six inches taller, and she could tell that his polo-style shirt and khaki shorts covered a fairly muscular frame. He waited for Camille to say something else but, when she pivoted to walk away, he spoke up to keep the conversation ongoing. “So, how long have you attended Believers Ministries?”

“Just about two years,” she said, stopping short and turning around again. “I assume you go to Pastor Bailey’s church?”

“I’ve actually been visiting for a few months. I’m new to the Tampa Bay area. My job transferred me here late last year, and a friend told me about House of Faith, but after today’s service, I think I might want to visit Believers Ministries a little more. I really enjoyed the bishop’s message.”

“That’s nice,” Camille said, looking around to see if any of her church members were watching.

“Did you find the person you seemed to be looking for during the service?”

Just then, Camille saw a petite middle-aged blonde woman approaching.

“Actually, I just did,” she said of Britain, a clothing buyer who often sold garments at the boutique where Camille worked.

“I got here a little after the service started, so I sat in back. I tried to get your attention but you were looking in the opposite direction.”

“I can’t believe I missed you. What did you think of the service?”

“It’s a lot different from Catholic Mass, but I really enjoyed it.”

They kept talking as if the man next to Camille weren’t there. He cleared his throat loudly to announce his existence.

“How rude of me not to introduce you,” Camille said. She paused. She didn’t know his name.

He reached into the pocket of his shorts and took out a silver business card holder. “Here’s my card. Maybe we can get together sometime and talk. You could tell me more about your church.”

He nodded courteously in Britain’s direction. “It was nice meeting both of you ladies,” he said, before heading in the direction of the kick ball players.

Camille looked down at the embossed card and saw the logo of a well-known consulting company with branches along the east coast. “Paul Stanley, financial manager,” it read. She tucked it into her purse.

“And what was that all about?” Britain had asked, as if she already knew the answer.

“That’s what I’m trying to figure out,” Camille said.

Camille looked up and spotted Trisha waiting, hands on hip, beside Camille’s car in the parking lot. She had called Camille’s cell phone three times since church ended.

“Where have you been?” Trisha asked, finally seeing Camille walk briskly across the asphalt.

Camille put up her hand to stop her friend midsentence. “You are not going to believe this, Trish.”

“What?”

“I’ll tell you at the restaurant; we can’t talk here,” she said. She introduced Britain, opened the car door, and slid into the driver’s seat.

Judging from the way Camille had behaved, Trisha almost thought her friend was on a top secret mission. Then she heard the truth.

“Girl, move into the twenty-first century please,” she told Camille at Rise ’N’ Shine. “Who doesn’t know a mixed couple these days?

“I dated a guy from India once and found him to be very interesting. Of course, he wasn’t the one to take to my family reunion,” she said. “The Johnston version of the electric slide might’ve scared him away.”

“I know that’s right,” Camille said, laughing.

Britain, who had been listening quietly, finally joined in the conversation. “I dated a black guy once, ya’ know,” she said proudly.

Camille hadn’t envisioned her prissy, often wound-too-tight friend venturing outside of her own race. “You’re kidding, right?”

"Yep. We met through a mutual friend, and I enjoyed his company and he enjoyed mine, and it was as simple as that," she said with a quick shoulder shrug.

"Frankly, I found him to be a lot more fun than a lot of my white boyfriends."

"Oh, really now?" Trisha said, throwing Camille a sideways glance.

Camille ignored Trisha's not-too-subtle slight on Britain. "So why didn't the relationship work out?"

"We always had a really great time together," Britain said with a little giggle, while putting her fingers to her lips for a silent "shhh." She paused for a response, but Camille didn't want to hammer her with a fornication speech, at least not yet. Trisha rolled her eyes.

Britain sensed she had crossed some unspoken line and picked up where she left off to relieve the awkwardness. "When it came down to it, Andre and I didn't have a whole lot in common. I don't think it had anything to do with our race. We were just two different people who didn't share the same interests."

"Could it be that you had different interests *because* of your race?" Camille asked.

"There definitely were some cultural differences, but I've dated white men I didn't click with either, so I don't see my relationship with him any differently."

"I bet his mother saw it differently," Trisha said, not quite under her breath.

"I never met his mother," Britain shot back.

"I wonder why."

Camille flagged their waiter and asked for the checks, hoping to end the unexpected standoff between her friends.

Britain forced a slight smile to show that Trisha's attitude didn't intimidate her. She remembered how black women strangers would turn up their noses when she and Andre went out together. She heard their gripes about white women taking *their* men, as if they held title to every black man on earth. Obviously Trisha fit into that category, although she tried to make herself appear open-minded by mentioning her Indian ex-boyfriend.

"I may not be one of the black sisters," Britain said lightheartedly. "But I think you should go for it, too, Camille."

Camille poured herself more coffee. "Since I've never dated a white man, maybe you can tell me what I can expect."

"All I can tell you for certain is that not all white men are alike, just like not all black men are alike."

"I agree with that," Trisha said, loosening up a bit. "And I say it's our turn to get in on this multicultural action. We are educated, smart women who don't have to wait around for a black man to wake up and take note of the queens that we are. We have options, so I say go ahead and explore, my sister."

Camille liked the sound of that, so much so that she raised her palm, beckoning Trisha, then Britain to give her a hand slap. After the laughter subsided, Trisha offered one last piece of parting advice.

"One thing I learned from my little expedition, though," she said, before taking a sip of her hazelnut coffee. "Be careful. In the long run, a man is a man is a man, no matter what color his skin happens to be."

Camille had looked at Paul's card at least twice a day since Sunday, trying to decide if she should call him or not. She hadn't mentioned it to her mother, who was progressive in a lot of ways, except when it came to her daughter seeing a man who wasn't black. For some reason, the black woman/white man thing remained taboo in some circles, even Christian ones.

She broached the topic with Pinky one morning when the two met for their occasional breakfast. "Did you happen to notice me talking to a man after service on Sunday?"

"That white man?"

"Yes, that *white* man, if you must put it like that."

"I saw him talking to you and give you his card. I didn't think too much of it other than he was trying to market his business or something."

"Actually," Camille said, "he asked me out."

"Asked you out? On a date?"

"Pinky, why do you sound so surprised?" Camille asked, masking her own doubts. "Look around. There are plenty of mixed-race couples these days."

"I know. I see it more and more. But I'm from the old school, so it's kind of hard for me to think of a reason that a beautiful black woman like you wouldn't want to be with a fine upstanding black man."

The response caught Camille off guard.

"Who said I didn't want to be with a black man? I'm ready and waiting for any decent black Christian man to come my way. But he hasn't, so why should I limit myself?

"And, Pinky, I have to say that I'm surprised at you," her tone growing defensive. "Weren't you the one nodding in church on Sunday when Pastor Bailey preached about how God pays no attention to skin color?"

Camille waited for a response, but none came, at least not for several moments. When she did speak, Pinky's words were slow and careful.

"I'm not saying you should limit yourself. I just think you'd have a lot more in common with a man who can relate to the problems you encounter as a black woman in a society that is still not color-blind, no matter how much we'd like it to be."

"Well, all this talk is too soon anyway," Camille said, wanting to change the subject. "I might not even like this guy. I haven't even called him yet."

"And you better not call him," Pinky said.

"Excuse me?"

"You heard what I said. You. Better. Not. Call. Him.

"You young folks may have your own way when it comes to dating different races or dating over the computer or whatever else is in style these days. But one thing I know that'll never change: A woman needs to let a man pursue her if she expects the matchup to be anything close to the way God intended. Don't start out running the relationship by calling and sending him text messages all day long, then expect him to step up one day down the road and be the leader. If he's going to be the head of the relationship, he needs to pursue you from the start, and that means more than just handing you his business card. That's way too easy."

Camille flipped through the channels, barely taking note of the programs that flashed across the screen. At the boutique, she had pushed her newest designs all day. Now she just wanted to mellow out on the couch, the TV dialogue serving as white noise to her rambling thoughts. Nearly a week had passed and she hadn't called Paul. Per Pinky's advice, she had no plans to do so. Not that Pinky's word had to be the end-all of the matter. In truth, Camille didn't feel comfortable calling him anyway with what little she knew of the man.

In retrospect, she had only made such a show of meeting him because it'd been so long since anyone at church asked for her number. Not that most women in her situation would blame her. An educated black woman, thirty-five years old with no husband and no kids—statistics said she would die single. The chances of her getting married looked about as likely as a modern-day parting of the Red Sea.

TV and magazine reporters researched the issue. People made documentaries about it. Why do fewer black women get married than white women? Plenty of panel discussions and magazine articles mentioned it, too. Camille listened and read as much as she could take. More black women have college degrees than black men and won't settle for the lesser educated. Or too many black men are in prison. Then there's the spread of AIDS in the black community.

The truth was probably as complex as getting integration in the churches. And, for Camille, the statistics were probably worse, considering the added criteria that her man be a Christian. When she broke up with Blackwell and committed her life to God, she assumed He would send her the right mate. Not long into her Christian makeover, she realized the church had far fewer potential catches than the nightclubs.

She even subscribed to a couple of dating websites, keeping that to herself, of course. You could never tell what people in church would say about her glamorized photo and biography on CouldBeTheOne.com and ChristianLoveMatch.net. No doubt, someone would recite the Scripture that speaks of a man finding a wife—as opposed to a woman finding a husband. But Camille had already thought of that one and settled the matter by refusing to initiate communication with men on the websites. Let him "find" her by sending an e-mail first, and she would respond if she saw fit. She got some hits, although mostly from men who had posted fake pictures of other good-looking men in place of their own and older sugar-daddy types with screen names like BigPoppa and SugaFoot.

Then entered Paul, a nice-looking single man who seemed to have a decent career and who had the gumption to pursue her. In person. But would she ever see him again?

She knew better than to spend her days worried about a man. After all, she had a career with goals to achieve. In the months since Blackwell, she busied herself with an idea for a new clothing line that she would design and showcase in the boutique then eventually send to designers in New York City. She was determined to get closer to God. She spent more time in prayer and studying the Bible than she ever had. The singles ministry became a social outlet. Now one of the leaders, she organized outings and occasionally facilitated discussions. Damian regularly called on her to lead the group in a closing prayer.

But every so often she wondered if something were wrong with her. Was she not attractive? Had she made a mistake in giving up on Blackwell so easily? Would her Christian man ever come along?

This particular Friday night, she had thought about calling a girlfriend to hang out with, but she knew neither Tonya nor Trisha were what she needed, or rather what she wanted. Friday night in front of her TV, scrolling to find a good docudrama on the A&E network, Camille paused, closed her eyes, and said a quick prayer. "God, whoever it is that You have for me, please send him—quick."

Pinky spotted Paul first at church Sunday. She tapped Camille who stood beside her as usual. His presence hadn't surprised Pinky who expected to see him there. Too early to tell whether anything would ever happen between he and Camille. Either way, Pinky knew God was using his presence to teach her something, too.

She had felt uneasy ever since her conversation with Camille. Her concerns about Camille dating a white man revealed that something hadn't settled right in Pinky's views on race. She had talked about how everyone is equal in God's eyes and believed it in theory. But when the issue became personal and involved someone she knew and loved, Pinky's true feelings came out. She retrieved her notes from Pastor Bailey's sermon and reread the part where he'd said that believers are one in God's eyes. The message seeped into her spirit, and Pinky felt ashamed of herself for discouraging Camille's potential matchup. The color of Paul's skin literally paled in comparison to the importance of his character. It's like Pinky had told people herself, "You can't get to the gift unless you take off the wrapping."

Now she noticed how Paul eyed Camille from his seat across the aisle and how Camille looked his way and smiled every now and then.

"Excuse me, Pinky," Camille said when the service ended.

She pranced over to Paul and they chatted as the sanctuary emptied. Pinky watched as Trisha joined them for what looked like a brief introduction to Paul then said her good-byes and headed out the door, leaving the two alone again.

"That looks interesting," Sister Madeline said to Pinky with a slight nod in the direction of Paul and Camille. "You know whether something is going on between those two?"

"Nothing yet," Pinky said. "We'll just have to let the Lord decide."

At Rise 'N' Shine, several waiters waved at Camille as she was escorted to her booth. "You must come here often," Paul said.

"At least a couple times a month. I love the whole wheat and banana pancakes here."

She hadn't planned on coming back this Sunday, though, nor had she intended to talk with Paul for such a long time after service. Plenty of eyes had watched and Camille could only imagine the gossip surrounding the scene.

In the middle of the sanctuary, they had talked about how much they enjoyed the worship team that morning and Paul commented that one of the songs really touched him, which led to a discussion about gospel music and which of the latest CDs was worth buying. After a while, Paul suggested they go someplace nearby for lunch. Camille suggested Rise 'N' Shine.

But Paul sensed her restlessness from the time they stepped through the door.

"Are you uncomfortable being seen with me?" he asked finally.

"Of course not. Uncomfortable? Me? Why would you think something like that?"

"Maybe it's the way you're constantly looking over your shoulder. At first I thought you were watching for someone again, but I'm beginning to wonder if you're checking to see if anyone is watching us."

Camille's mouth dropped open, but Paul just kept talking. "Is it because I'm white, is that why you're so on edge?"

"Paul! Absolutely not! How could you think such a thing of me?"

Camille had upped her voice at least an octave. Even she heard the fakeness in her tone.

"Look, Camille, I'm just a guy who knows a beautiful woman when he sees one, whether she's white, black, Asian, or whatever. Yeah, I'm a white guy—I go sailing. I watch NASCAR races."

Camille stifled a laugh, and he was happy to have lightened the mood.

"I have dated women from different cultures, including African-American women, and to be honest with you, I manage to find something fascinating in each one of them. What's hard to find, no matter the skin color, is a woman who's dedicated to her relationship with God. That's what caught my eye when I saw you last week praising the Lord. Well, that, and the fact that you really are beautiful. It's hard to believe that some man hasn't already snatched you up."

"Paul, you are so sweet," Camille said, before taking a moment to craft her next words. "You're also right. I have been uncomfortable with the thought of seeing you again. I know that mixed-race couples are not uncommon these days and, believe me, I have no problem with that. The thing is, no white man has ever asked me out, so it came as a surprise. I guess I haven't handled it well."

Paul reached across the table and gently placed his hand on top of Camille's.

"I totally understand," he said. "How about we focus on getting to know one another as friends? That wouldn't make you uncomfortable, would it? I know from last Sunday that you have at least one white friend," he said playfully.

"In fact, I have several," Camille said. "And, yes, you and I as friends would be nice."

"And comfortable?"

"Yes, comfortable, at least for now."

Their waiter stopped by to check on them. "More coffee?"

"None for me," Paul said.

Camille declined, as well. That's when she noticed the waiter glance at Paul's hand still resting on top of hers. She detected him raising his eyebrows in surprise ever so slightly. Camille slid her hand from beneath Paul's and reached for her purse, pretending that she suddenly needed something inside.

THINK ABOUT IT

1. In what way is Camille living in the pink in this story?
2. What are your views on interracial dating? Have you personally dated outside of your ethnicity? Would you? Why or why not?
3. With some exceptions, many churches today remain segregated. What do you believe are some reasons behind this? Do you think that church leaders should make diversity a priority in their sanctuaries? Why or why not?
4. Read Galatians 3:26–28 (NIV) below and discuss with a group what the passage means and how it might relate to your experience in relationships with coworkers, significant others, church members, or any other situation where you interact with people of a different race or culture: *You are all sons of God through faith in Christ Jesus, for all of you who were baptized into Christ have clothed yourselves with Christ. There is neither Jew nor Greek, slave nor free, male nor female, for you are all one in Christ Jesus.*
5. Despite God's view of equality, Pinky noted that the society we live in still sees vast differences between people of different

ethnicities. How much do you think the realities of society should play into our personal decisions in selecting a mate?

6. Are you a single woman over thirty-five who desires to be married? Think of ways you can turn your focus away from the absence of a mate toward productive activities that give your life purpose.
7. Camille had some spiritual reservations regarding online dating. What are your views on this method of meeting men?

WONDERFULLY MADE

THE TABLE was a circle of laughter. Even the waitress couldn't stop giggling as she balanced a plate of shrimp ravioli on her palm. She just set it in the middle of the table—there was too much excitement, too many hands gesturing, too many voices issuing requests.

The two couples celebrated the New Year with an intimate dinner party and lively discussion, getting worked up over meaningless debates about people they had never met.

The first probing question to be answered: Could Whitney Houston make a true comeback and shine again like her star power in the 1980s?

From there the conversation progressed to Al Sharpton—a savior for the oppressed or a political clown?

Then to spiritual things: In his heyday, could Billy Graham outpreach T. D. Jakes?

"Are you out of your mind?" Roland said. "Billy Graham was a good man and all, but T. D. Jakes could preach a whole sermon, crack five jokes, sing an old gospel hymn, and lay hands on ten people in the time it took Billy Graham to read 'Jesus wept.'"

Brianna lifted her palm in front of his face as if to shut him up. "See, that's the problem. We are so concerned with presentation that we lose focus of what's really important. Substance," she said, playfully staring her husband down. "No, Billy Graham was not decked out in a baby blue three-piece suit with matching shoes. He did not walk across a stage five times with a towel, heaving and sweating. But I've watched recordings of his stadium revivals, and the man could preach. Thank you."

Jessey took a sip of Perrier then added her two cents. "Both of you have a point. You can't argue with the fact that Billy Graham was a great preacher. People—black, white, Hispanic, whatever—packed football stadiums to hear the man talk about God. No, he was not as dynamic as Jakes, but you can't say he was any less effective."

"Again, Jess, we're on one accord," Eric said to his girlfriend. "You can't deny that Jakes is a profound preacher. He can be a little flashy, but don't get it confused, he teaches God's Word. That's why people want to hear what he has to say. That's why he can pack stadiums, too."

Jessey nodded and rubbed Eric's back.

But Roland's light had dimmed. He pushed his chair back and excused himself from the table. Brianna nervously took a sip of her flavored iced tea.

"Is something wrong, Brianna?" Jessey asked, noticing the tension between them. "Roland seemed a little upset just now. Was it something that we said?"

"No, of course not," Brianna said, searching for an excuse. "It's just been a long week for him at work."

"You must get some kind of pleasure out of making me look stupid in front of my friends," Roland said after shutting the front door and entering their living room. He hadn't spoken a word on the ride home, always preferring to wait until securely behind closed doors to unleash his anger.

"I can't believe you disrespected me," he went on, his temples bulging. "Did you see how Jessey agreed with her man? That's what you're supposed to do. Not try to make him look like a fool!"

Brianna avoided getting defensive, which would only make matters worse.

"Honey, I'm sorry. I didn't mean anything by it. It was all in fun," she said, backing up, then turning and walking quickly down the hall to their bedroom. It sounds silly for a grown woman, but when she got scared, she locked herself in the bedroom closet. Alone and kneeling in the darkness, she felt safe.

She wouldn't make it there this time. "Where you going? To the closet like a five-year-old?" Roland said, growing angrier. "Don't you turn your back on me. You already disrespected me once tonight. Not again, not in my own house!"

He caught up to her, clamped his right hand on her left shoulder, and swung her around with a force so strong her whole body turned and she reeled over the coffee table onto the floor. She felt his hard-heeled Cole Haans kick the side of her waist, then his hot breath on her cheek. He had stooped to the floor and was looking at her limp body with an expression of disgust.

"You hear me when I say this, and you hear me good," he said, roughly grasping her chin between his thumb and forefinger. "I don't ever want to be put to shame like that again in front of my friends. I knew I shouldn't have married you in the first place, but here we are. Now, you want to roll with Roland? You want to be the woman on my arm? You better get yourself together."

With that, he released the grip on her chin, stepped over her, and walked to the bedroom, slamming the door behind him. Brianna whimpered on the floor for a while then gathered herself. She got a blanket and pillow from the linen closet and fashioned a bed on the couch.

“What’s up, Mother-in-law?” Roland said, wrapping his arms around Sister Pinky in the church lobby just before service began.

“Hi, son,” Pinky responded playfully. “You know you’re looking handsome this morning.”

“Thanks, Mom, but the only one I’m trying to impress is this beautiful woman right here,” he said, placing his hand on Brianna’s back.

Pinky noticed her daughter squirm slightly when he touched her. “What’s wrong, baby?”

“Nothing, Mama,” she said, forcing her lips into a tight smile. “I’ve just been a little tired, that’s all.”

“Oh? You sure that’s it? I saw you all walking up from the parking lot and it looked like you were limping a bit. Something wrong with your leg?”

“No, not really. I was just—”

Roland interrupted. “Not watching where she was going, she fell over the coffee table last night, hurt her back. You know how clumsy your daughter is,” he said, chuckling.

“Well, she always has been uncoordinated,” Pinky said. “Bri, remember that time you fell trying to do a pyramid on the cheerleading squad in high school?”

Brianna smiled along with the joking for a moment then started toward the sanctuary when Willie made his way through the crowd to give her a hug.

She avoided eye contact with him. If anyone in the family could see through her façade, Willie could. The two had similar laid-back personalities and quickly connected after Willie and Pinky married.

“What’s wrong, darling?” he asked, immediately sensing her distress.

“Oh, nothing, I just—”

"She just fell over the coffee table last night," Roland said. "She'll be all right."

With his hand still on her back, he nudged Brianna into the sanctuary, and they walked to the very front where Roland liked to sit. The praise team had just begun to worship, so he found his seat but remained standing, clapping and singing along with the melody. Bishop Everett, sitting in the pulpit, fondly observed the sight of a man unashamed to praise God.

"Something is wrong with Brianna," Willie said to Pinky later that evening at the dinner table. "Seems to me like the past year or so, basically since she's been married, she's lost the life in her spirit. Plus, she's always hurting herself. Remember awhile back when she broke her arm? And then she'd sprained her finger once, and that time she slipped on her porch in the rain and bruised her face all up?"

"Yeah, I know," Pinky said. "I thought about that this morning when she said she fell."

"That just didn't sound right to me," Willie said, "didn't sound right at all. How can you fall over a coffee table in your own house? It's in the same place it's always been. What made her forget that and fall over it all of a sudden?"

"Sounds like she's not thinking straight these days. Brianna has always been shy, and I thought Roland's personality would help bring her out of her shell. But I'm beginning to wonder if she's intimidated by the fact that he's so outgoing and so charming—we can all see that's a charming young man."

"Pinky, I know you really like Roland, but I'm starting to think something more serious is going on."

"Like what?"

"Like he ain't the prince you think he is. I see the way he acts around her. The man barely lets Brianna finish a complete sentence without butting in. What's he afraid she's going to say? By the way, have you even noticed that your daughter hardly ever stops by the house without him anymore?"

"What are you trying to say, Willie?" Pinky asked defensively.

"I'm saying what I should've said long ago. I think that man is putting his hands on Brianna, and I'm tired of sitting back while you grin and gloat over him like he's the best thing since sweet corn bread!"

"Willie Pinkston, you done lost your mind!"

"No, I haven't lost my mind, but you might want to send a search team out for yours. You spend your time counseling all these other women at church, discerning when something's wrong, but what about your own daughter? She is a beautiful, intelligent woman, not the clumsy, bumbling fool you and Roland make her out to be. She tripped and fell over the coffee table—you believed that? Woman, please!"

"You think you know my daughter better than me? Well, excuse me, but I thought I was the one who raised her all by myself. I thought I was the one who sat up at night with her when she was sick," Pinky said, pointing at her own chest and raising her voice. "Where were you, Willie, since you know so much? Where were you?"

Willie lowered his tone, seeing the argument had gotten out of control. "Look, Pinky, all I'm trying to say—"

"Never mind what you're trying to say. This is what I've got to say: I raised two lovely, God-fearing, strong young women. The first time a man even tried to hit one of them, he would be answering to the police or answering to me because I would know about it. You understand me? I. Would. Know! No way in the world my babies would sit back and let some man beat up on them."

"How can you be so sure about that?" Willie said, allowing his mouth to keep moving before good sense could stop it. "Especially since you did."

Immediately, Pinky turned and walked off. The words picked at painful scabs from her past. She heard Willie mumble something about being sorry before she shut the door to the bedroom and lay silently across the bed.

If only we could rewrite the past, at least the worst parts anyway. Pinky, for one, would take an eraser to the periods when she shacked up with men, especially *him*—the one she never mentioned by name, the one few people knew about, even the young women she talked to at church.

She and her daughters' father had been apart for several years and the loneliness overwhelmed her. She couldn't remember the last time a man had asked her out on a date. An older woman at the church she attended in Jacksonville had the solution: her nephew. She introduced him and Pinky and, two months later, the man had moved into Pinky's two-bedroom apartment.

The hitting started with a backhand slap for a comment Pinky made the first week he moved in. She had a mind to throw him out, but he cried and apologized and said the words she'd been desperate to hear—"I love you so much." She knew that would be the last time he hit her. Until the next time. Soon, they argued every day. He called her fat, insulted her cooking, criticized the way she raised the girls.

Pinky sent her daughters to their room when the yelling got out of control. Brianna was ten at the time; her little sister, Jasmine, seven. Thinking back now, Pinky questioned whether she had really shielded them from the violence or if they had figured it out.

She sat up in bed, reached for the phone on the nightstand, and dialed Brianna's number.

"Hello?"

"Hi, Roland," Pinky said. "I'd like to speak to my daughter, please."

"Sure thing, Gorgeous, she's right here."

After a few moments of muffled voices, Brianna answered.

"Hi, sweetheart, I've been thinking about you and realized we hadn't had any mother-daughter time in a long while. Can you come over soon, maybe tomorrow evening after work? I can cook up your favorite lasagna just the way you like it."

"You want me to come by the house tomorrow for a mother-daughter night?" Brianna said, repeating the request so that Roland could hear. He shook his head no. "Well, I'd love to but I need to check—"

Roland grabbed the phone from her. "Hey, Pretty Mama," he said with his trademark upbeat tone. "Brianna and I have plans to meet some friends for a quick bite tomorrow. But we can stop by to see you and Pops over the weekend."

"I see," Pinky said simply. "I see."

Pinky only pretended to sleep when Willie settled into bed, so she could avoid talking to him. Her body ached—her back, her arms, and neck. The intense stress probably caused it, although Pinky wondered if her body somehow had tuned into the abuse her daughter endured.

She eased from bed and trudged to the family room where she kept her photo albums. She found a picture of Brianna when she was ten, wearing a white frilly dress with lace bobby socks and black patent leather baby doll shoes. Her hair was in a ponytail tied back with pink ribbon and Pinky had parted a bang in the front, just the way Brianna liked it. She had won first place in a writing contest at school and was nervous about giving her presentation during a special program. You could see the scissor marks on the left side of the photo where Pinky had cut out that man's face.

Who had she been fooling? Of course the girls knew about the abuse. With all the yelling and cursing, how could they not? Had they heard the time when he threw her into the bedroom dresser and all her jewelry and perfume bottles crashed to the floor and she hurt her tailbone and cut her foot on the glass? Had they been roused from their beds the night he choked her on the bedroom floor and she couldn't breathe and one of the neighbors called the police?

The relationship lasted a little less than a year when the woman who introduced them asked about the bruises Pinky had tried to hide with makeup. She apologized for bringing them together and begged Pinky to leave him, even prayed with her to let it go. Eventually, the woman's encouragement overrode Pinky's insecurity and brought out her natural scrappiness. She devised a plan to leave him for good, with as little drama as possible. She asked her boss at the phone company for a transfer from Jacksonville to Tampa, about three hours away.

A few weeks passed in straightening out the details. The Lord even worked it out where the apartment lease ended that month. And one day while he worked, Pinky took the girls and left. She ran into him in the grocery store a few years later when she returned to Jacksonville to visit family. By then he had another woman following him around and didn't bother speaking to Pinky as he walked by.

Cutting his face out of photos was easy, but she couldn't undo the damage instilled in her daughters' minds. What kind of example had she set? Equally as bad, why hadn't she seen through Roland's act?

Brianna was thirty-six when she met Roland, and Pinky prayed she wouldn't let another good man slip away. The first time Brianna brought him over for dinner, Pinky could tell it was Roland Caldwell's charm, not his looks, that attracted her daughter. If he passed by on the street, no heads would turn, so he leaned on his personality and intellect to make up for what his DNA lacked. He worked in the engineering department at Gemstone Homes, a development company that designed and contracted to build subdivisions. Brianna worked in human resources for a firm that contracted with Gemstone. He noticed her one day during a business meeting, started a conversation later in the hallway, and followed her back to her office. Their talk led to books, and he impressed her a week later when he returned with a well-worn copy of Max Lucado's *And the Angels Were Silent.*

Brianna, on the other hand, had the looks. Clear mahogany skin, high cheekbones, and light brown eyes. Her hair draped past her shoulders, jet black—and real, not weave. Average height and a perfect size 8, she didn't even bother working out to maintain her slim waistline and slightly curved hips. "It was all in the *genes,*" Pinky told her once, pointing to Brianna's shapely figure in a pair of fitted jeans.

Months later, when Roland approached Pinky and Willie to ask for their daughter's hand in marriage, the words barely left his lips before Pinky shouted, "Hallelujah!" She had been so happy that day. Jasmine already had a good husband. Now Brianna would step into that next level of life, too. At least that's what they all believed at the time.

The more Pinky thought about it, the more guilt settled in. She knew she had to shake it off and use her energy to help her daughter, instead of condemning herself for the past. Pinky looked at the clock: a quarter till five. She went to the kitchen and fixed a pot of coffee, then took some ground beef, sausage, ricotta cheese, and tomatoes from the refrigerator and her lasagna noodles and seasonings from the pantry.

No man could stop her from talking to her own daughter.

Pinky walked to the main reception area at the firm where Brianna worked and asked for directions to the human resources department. She hadn't called. She just packed lunch for two into Tupperware containers and arrived a little before noon.

From her glass paneled office, Brianna had to look twice to believe her eyes. Yes, that was her mother stepping off the elevator. Brianna raised her arm to catch Pinky's attention and waved her back to the office.

"Mama, what in the world are you doing here?"

"Hi, baby," Pinky said, giving Brianna a hug. "I thought I would surprise you since you couldn't come over tonight."

Brianna looked down at the bag of food and couldn't hide her pleasure at the thought of her mother's cooking. She suggested they walk a block from the office complex to Eden Park. On the way, Pinky told Brianna about the goodies in her bag: homemade lasagna, a crispy vegetable and bean salad, fresh Cuban bread, brewed sweet tea, and her special recipe red velvet cake.

"Mama, you must've been up cooking all night."

"As a matter of fact, I was," Pinky said, as they settled at a picnic table in a small pavilion. "I was worried about you."

Brianna looked up from the table, confusion on her face.

"Let's enjoy our food first," Pinky said, lightening the mood. "Then we can talk about some other things. How's work?"

For the next twenty minutes, Brianna updated her mother on projects at the office and a few irritating employees. The small talk made Pinky realize what little she knew about her daughter's world these days. Then Brianna's cell phone rang just as they savored their last bites of cake and Pinky was about to disclose the real reason for her visit.

"I'm sorry, Mama, but I have to answer this. It's Roland."

"Hi, honey," Brianna said, before pausing to hear him speak. "It's so nice outside that I decided to eat lunch at the park today. That's why you couldn't reach me at the office."

Pinky studied her daughter's face as she spoke and noticed the care she took in saying just the right words. She heard a slight tremble in her voice and Pinky remembered twenty-five years earlier when she had the same carefulness and fear about her, that same tremble. How could she have missed seeing these signs before?

"Why didn't you tell him that I was here with you?" Pinky asked after Brianna hung up the phone.

"You know how Roland is when it comes to you," she said, trying to think of a quick answer. "He'd probably try to come over here so he could see you, too, and interrupt our time together." Time to change the subject. "So . . . what did you want to talk about?"

"Brianna, I was thinking last night about my relationship with Louis—you remember Louis, right?" she said, mouthing his name for the first time since she could remember.

"Of course, Mama, who could forget him?" Brianna rolled her eyes.

"I never talked to you girls about our relationship, but now that you're grown, I think you can better understand. You see, Louis used to abuse me, physically and verbally. I tried so hard to shield you girls from the truth, but last night I was wondering whether I failed."

Pinky looked at Brianna's face and didn't see the surprise she had hoped she would. "You already knew, didn't you?"

"Yes, Mama, we knew. Jasmine and I would lock ourselves in our bedroom closet when you two fought. We knew he was hurting you." She paused, trying to stay in control of her emotions. "One time, I looked through the peephole and I saw him on top of you, choking you, and I was so scared. Mama, it was me, not one of the neighbors, who called 911 that night. I begged the operator not to tell you that I had called because I didn't want to get in trouble."

Pinky threw her arms around Brianna and held her tight. At least a minute went by, but she wouldn't let go. Still embracing her, she said into Brianna's ear, "Last night, I was thinking that if I had set a better example for my babies, then you wouldn't be putting up with a husband who's doing the same thing to you that Louis did to me."

Brianna froze. She unwrapped her arms and backed away to look Pinky in the face. "Wha . . . what did you say?"

"Brianna, it's time to stop pretending now. I know what's going on. I just realized it last night, but now I know, and I'm not going to stand back and let it continue," Pinky said, careful to maintain a soft and loving tone. This was no time to judge. “Do you know how beautiful you are? Do you know that you were made in the image of God? You are fearfully and wonderfully made, much too precious to let some man bring you down and hurt you, even if he is your husband.”

Brianna gasped and put her hands to her mouth. She felt the strangest mix of fear and relief. Finally, someone knew what she was going through, someone who could relate.

“Now, listen,” Pinky continued. “We can’t let this go on for another minute. You need to take the rest of the day off, go home to get a few things, and come over to our house. You can live with Willie and I for as long as you need to and—”

“Mama, I can’t,” Brianna said, shaking her head.

“Oh, yes, you can,” Pinky said matter-of-factly. “I can’t even stand the thought of that man having a chance to put his hands on you one more time, so we are going to walk back to that office, then I’m going to follow you to your house and we’ll get as much of your stuff as we can fit into our cars while he’s still at work. Don’t even worry about who’s going to get the house and all that right now. That stuff can be worked out later. Your safety is first. So—”

“Mama, I can’t leave him, not now.”

“Baby, the Devil is a liar—”

“Mama, you know God hates divorce.”

“And He hates husbands who beat on their wives, too.”

“But, Mama,” Brianna said, searching for the right words to say, “I’m three months pregnant.”

Roland was waiting for Brianna when she walked through the door that evening, unusual since he typically arrived later than she did.

The first thing he said: “So, how was your lunch in the park?”

Brianna knew something was wrong, but played along anyway. "It was fine."

Did Mama already say something to Roland about their talk? Her mother had been furious when Brianna refused to leave with her. She had pleaded, saying that she, Willie, and Jasmine would help her through the pregnancy. Brianna wouldn't budge. She wanted her children to have both parents. Plus, Roland had always wanted a child, and she was waiting for just the right time to tell him. Once she did, Brianna hoped the baby would bring out the goodness in him.

"Just fine, huh?" Roland was saying. "It looked a little more than fine to me."

He walked slowly toward her. "I decided to do a little drive-by and make sure you weren't lying to me about going to the park. That's when I saw you and your mother walking back to the office, arguing and crying. What was that all about?" he said, the veins bulging in his forehead. "Were you telling her lies about me?"

Brianna slowly backed away from him. "Roland, you've got this all wrong," she said, her voice shaking. "Mama just stopped by to tell me about some problems she and Willie are having at home."

"Then why didn't you tell me she was with you when I called?"

"I . . . I didn't mention it because she asked me not to tell anyone about their problems."

"Don't you lie to me."

Brianna had backed up to just a few feet away from the front door. Her keys still in hand, she turned and bolted toward the driveway. Roland came after her and grabbed hold of her blazer, ripping the sleeve, but stopped the chase once Brianna reached the front yard. Mr. Jamison, a deacon at Believers Ministries, was sitting on his porch across the street and stood up when he saw Brianna's frenzied running. Roland spotted Mr. Jamison, calmed himself, and waved as if all was well.

"Hey, Mr. Jamison," he yelled.

"Hi, son. Everything okay with the little lady there?"

Brianna's car jerked out of the driveway, leaving tire skids on the pavement.

"She's fine," Roland said. "Just running late. You know how women are."

Once back inside the house, he tried to figure out what to do. He knew where Brianna was headed and, for the first time in a long while, he didn't know his next move.

"Don't you worry about a thing," Willie said, while fixing Brianna a cup of hot green tea. "Your mother and I, the whole family, we'll all be here for you and the baby."

"That's right, sweetie," Pinky said from across the kitchen table.

"I know you'll be there for me," Brianna said, her mind weary from the events of the day. "Can you do one more thing?"

"Whatever you want," Willie said.

"Would you please pray for Roland?"

Pinky stiffened and sat back in her seat.

"Mama, I know it's not what you want to hear, but please don't judge my marriage by what happened to you. I know you hate Roland right now, but Ma he is a believer. He does know the Lord, and I know that if God can feed five thousand with two fish and five loaves, He can change my husband. He can save my marriage."

Pinky and Willie stared at her for a moment, then turned and looked at each other without saying another word.

Pinky grew more frustrated with every minute she waited outside Bishop Everett's office. She couldn't remember the last time she called his personal cell phone and requested to meet with him ASAP. Yet he wasn't waiting with his office door open when she arrived. His secretary offered Pinky a seat until he finished another appointment. Five minutes passed, then ten, then fifteen.

Finally, the door swung open and Deacon and Sister Moore walked out. They waved at Pinky, who was so consumed with her own thoughts she looked right on past them, saying only "excuse me," as she hurried past the secretary and into Bishop Everett's private sanctuary.

"Sorry to keep you waiting, Sister Pinky," he said, calmly looking up from the appointment book on his wide mahogany desk. "You sounded upset over the phone. What's going on?"

"Bishop Everett, I need you to talk some sense into my daughter Brianna."

"Sense into her?"

"Yes, sense. Good sense. Wisdom. Spiritual discernment. Whatever term you want to use. My daughter's life is in danger and I need your help because she won't listen to me, but I know she'll listen to you."

Pinky got up from her seat to walk off the tension building inside of her. She had told herself she wouldn't get emotional in front of Bishop Everett, but every time she thought about that man beating on Brianna, anger seeped through her pores.

"Pinky, you need to calm down so we can talk things through."

"You don't understand," she said. "That man has been smiling in my face and, all the while, putting his filthy hands on my daughter. He's been—"

Pinky stopped midsentence, noting the pensive expression on Bishop Everett's face. Something was missing: surprise.

"You already knew, didn't you?"

Bishop dropped his head for a moment then looked back at one of his most trusted church members.

"Listen, Pinky, I can't discuss confidential conversations that I have with other church members, but I will tell you that Brother Roland came to see me last night, apparently after Brianna had gone to your house."

"You have got to be kidding me! You mean to tell me that ugly stinker had the nerve to walk into this church after all he's done and try to get the upper hand by talking to you first?"

"Pinky, watch what you say," Bishop said, rising from his seat. "All I can say is that I intend to schedule a meeting with both Roland and Brianna to help them through this."

"You're not going to try to counsel them to get back together, are you?"

"I know you want the best for your daughter, Pinky, but you're going to have to let God have His way."

"God ain't got nothing to do with a man hitting on a woman, nothing at all."

"You may not like Roland right now, but he's still a child of God. He may have some serious issues, but—"

"*May* have some issues?"

"Pinky, neither one of us knows the whole story. You heard one side; I heard the other. We both know that the truth is somewhere in between."

"So he's got you fooled now, too, huh? Just like he's had me fooled all this time."

"Roland is not all bad, Pinky. I've watched him worship on Sunday mornings. I've seen him mentor younger men in the church. Your own husband, Willie, has seen him mature spiritually in the Brothers Keepers group."

"Spare me, Bishop. The man should be in jail for assault and battery. He's a manipulator. He tricked my daughter into marrying him. He fooled me into trusting him. Now he's swindling you into thinking he's a 'child of God.'"

"What is wrong with you, Laura Pinkston? We've been friends for years, but I don't even know the woman I'm talking to right now. The Pinky I know realizes that every Christian carries his own baggage. That's why Jesus said, 'Let he who is without sin cast the first stone.' You sure you want to be the one throwing stones these days?"

"What happened?" Willie asked, following Pinky from the garage door into the living room.

"What happened was that man got to Bishop before I could. He called the bishop yesterday after Brianna came over here."

"What'd he tell him?"

"Don't know. Bishop wouldn't tell me. Whatever he said, he's got the bishop thinking there's still some good left in him. I guess men stick together no matter what."

"Now, Pinky . . ."

"It's the truth, Willie," she said, looking him straight in the eye, challenging him to disagree. "Anybody with a mustard seed of sense knows that a church is the most sexist place there is. You've got churchgoing men doing whatever they want to: cheating on their wives, abusing them, getting their girlfriends pregnant, molesting little girls *and* little boys. And what are the church leaders doing about it? Not a doggone thing. They're saying just what Bishop Everett told me, 'Nobody's perfect,'" Pinky said with a sarcastic tone. "Truth is they don't want to do anything about it because they're doing the same things themselves."

"You didn't tell him about the baby, did you?"

"No, of course not. Brianna doesn't want Roland to know right now, and I think that's a smart move. He'll just try to use the baby to get back into her life."

Willie knew better than to join in Pinky's monologue. In all honesty, he agreed with some of what she said. The night before, he had asked Brianna about pressing criminal charges, but she refused. She'd gotten away before Roland could strike her this time, so calling the police would only add drama to the situation without yielding results. Still, Willie thought it would be a shame if Roland got off with no punishment at all, other than a stern talk from the bishop. He didn't mention his feelings to Pinky, knowing they would only give her fuel to keep the banter going. When her rant died down, she stomped into the living room and asked where Brianna was.

"She left about an hour or so ago," Willie explained. "Said she had to get out of the house for a while."

He watched Pinky settle onto the couch and start thumbing mindlessly through a magazine to pass the time. As even-tempered as she was when it came to advising other people about their problems, she could be high-strung and unreasonable when it came to her own family, especially her daughters. This time, Willie worried that her meddling would cross the line with Bishop Everett and damage her relationship with him and Madeline.

He went into the kitchen and poured a cup of hot green tea that he'd let steep on the stove then headed back into the living room.

"Darling, why don't you sip on this and relax awhile."

"Thank you, sweetheart," Pinky said, reaching for the mug. Willie then turned and left the room. "Where are you going?"

"To my closet," he said, referring to the den where he kept his Bibles and other books and where he spent time alone. It was the only room in the house that he could call his own. "Somebody's got to stop complaining and start praying."

Brianna drove about forty minutes to a nature park on the other side of the county. It was a weekday—only a few people walked along the trail where little critters skittered about in the wilderness area. She noted how the trees stretched to the sky and watched as the sun set, casting an amber glow over the entire scene. She felt the bulge in her stomach, ever so slight now, and thought of the miracle inside of her to be birthed from a tiny seed.

How could a God who cared so much about the details of His creation allow her—allow her innocent baby—to be in this position?

She had prayed before accepting Roland's proposal. "Please, Lord, show me if he is the one You've chosen for me. Show me whether I'm making the right choice."

All the signs said go forward. Roland loved going to church and seemed mature in his spiritual journey, having memorized more Scriptures than Brianna ever had. And one night, down on her knees, Brianna could have sworn she heard God speak to her. Not an audible sound, just a sudden awareness, a sense of peace assuring her of God's approval. No, she couldn't leave Roland, not yet. When a woman believes she's hanging on to a word from the Lord, she'll weather a typhoon before she'll let go.

But Brianna had someone else to think about now, her unborn child. She had been so afraid the night Roland knocked her over the coffee table. She could have miscarried, and she couldn't take that chance again. With her thoughts conflicted, she settled onto a bench on a deserted part of the walking trail, shut her eyes, and began to pray. "Lord, I need to hear from You," she said. Surrounded by the nature that He created, she hadn't felt so alone yet so close to Him in a long time.

"You are the God of all creation, the Mastermind of the universe. I need You so much right now. Please, Lord, show me what to do."

She had no idea how much time passed as she sat there meditating before a wave of God's love washed over her. She wished she could stay forever in this place of serenity, away from all of her doubts, away from other people's advice and opinions.

Her mind felt at rest and something clicked inside. She still didn't know the answers to all of her questions, including whether her marriage would ultimately survive, but her spirit told her what to do for the moment. Just then, her cell phone vibrated in her pocket, as it had done constantly all evening. This time, she grabbed it and looked at the display case. Roland.

Word spread quickly among members of Believers Ministries that Brianna and Roland had separated. As the rumor went: The couple got into a big fight in their front yard, and a neighbor ran across the street to break it up. That's when Brianna sped off to her parents' house, prompting Pinky to storm into the bishop's office, interrupting a meeting with Deacon and Sister Moore and demanding that he kick Roland out of the church.

Pinky blamed the church secretary, the Moores, and one of Brianna's nosy old neighbors for planting the seeds of gossip, which people watered with their own twists, making the lies and half-truths more outlandish with each phone call. All day long, members she hadn't held a conversation with in months called "just to see how she was doing," obviously hoping she'd open up and fill in juicy details. She didn't.

Then Madeline called. "I shouldn't be telling you this but we've been friends for so long that I felt it best to let you know," she said.

Pinky steadied herself. Madeline's voice sounded slightly above a whisper, so Pinky knew her friend's husband didn't know about the call. Over the years, they had shared family secrets that Willie and Bishop assumed had remained between married couples. If only they knew.

"What is it?" Pinky asked, her voice quieting to match Madeline's.

"Glenn just got another call from Roland, an emergency call, so to speak. Apparently, Brianna has agreed to talk to him, but only if Glenn is there with them. So, they're all meeting at the church in an hour."

After a quick thank-you, Pinky hung up, scurried to the kitchen, and grabbed her keys from the hook by the door, just as Willie stepped out of his den and asked where she was going.

Pinky repeated Madeline's news then opened the door to the garage.

"Wait a minute," Willie said, putting his hand on her shoulder. "You told me about Brianna and Roland, but you still haven't told me where *you're* going."

"I'm going to the church, of course," Pinky said, getting irritated. "Where else would I be going?"

Willie stepped in front of her and gently shut the door. "No you're not."

"What is wrong with you? You know I've got to get down there to see—"

"Now, Pinky, I've had just about enough of this. You are not going down to that church. Yes, Brianna is your daughter, but she's still a grown woman. She's in a very difficult place right now and our job is to support her, to be there for her, and to trust her and God that she'll make the right decision."

"She hasn't made the right decision all this time."

"Oh, hush, Pinky. Just hush!" Willie wasn't known to raise his voice, so Pinky knew she had completely worn out his patience on the rare occasions when he did. "How do you know what the right decision is anyway? You've been marching around here like you've got all the answers. Well, you don't. And, I'm sorry to tell you that you can't fix this, Pinky. This one is out of your control. It's between Roland and Brianna and God."

Pinky stood there for a moment. Half of her wanted to slap him, but the other half knew he was right. She walked away from the door, put down her purse, and placed her keys back on the hook.

"Well, Mr. Pinkston, I suppose you have a point," was all she could say. She walked silently back to her bedroom and shut the door.

The two people now sitting in Bishop Everett's office hardly looked like the content couple he'd watched on Sunday mornings. Roland hadn't shaved, his shoulders slumped, and he barely held his head up. Brianna seemed slightly more composed.

Bishop had counseled couples in abusive relationships before and seen outcomes go either way. This time was different. This was Brianna, Pinky's daughter, whom he had known for years. This was Roland, a young man who had appeared genuine in his quest for the Lord. Before their problems came to light, Bishop had even considered asking them to get involved in a new ministry for young married couples.

Bishop spoke first. "Brianna, first I'd like to say that I know you are deeply hurt. I personally want to tell you that any abuse you may have suffered was not God's will for you. He still loves you more deeply than any man ever could. Sometimes things happen that we can't explain, but that doesn't diminish God's love. And aside from that, your family loves you and I, as your pastor and friend, love you. I want you to know that in the future you can come to me with your fears and I will do everything within my power to help you. Do you understand that?"

She nodded. His words had provoked a fresh batch of tears, and he handed her a Kleenex.

Then he turned to Roland. "You're the one who called this meeting. You wanted to say something to Brianna. What is it, son?"

Roland squirmed in his seat, searching for the right words. Bishop Everett questioned Roland's sincerity. The night Brianna left, Roland told him that they had gotten into a big argument and he lost control because she kept nagging him, almost provoking him. Bishop knew better than to believe Roland had lost control for the first time or that Brianna's nagging was the blame.

"I just want to start off saying to you that I'm sorry," he told his wife shakily.

Brianna, who had appeared strong when the meeting began, wilted like a rose in the sun after hearing the words she'd waited for so long. Bishop scooted his chair next to hers and put his arm around her. Roland stayed put and looked around the room uncomfortably.

After she composed herself, Bishop spoke again.

"Brianna, I'm advising you to put your safety first and to stay, for now, with your parents where you are protected and where you can relax and be around people who care for you."

Then he turned to Roland with an expression of ruthless sincerity that neither Roland nor Brianna had ever seen from him before. "I need you to know, son, that I love you, too, because you are my brother in the Lord's eyes. But if you so much as threaten this woman or do anything to hurt her again, you won't need to be afraid of the police; you'll need to fear me. I won't think twice about whipping a man weak enough to hit a woman. Do you understand, son?"

Roland nodded reluctantly.

Bishop continued. "I've been thinking about this situation very hard and, because of my relationship with both of you, it would be wise to recommend that another pastor who is very experienced in this area counsel you from here on. That is, if you want to be counseled.

"This," he said turning to Brianna, "is my most important question tonight. Since Roland has called this meeting, it seems that the choice is yours. Do you want to try counseling in hopes of saving your marriage?"

Brianna looked downward and fiddled with the Kleenex in her hands. Of the three in the room, only she knew about the child she carried. Only she knew what that inner voice told her in the park.

She looked back up at Bishop. "Yes," she said. "I would."

THINK ABOUT IT

1. Have you or a woman you know been subjected to domestic violence? If so, did you talk with others about it or did you talk with the victim? Why or why not? Write down your experiences in a journal or, if you feel comfortable, share them with your group.
2. Why do you think Pinky was so ashamed of having been abused? In what ways do we as women in general perpetuate the hush-hush nature of domestic violence? How did the situation reveal both Pinky and Brianna had been living in the pink?
3. Do you believe that men or women who abuse their mates can change? Have you witnessed such a transformation? If so, share that experience with your group, without using names.

4. Do you agree with Pinky that there is a culture of sexism that still exists in churches today? Why or why not?
5. We often look at other people's lives from the outside and think they have it all together. In reality, we don't see the problems that many married couples face and their struggles to remain a family. Take time right now to ask forgiveness for being envious of others' lives. Then thank God for the ways He has blessed your life.
6. No mother is perfect, but how can we set better examples for our daughters and sons, exposing them to relationships in which men and women truly love and respect one another?
7. Read and meditate on Psalm 139:14 (NIV): *I praise you because I am fearfully and wonderfully made; your works are wonderful, I know that full well.*

A WIFE'S DREAMS

HE DABS HIS FOREHEAD for the third time in fifteen minutes, the white handkerchief a prop in his crescendo. His voice dances rhythmically through the sanctuary, "He died! On an ooooold RUG-ged cross." An organ punches melodies in the backdrop. Amens and hallelujahs add life to the chorus.

"Preach, Pastor!" shouts a lady in back.

Sister Hopewell sits calm and straight-faced the whole time, hands in lap, legs crossed at ankle, eyes focused but deadened. No need to listen, not really. He preached the same sermon at a backwoods church up in Louisville, Kentucky, last year, and ten years before that at the revival in Eatonville, Florida, where they met. He captivated her, too, back then, strolling the aisles, picking people to pray for like a modern-day Ezekiel. She almost fainted when his warm palm covered her forehead, his commanding baritone bellowing in her ear, "Lord, help her see Your will," he prayed. "Don't let her go astray, Father."

At home later that night, she stared at a pile of short plays, about a country family corrupted by wealth, about a corporate executive turned madam, about the gangster's son rising to stardom. Someday, marquees would boast Destiny Austin's latest work. She had imagined neon lights and royalties when Hollywood bought the rights. Until the day the prophet came. Dreams and God's will don't always mix.

He called the next day. "How about lunch?"

He had asked where she wanted to go but made a quick decision when she wavered. Over sandwiches he talked about his calling, to preach for his own congregation someday. He planned to work his way through the ministers' circuit and into a permanent position as assistant pastor of an established church, and then prove himself capable of shepherding his own.

In the months to come, he would put his arm around her and talk of his future—their future—and she would lean her body snugly, securely into his. He said he'd give his life for hers if it ever came down to it, the kind of love a real Christian man should have for a wife. Her insides tingled, almost like she was at the upside-down part of a roller-coaster ride and feeling excited and fearful all at the same time.

A courtship and an "I do" later, fate revealed itself as roller-set hair and matte lipstick, tailored two-piece suits with matching hats, closed-toe pumps, and handbags. The pastor's wife in the portrait of a happy couple adorning handouts for Believers Promised Land Church.

Now she knows his scripts so well she could preach them herself. Tell the story of Jacob the trickster, of David the adulterer, of the woman at the well who was living with a man. Redemption. Forgiveness. Deliverance. Then enters the feverish pitch, the sweat, the hanky, the sip of water, the people proclaiming instant transformation. Some bowing to God, some worshiping a man with a title and a dry-cleaned suit.

If only they knew the typical in him, like last night when he took his empty plate to the dishwasher and left hers right there on the table. She'd shopped for the food, cooked it, even served it with garnish like at the restaurants, and he couldn't pick up her plate and take it to the kitchen, too?

"Whaaat?" he asked, realizing her attitude hours later. Clueless.

Look at him, just preaching his heart out today, getting these folks fired up with talk of a multitasking God: "He's your doctor in a sick room! He's your lawyer in the courtroom!"

Another shout: "Thank You, Jesus!"

"Whatever," Sister Hopewell mumbles so no one else can hear. "I wish somebody were a busboy in my dining room."

Long ago, Sister Hopewell stopped weighing the love in her marriage versus the convenience. Why bother? Convenience would win the tilt every time. She wondered whether it always had for him. The preacher's wife, after all, is necessary. She cheats temptation. She scares away jezebels stuffing shapely hips into short skirts. She is the helpmeet, the Eve. Plus, the church couples need counseling. Not much a bachelor pastor can tell a married man with his own house and kids.

He always introduced her when they traveled: his "lovely wife" and the mother of his children. She would stand and smile and give a courteous nod like a contestant in a beauty pageant. He made note of how God had blessed his family. As the story was told, he'd started out studying the Bible every day, visiting the shut-in, stopping by choir practice, and securing the bank loans, while his wife punched numbers as a data clerk, her paycheck offsetting meager Sunday collections. Excitement would transform the story into sermon somewhere around here: "Then (hallelujah!) the flood trickled in with men who did drugs, who used to cheat on their wives. (Hallelujah!) Women tired of searching at nightclubs found what they were looking for at church. (Praise Jesus!) People who had worshiped their careers or even themselves bowed their knees to the Almighty God. Soon, their friends and lost cousins came in. More families came in. The sinners turned into saints as quickly as

Jesus turned water into wine. (Thank You, Lord!) I tell you, crimson stains were washed white as snow!"

As the years passed, the wife went from wannabe playwright to a full-time pastor's quietly submissive better half, then back to playwright again, in so many words. This morning, she recalled the evolution. Like the night a few years ago when she got mad at Vincent and went running to the closet where she found the old box with her work beneath a case of blank baptismal certificates. She skimmed the one about the madam leading the double life. It was so full of clichés that she laughed. How could she have thought that anyone would pay to see these? She thought about feeding them to the paper shredder, but decided to keep them, although she didn't know why at the time. She tucked the plays back into the box and shoved it to the rear of the closet. Then she crept beneath the covers, next to her snoring husband. She watched the rhythm of his chest heaving up and down and wondered if marrying him had taken the breath out of her own dreams.

"Sister Hopewell," she hated that name, just as much as all the other formalities of ministry. The demure posture she was expected to hold. The celebrity status church members heaped on her for what appeared to be her grandest achievement: marrying Vincent Hopewell. The younger girls strived to hang around and serve her in the most basic tasks: "Do you need some help carrying your Bible?" Then there were the haters who scrutinized everything from the slightest mispronounced word to her hairdo; secretly coveting a life they knew nothing about. She overhead two saints in the ladies room once:

"Did you see Sister Hopewell's hair this morning? I don't know where she got that Marilyn Monroe hairstyle but she needs to give it back, quick."

"Amen to that! And did you see her face during the pastor's

sermon? Something's not right in that house, if you know what I mean."

Thank God for the power of restraint that held her in that restroom stall to hide until they left. That happened a few years ago, just before she and Vincent separated and sought marriage counseling. He was still assistant pastor at Believers Ministries International then and their separation sent rumors at the megachurch into a tailspin. People they barely knew weighed in on the odds of the couple staying together. She'd just given birth to their second child, Vincent Jr. Rumor had it that she planned to take the baby while her husband would take their daughter, Priscilla. Another lie had it that she and Bishop Glenn Everett had an affair. Not an inch of truth to it, but once church folks get hold of a scandal, they'll nurse it till either a juicier story breaks or Jesus comes back, whichever comes first.

The Hopewells met Dr. Rita at a Christian counseling center on the outskirts of town. A gangly woman who favored dark-colored pantsuits that were slightly too short, she stared blankly into their eyes as they answered her questions. Unnerved, the pastor typically responded as succinctly as possible. What was his parents' relationship like? Good. Before he died, his father had worked hard every day of his life, took care of the family, and loved and respected the Rev. Hopewell's mother who honored God and nurtured her children. The reverend preached of them often and hoped for the kind of marriage they had.

Sister Hopewell, on the other hand, couldn't stop talking about her daddy. He'd called her "Baby Girl" well into her teens. Every Friday when he came home from work assembling car parts at the factory, he brought her a treat: a candy bar and sometimes lavender and pink barrettes for her ponytails. Once, he brought a journal decorated with yellow tulips. She wrote a make-believe story in it about a girl and her favorite doll and presented it to her parents for Christmas. They carried on like it was the best story they'd ever heard. One day, her father went to work and never came home.

Her mother got the call just before lunchtime on a Monday afternoon. There had been a terrible machine accident. Baby Girl was seventeen at the time. She went to the Dollar Store and bought one of those journals to write out her feelings. In time, she was writing poems, then short stories and plays.

Of course, the pastor knew the details of his father-in-law's death, but he knew nothing of a journal and writing and plays and such.

"Why didn't you ever say anything?"

"Because it was a crazy childhood thing," she'd said dismissively.

From there they talked about why they argued more than they made love.

Sister Hopewell: He doesn't appreciate me, never considers my feelings. He's trying to re-create his parents' marriage. All he needs is a showpiece and a maid.

Pastor Hopewell: Many women pray to live the life I give her. She spends her days volunteering, meeting friends for lunch, and taking care of the children, the home, and a little church business every now and then. What is she complaining about?

"We are not getting divorced," he said during one session. "What would we tell the church? I've counseled a quarter of them through their own marital problems, but we can't figure out our own?"

"That's what you care most about, isn't it, what the people at church think?"

"No, I care most about saving our marriage. But the fact is that I'm a pastor and I am called to live a life that pleases God, a God who hates divorce, by the way."

Nothing to say to that, Sister Hopewell turned her head. Every time an argument seemed to head to the root of the problem, her husband recited a Scripture to shut down a discussion he might otherwise lose. And he succeeded. No way would she go up against him in a battle of God's Word.

Dr. Rita wouldn't be pulled off track, though. "Let's get back to what specifically is going on between the two of you and leave out the biblical references for now.

"Destiny," she said, then stopped abruptly noticing a startled look on her client's face. "Is there a problem?"

"No, not at all. It's just that I'm not used to anyone, except my husband and my mother, calling me by my first name. It's very refreshing."

"And why is that refreshing?"

"Because that's who I am and, somewhere along the way, it seems like the Destiny in me got lost."

"But where did she go?"

Destiny paused. She could see her husband's confused look from the corner of her eye, but determined she wouldn't be swayed. "A big piece of Destiny faded into her husband and her children, trying to be what they needed. A little bit went to the church, to meet the people's expectations."

"And the rest, or is there no more left?"

"To tell you the truth, I'm not sure. I don't know if any part of the woman I used to be is still around."

"If she were, what would she be doing right now with her life? Would she be married? Would she have children? Would she have a career?"

"She would probably be writing," Destiny heard herself say sheepishly.

The pastor could no longer contain himself: "Writing what?"

Destiny gave him a sideways glance and continued talking to Dr. Rita, as if the question had come from her.

"I'm not sure what, but she might be writing a book or a play or whatever else God gave her the ability to write. She would have the opportunity to use her talents just as her husband is allowed to use his," Destiny said matter-of-factly.

After the counseling ended, Vincent periodically hired babysitters to watch the children and took his wife on spontaneous outings to swank restaurants or, her favorite, a stage play at the theater across the bay. Destiny took Dr. Rita's advice and shared her feelings more often. In the past, the pursuit of her goals seemed almost silly in light of the higher calling of the church. But after Vincent started Believers Promised Land, she began to see how maybe the two could work together. She organized some of the church teens and a few creative adults to start a drama ministry that presented plays and short skits throughout the year. Vincent encouraged it, impressed by the clever and entertaining plots his wife crafted. His favorite play was the one about a megachurch minister who had become corrupted by wealth and raked in more and more tithes until God changed him.

"Sister Hopewell," one of the older members asked after the spring play. "Where've you been hiding all this talent?"

"It's been tucked away in a little box for a long, long time."

Superstardom didn't matter as much now that her star shined someplace, even if only at a medium-sized church in Tampa. Even if only between driving the kids all over town, keeping a clean house because "you never know who'll stop by," gathering donations, feeding the homeless, and organizing the women's ministry.

Another part of Dr. Rita's advice had been harder to practice, at least on a continual basis without falling back into old habits. And three-quarters of the way through today's service, Destiny is thinking how sometimes the simplest things give people the most trouble.

She watches as two people walk to the front altar and agree to commit their lives to God. Her husband prays over them, while the praise team sings. Sister Hopewell hums along, at first out of obedience to the part, and then finds herself lulled into the harmony of "Great Is Thy Faithfulness."

The final prayer. The benediction. The people form a line to hug their spiritual shepherds.

The crowd dwindles, and one young woman stands before her. She smiles widely in admiration, wanting perhaps to be just like the pastor's wife.

"Sister Hopewell, I just love those shoes! You're always so put together."

Sister Hopewell looks down at the patent leather sling-backs, a perfect complement to her black and gray boucle suit.

"Thank you," she says. "You're too sweet."

Then her husband's fingers touch her shoulder. "Ready?"

The pastor and his wife stride to their car in their designated parking space. He opens her door and situates himself behind the wheel. She stares out the window.

He speaks first. "Still upset about last night?"

THINK ABOUT IT

1. Why was Destiny unhappy with her life and who, if anyone, was to blame? How was she living in the pink?
2. For much of the story, she plays the "role" of a dutiful preacher's wife. Do you ever do things to fit the "role" that others expect you to play—at home, at work, at church, at extended family gatherings? If so, why? How can you change to reveal more of the woman God intended you to be?
3. If you go to church, think of how you view your leaders. Do you see them as real people with feelings and flaws like everyone else?
4. Ecclesiastes 4:12 (NIV) says: *Though one may be overpowered, two can defend themselves. A cord of three strands is not quickly broken.* If the "strands," so to speak, were husband, wife, and God, why do you think so many Christian couples get divorced today?
5. Communication is key in strengthening any relationship, be it a

married couple, friends, or family members. How does Destiny's lack of communication about her desires and feelings lead to resentment toward her husband?

6. How might Destiny's relationship with her father have contributed to what she likes most about her husband? How has your relationship with your father, or the lack thereof, contributed to the traits you find attractive in men?
7. Are there dreams unfulfilled in your life or talents left untapped? If so, what are they? Write them down on a sheet of paper. Ask God if it is His will that those dreams be realized in your life and, if so, to open a door for you to walk through to your spiritual destiny. If not, ask Him to help you continue finding contentment with the blessed life you live today.

SISTER'S KEEPER

JAYSHELL STOOD BEHIND the 75 percent off rack in the shoe department, pretending to be interested in size 9½ purple snakeskin mules. Time inched along. She had to be at a meeting soon, but for the last ten minutes she'd been held hostage in Pineview Mall.

The obstacle to her exit stood five yards away at the makeup counter and right in front of the door to the parking lot: Maxine.

Name should have been Waxine, as far as Jayshell could tell, for all the concealer and powder she shellacked on her face each day. No surprise to see her here, testing the latest lip liner and gloss, smoothing liquid foundation on her cheeks, scrutinizing her butterscotch complexion in the mirror.

From between steel racks, Jayshell eyed Maxine's freshly styled bob, her silver dangle earrings with matching neck choker. Her trendy black linen blouse and slacks. The black and white sandals with gold straps. The toenails shaped and painted to match the French manicured acrylics on her fingertips.

"Yes," Jayshell mumbled, "she thinks she's all that."

But Maxine hadn't seen *her*, and Jayshell wanted to keep it that way. Looking at her watch, however, she decided a meeting seemed inevitable, unless she wanted to be late. A face-to-face would be awkward and fake. She would have to pretend that she and Maxine liked each other. She mentally constructed a quick conversation. Of course, she would start with a big grin and a "Hey, girl!" Then she'd have to come up with something polite and witty: "I love that lip gloss on you, but don't go crazy and spend your tithes out here! See you later."

Puh-lease.

Just then, Maxine put down that shimmer eye shadow and walked away. Jayshell sighed with relief and darted in the other direction toward the door as soon as Maxine's cute little toes hit the mall's main hallway. She still had fifteen minutes to get to her Christian book club and she had managed to avoid the wax lady.

For now.

Staying away from Maxine Short would be much harder tomorrow. It always was, on Sundays at church.

"God bless you!" Maxine said over and over again, embracing one person after the next. It was meet-and-greet time at Believers Community Church. Time to say "Hello" to people you hadn't seen all week and give them a big hug. Time to let them know that the "Jesus in you" loved the "Jesus in them." The praise team sang and the Spirit of God was high that morning. Hallelujah!

Maxine loved this place. Not too big, like the main Believers Ministries campus where you can barely get to know anybody. But not so small that there's really no one else to get to know. "The BCC," she called it for short. Maxine had a bad experience at the main campus and after visiting the BCC she never went back. She had been a member now for several years, since she was a babe in Christ without real knowledge of the Holy Spirit. So much in her life had changed since then that she counted herself among the mature saints now. The BCC felt like home, many of its members like family. As they hugged, Maxine sensed sincerity in their embraces. She gave a few of the younger girls a peck on the cheek.

She stayed within the section of chairs where she always sat, though. Her mother always taught Maxine to "stay in your place" and right here was hers. These were her friends, the people she knew and loved. She didn't want to chance bumping into somebody whose cheek she cared not to kiss. Someone like Jayshell.

It had been a close call the day before at Pineview Mall. Maxine stood at the makeup counter, trying to find a shade of eye shadow to match the glitter in the suit she wanted to wear to church today. She was testing Beautiful Bronze in the mirror when she saw a reflection of Jayshell nearby looking at cheap shoes.

"Bless her heart," Maxine had muttered condescendingly. Jayshell, a clearance sale shopper, just didn't have the sense of style to compete on Maxine's level, although at times it appeared the girl tried. Not yesterday, though. Maxine couldn't see everything from the mirror, but it looked like Jayshell had on a pair of jeans and a simple white cotton shirt. She'd pulled her hair back in either a bun or a ponytail, and her face looked Plain Jane.

She hadn't wanted to risk Jayshell spotting her and coming over for pointless small talk. Maxine put that eye shadow down and walked briskly out the door without saying a word. She got her makeup somewhere else.

But the BCC was where she got her hugs.

"God bless you," she said, wrapping her arms around another member.

"Oh, He's got a blessing for all of us. For you, too," said a familiar voice, just to Maxine's right. "All you got to do is get in His will and stay there."

Maxine looked up and saw Sister Pinky, who often visited the satellite congregations, although she usually came for Bible study or a special service during the week. Considered multitalented, Pinky could oversee children's church, give a word of encouragement, visit a nursing home, and cook in the church kitchen. Whatever the need was, wherever it was, she could fill it. For that, most women, young and old, respected her—even the few who didn't like her.

But something about Sister Pinky's words of blessing made Maxine uneasy this morning, like Pinky was trying to tell her something rather than convey mere joy in the Lord.

The music quieted and people headed to their seats. The pastor stood to preach. Maxine sat down and glanced to the left, spotting Jayshell on the other side of the sanctuary with her Bible opened. Jayshell already had pulled out her pen and notepad, like she couldn't wait to get down to studying God's Word. Maxine rolled her eyes and turned away. She unzipped her leather Bible case and stared straight ahead.

Sister Pinky went home and started to plan one of her sisters intervention sessions, hoping she could get everything in place by the following Saturday. That wasn't a lot of time, but Lord willing, she could make it work. She always trusted God's voice when she heard Him telling her to do something. Just like this morning. She preferred her own church on Sundays, but something in her spirit said to go to Believers Community. She combed through her curly Afro, slipped on a comfortable smock-style dress, her low-heeled shoes, and headed straight across town. God would surely reveal whatever He wanted her to see or do, that much she knew. And not forty-five minutes after she got there, Pinky saw the cause of her mission.

The hugs tipped her off.

First came Jayshell Sweet, walking around grinning and hugging everybody during meet-and-greet. She approached Pinky and squeezed tight. Pinky wouldn't have thought anything amiss had Jayshell not looked up, caught sight of Maxine Short's back, and quickly turned away. Instead of walking forward, a straight shot to her chair, Jayshell pulled a Jonah and went the opposite direction.

She nearly walked around the whole sanctuary just to get back to her seat.

Then came Miss Short who acted like a child locked in an invisible box who couldn't go beyond the square of seats around her. Just to shake things up, Pinky walked up from the rear of the sanctuary and stood in her path. Maxine obliged with a "God bless you" and a stiff hug.

Sister Pinky scrutinized both ladies when she sat down. She saw Jayshell bend to pick up her Bible, then glance over at Maxine to see what she was doing. Just as Jayshell turned away, Maxine looked over at her and rolled her eyes.

The typical woman rivalry. Pinky had seen and handled so many over the years, she could diagnose the cause before even talking to the women involved. Judging by the secret glances they traded, this one appeared to be induced by jealousy—the most common root, especially when it came to churchwomen desperate enough to fight over a few positions of prestige. Either one or both wanted something the other had.

"Lord, when are we going to be secure enough in who You made us to be that we don't hate our sisters for simply being who You made them?" Pinky mumbled.

According to the pastor at Believers Community, Jayshell and Maxine were two of the most talented women in the church. He mentioned their names often in leadership meetings. Pinky had seen them both at previous prayer services and women's fellowships with their hands lifted in surrender during worship. She watched them work in ministry—Jayshell teaching Sunday school, Maxine singing on the praise team. She had witnessed Maxine's transformation firsthand, from a few years back when she played a married man's "other woman" till today when people saw her as a woman of God.

But the Devil walks around looking for people he can devour. He often gets lucky with women who think they've reached their spiritual peak but really live dangerously in the pink, which seemed to be where Maxine and Jayshell had settled. Now it would take an intervention to straighten out this mess.

Step One: Pinky would have to figure out who was the stronghold, the one who initiated this war in the first place. Somebody had to start it, typically the more insecure of the two. Pinky would have to identify her and soften her heart. Since she already had a relationship with Maxine, Pinky decided to call her first. A few strategic questions would reveal if she were the initiator or Jayshell.

Step Two: Once she had softened the initiator, Pinky would get Jayshell and Maxine together in the same room and let God do the rest. She had conducted these sessions countless times, so much so that when she called the pastor he knew exactly what she had planned and freely gave the phone numbers for Jayshell and Maxine.

Maxine knew she sensed something different during her encounter with Sister Pinky on Sunday, so hearing her voice mail message only reinforced that she was up to something. In her message, Pinky said seeing Maxine at church reminded her that they hadn't talked in a long time. They really needed to catch up.

Of course, Maxine would return the call. Her life had transformed all because Pinky invested time in her when everyone else talked about her. Not that she didn't deserve it. She knew the man was married when she noticed him looking at her during praise and worship. He gave her the look that never changes whether a man is at a pool hall, walking down the street, or, yes, sitting in the pews at the house of God. Back then, the look inspired Maxine to wear her skirt a little shorter and switch her hips a little harder when she walked down the aisle to her seat. Didn't matter whether he was married—as long as he didn't mind his wife neither did she.

After the whole congregation found out, Maxine might have moved on to the next church and pranced around in front of another husband with the look, if it hadn't been for Pinky. Maxine knew her by reputation only, but Pinky called and talked to her a long while about dignity and self-respect, about real godly men. She broke up with Brent and took Pinky up on her invitation to attend the BCC. Pinky even escorted her there a couple of times. She introduced Maxine to the praise and worship leader after hearing her sing along with the radio on their way to church. When she got comfortable attending on her own, Pinky stopped going, although she periodically called the pastor for an update on Maxine's spiritual progress.

Maxine scrolled down to Pinky's name in her cell phone contact list and placed the call.

"Pinky? Hi, it's Maxine. I got your message and wanted to call you back. It was good seeing you, too, on Sunday."

"Yes, baby, thank you. Since we haven't talked in a while, I thought this would be a good time to catch up. Plus, I wanted to tell you about a workshop I'm putting together next weekend."

She organized the event to help a few talented women get further along in their spiritual journeys. Maxine, she thought, would be a good candidate. Despite the vague description, Maxine accepted the invitation. She couldn't say no to Pinky.

That out of the way, Pinky narrowed in to accomplish Step One of her plan.

"I'm so glad you're hanging in there with the Lord. I know Pastor Hopewell thinks well of you. He's always mentioning your name, as well as another young lady there: a Miss Jayshell Sweet. In fact, I met her briefly on Sunday. You know her?"

Over the phone, Pinky couldn't see how Maxine curled her top lip in mock disgust when she heard Jayshell's name. She straightened it, though, in time to turn on a high-pitched sweet voice.

"Jayshell? Of course I know her! Everyone at the church does. Just like her name, she is such a sweet person. She teaches Sunday school, you know."

"Oh, really? So you two are friends?"

"No, I wouldn't say we're friends. I haven't had the pleasure of getting to know her personally. But from what I can tell she's a wonderful woman."

Pinky called the bishop and left a message on his voice mail. She had an idea and would need his permission before moving forward with the intervention. If he gave the go-ahead, things would fit together nicely, especially now that Pinky had figured out Maxine started the conflict. That much rang clear in the phone conversation.

Make no mistake; there are two ways to tell whether a woman is jealous of another woman. In Tactic No. 1, Woman A always has something negative to say about Woman B, hoping to downgrade everyone else's opinion of her. In Tactic No. 2, which is common among supposed classy ladies like Maxine, Woman A overly praises Woman B in front of most people because she's too smart to reveal her jealousy by using the more obvious strategy in the first tactic. She overcompensates, instead, extolling Woman B's good virtues and proclaiming how wonderful she is—although curiously not wonderful enough to be her friend. However, when she gets around her real close girlfriends, she talks about Woman B like a dog.

Pinky could see right through Maxine's empty compliments. That's not to say that Jayshell had no blame in this, too. But in Pinky's experience, the initiator usually drove Woman B to dislike her and start acting out in the same manner. In the years that the Lord called her to counsel women, Pinky learned that the most talented, intellectual, charismatic, and sweet girls could find something in themselves to be insecure about. They would become like that lion, looking for a way to devour any woman who had whatever they lacked. To make this all right in their minds, they conjured up reasons to justify disliking the other woman—she's fake, she thinks she's cute, she's self-righteous, she's stuck up.

Pinky, for one, had been on both sides of the issue. At one point in life, she played Woman A; at another, Woman B. From experience she knew that the hardest part of her intervention, would be getting Maxine and Jayshell to acknowledge their jealousy, even to themselves.

Jayshell grew leery about the upcoming church workshop. It seemed so mysterious when Sister Pinky called to invite her. She said she picked Jayshell to participate in a small women's workshop because she was anointed and had potential to do great work for the Lord. Yet, no one else at church that Jayshell asked had gotten an invitation.

"It was an honor to be asked, so I guess I should be grateful," she told her friend Lisa over the phone, "but I can't imagine who else will be there."

"You know Miss Thing will be," Lisa said, referring to Maxine. "She's always up in the pastor's face and leading songs on the praise team to convince everybody how saved she's become since her, shall we say, 'exploits' back in the day. So if you got invited, you know she did, too."

"Why did you have to bring her up?" Jayshell said, trying to hide the fact that she had thought the same thing.

Once upon a time, Jayshell actually admired Maxine, who seemed to have it all together. Jayshell had even asked for her business card and called her a few times. Though polite, Maxine never had much to say, which Jayshell took as a hint that she didn't want to be bothered. It seemed that Maxine thought herself too good for the likes of Jayshell.

"I don't know if she's coming or not," Jayshell said into the phone. "Doesn't make me any difference either way."

Pinky's conversation with Jayshell revealed a certain sincerity and genuineness in the young woman. Her love for the Lord shined even over the phone. Maxine must have noticed that light, too. Jayshell's brightness likely made Maxine feel inadequate because of her own dark past. The key would be to help Maxine shine her own light brighter, rather than trying to diminish Jayshell's.

The bishop returned Pinky's phone call, as did the pastor of the BCC. Both gave her new idea the go-ahead and she told Maxine to meet her at nine, so they could talk about a new program before the workshop at ten. Maxine walked into the room Pinky mentioned just a little before the top of the hour. It was empty, with the exception of one round table in the middle and three chairs.

"I had the deacons clear out the other tables and chairs," Pinky explained. "For what we're doing, we won't need much."

"So, what's the setup going to be for this workshop?"

"We'll talk about that a little later," Pinky said. "Right now, I want to tell you about a new ministry group that the bishop, your pastor, and I discussed. I think you should play a key part in it."

"Really?"

"Definitely. It's going to be a group for women currently involved with or who have previously dated married men."

Maxine sat straight up in her chair like she'd been zapped with a bolt of electricity, but Pinky just kept right on talking.

"We'll open up the group to all churches in the Believers Ministries family, and to other women in the community as well. Just like some of our support groups, the one for sexual abuse victims for instance, this would have a high level of confidentiality. We've talked with a member over at Believers Promised Land, Gloria Sherron, who is also a licensed counselor and does a lot of work with women. She would head up the group, but she'll need an assistant. That's where I'd like you to come in."

"Whoa, Pinky, I don't know about this."

"You don't know about this? How about I tell you what I know. I know that you are not alone in what you did. Adultery is happening in churches all around us. It's going on between the choir members and the guitar players, between the ushers and the hostesses, even between the pastors and the women in the balcony. It's a shame, and shame don't go away just 'cause you don't talk about it.

"Here's something else I know: Everybody in this church already heard about what happened between you, Brent, and his wife, Joy, and you can't erase that. Only thing you can do is build on it. God turned your life around, gave you some respect. Now is the time to bring Him glory by helping other women who are as lost as you were."

Maxine rested back in her seat and her expression softened. "Since you put it like that, maybe I could help in some way. I just never saw myself doing something like that. I assumed my calling ended in the choir."

"Baby, you have so much to offer this world, you just have to recognize it," Pinky said. "As long as you don't get stuck worrying about what other people think or whether their gifts are better than yours, God's light will shine in you wherever you go.

"Don't let your past be your shame, Maxine," Pinky said, adding a glossy finish to Step One of the intervention. "Turn it around and make it your testimony."

Just then Jayshell walked through the door, and Maxine felt her lips tighten. A phony smile frozen on her face, Maxine looked directly at Pinky, who had walked over to the dry erase board. Behind her back, she heard the two women speaking to each other, "Hi, Maxine!" then, "Hey, girl!"

Pinky picked up a thick blue marker to begin Step Two. She wrote on the board in big capital letters: MY SISTER'S KEEPER.

Then she turned toward her students. "Everyone's here. We can get started."

"You mean we're the only ones coming?" Maxine asked, determined not to look at Jayshell. Sister Pinky hadn't said as much during their phone conversation, but Maxine assumed a lot of church members were coming.

“This is it,” Pinky answered. “I like to keep these workshops small.”

Maxine didn’t like being so close to Jayshell. The woman seemed self-righteous, the kind of person who never did anything wrong and who looked down on other people. Maxine got tired of Jayshell’s perfect angel routine Sunday after Sunday. But the idea of helping in this new ministry for adulterers somehow gave Maxine a new perspective. She didn’t have to be squeaky clean like Jayshell to be special.

Pinky sat back down at the table for three and opened the tattered pages of her Bible to Genesis 4:1. Totally confused, Maxine and Jayshell looked at each other, as if silently asking, “What is wrong with this woman?” For the first time, they were on the same side.

“I’m sure you both know the story of Cain and Abel? Just to refresh your memory, let’s start reading together.”

Jayshell had her notepad, but forgot her Bible in her car. Maxine opened hers and placed it in the center for them both.

In unison, they read about Adam and Eve having two sons, Cain and Abel. They read about Cain’s fruit offering to God and Abel’s offering of the firstborn of his sheep. They read how God liked Abel’s offering but not Cain’s. Cain got angry and killed Abel. Then the Lord asked Cain where Abel was, and Cain pretended not to know, saying, “Am I my brother’s keeper?”

“Stop right there,” Pinky said. “We see here that Cain and Abel were the first two brothers born on Earth, born of Adam and Eve. One of them did something to please God and the other didn’t. But instead of working to improve himself, Cain got jealous and killed his own brother.”

Jayshell and Maxine felt like children in Vacation Bible School. They stared blankly at Pinky, wondering what this lesson had to do with them.

“You see, Cain thought his brother was the problem, but in reality the problem lived inside of him: jealousy.

"Cain didn't have compassion for his brother, which is probably why he killed him so easily. He didn't care about his brother's welfare. That's why he said to God, 'Why should I know where my brother is?'"

Pinky pointed again to the words she'd written on the board. Jayshell and Maxine turned to read them: MY SISTER'S KEEPER.

"You two are sisters, at least that's what the Bible says about Christians," Pinky said. "Cain and Abel had the same blood, but you two have something even stronger—the same Spirit of God. We agree on that?"

Jayshell and Maxine threw each other uncomfortable glances, then turned toward Pinky and answered yes to her question.

"Well, praise God. Now, I'm going to ask you a few questions that I want you to think about and discuss with one another for as long as you need. You can talk about it here today, you can go to lunch and discuss it, or meet sometime next week, whatever you want to do."

Then Pinky read questions scribbled on a sheet inside her spiral notebook. Maxine and Jayshell copied them on their pads:

Have you taken the time to get to know your sister in Christ?

What needs to change within you to have a better relationship with her?

Do you care about her well-being?

Are you your sister's keeper?

With that, Pinky gathered her notebook and Bible, got up from the table, and scooted in her chair. She walked over to the board, picked up an eraser, and wiped it clean. Then she turned around to see two confused faces staring at her.

"I know you two were expecting something more today, but my work here is done. Now it's up to the Holy Spirit to do His work in you. God has blessed you each with gifts and talents, just as He did with Cain and Abel. Think about the work they might have accomplished if only they worked together."

Pinky gave them each a tight hug. Then she walked out the door, leaving them alone.

The room fell silent for a full ten seconds.

Maxine broke the quiet. "Excuse me, but is this an episode of the old *X-Files* or *Punk'd* or something?"

They both started laughing.

"Is she going to come back later and check our answers to these questions or what?" Jayshell asked through giggles.

"I don't know," Maxine said, "but let's try to answer them just in case. For me, the answer is no to the first question about taking time to get to know you. I don't know you well at all."

Jayshell was surprised by Maxine's honesty. "Look, I didn't have breakfast, so I'm hungry," Jayshell said. "Why don't we go grab something to eat and, maybe, find out a little more about each other."

"Sounds like a plan," Maxine said, getting up from her seat. "I'll drive. There's this little brunch place I like not far from here, right inside Pineview Mall."

THINK ABOUT IT

1. How were both Maxine and Jayshell living in the pink?
2. Jayshell and Maxine didn't really know each other, yet they'd decided not to like one another. What criteria do you use when deciding to let another woman into your circle of friends? What role has jealousy and/or envy played in the elimination process? What role do your own insecurities play?
3. Have you ever been just plain jealous of a female coworker, relative, friend, "sister in Christ," etc.? If so, how did you

manage to overcome those feelings or how do you continue to wrestle with them today?

4. Why do women generally have a harder time than men accepting each other as we are?
5. Genesis 50:20 (NIV) says, *You intended to harm me, but God intended it for good to accomplish what is now being done, the saving of many lives.* What do you think of Pinky's idea to turn Maxine's shame into a good thing by allowing her to help other women through a support group? Is there something that happened in your past that might help others in the same situation today?
6. Read about the spiritual principle of "taming the tongue" from the book of James, below. Consider the things you say to or about other women in your life. In what ways should your tongue be tamed?

   When we put bits into the mouths of horses to make them obey us, we can turn the whole animal. Or take ships as an example. Although they are so large and are driven by strong winds, they are steered by a very small rudder wherever the pilot wants to go. Likewise the tongue is a small part of the body, but it makes great boasts. Consider what a great forest is set on fire by a small spark. The tongue also is a fire, a world of evil among the parts of the body. It corrupts the whole person, sets the whole course of his life on fire, and is itself set on fire by hell. (James 3:3–6 NIV)

7. Think of other women you interact with regularly. Do you offer your help in times of need, listen to their worries, and pray for their well-being? In other words, have you been your sister's keeper?

A GROWN MAN

IT HAD BEEN MONTHS since Camille stopped speaking to him. Just like that. One morning he was with her. The next, she was telling him that she'd gotten a revelation about Christ and that their relationship needed to change. They couldn't sleep together anymore, so maybe they should just be friends, she'd said.

Friends?

How could they just be friends?

They had spent many nights in each other's arms. He told her things he rarely told anyone, like how he'd only met his father twice, how his mother drifted in and out of his life since he was six, and how much he adored his aunt who'd raised him. He liked talking with Camille because she could think through a situation, rather than just react, like he tended to do. Plus, she had class. She could be down-to-earth, playing a game of Spades at the July Fourth barbecue, then hold a conversation the next day at the company picnic about the federal stimulus package. Not to mention, she looked good. Silky skin the color of maple syrup. She was always put together—nails and short hair done, makeup, clothes trendy but tasteful—the kind of woman who made a man proud.

That all changed when she got spiritual. Used to be a time when they could be real with each other and have a good time without all the rules. They made their own decisions and lived how they wanted. But Camille changed when she hooked up with the super-saints at Believers Ministries with their churchwomen's rule book of no's.

No nightclubs!

No drinking!

And definitely no sex!

Camille had even stopped buying the latest music artists, preferring to listen to gospel CDs. Blackwell tried to listen to John P. Kee, Kirk Franklin, and Martha Munizzi, but as far as he could tell, their upbeat tempos were just corny knockoffs of Billboard's Top Ten, so why not just listen to the real thing?

Let Blackwell tell it, his experience with Camille explained why so many Christian women are single. Always running to another woman to tell them what to do, or in most cases, what *not* to do. He could hear the sisters gabbing away: "Girl, don't you let him . . ." "He is no good." "If I were you, I'd leave him now!"

Problem No. 1: Most women giving the advice don't even have a man.

Problem No. 2: The rest of the advice-givers are old, like Sister Pinky, and haven't gone out on a date in thirty years.

It ended for good the day Blackwell went to Camille's house to talk things out. He didn't want the relationship to end. She was acting like he were some no-good heathen. Didn't she remember the times they went to church—together? Maybe he needed to set aside his pride and tell her how he felt.

"I'm in love with you," he'd said, surprising even himself with the degree of vulnerability he showed. He admitted growing slack in his church attendance but he was willing to start going more regularly if that's what she wanted. "I know we can work this out."

"Blackwell, you're a nice guy," she told him, "but you don't love me."

Blackwell opened his mouth to assure her that he did, but she cut him off.

"No, you don't *really* love me," she continued, this time shaking her head. "You know how I know? Because God is love, and you don't know my Lord, therefore, you don't know what real love is; you can't."

She said this so matter-of-factly that he could tell it wasn't something she came up with herself. It sounded like the usual speech derived from the women at church who controlled her life these days.

His ego crushed by the sound rejection, Blackwell said nothing more before getting up from the kitchen table and walking out the door.

Willie Pinkston stood at the front of the church meeting room to start the monthly Brothers Keepers gathering for men. He went down his list of members, pausing at those who hadn't attended in a while. Blackwell Spencer? No answer. Willie marked a line through the name. He was concerned about Blackwell who used to be a regular. A few other churchmen his age, in their thirties and forties, hung out together.

"Anybody seen Black?"

"I haven't seen him in a couple of weeks, Pops," Eric said, calling Willie by the nickname that younger men in the group gave him. He dressed and acted like the father some of them never had. His skin was like black opal, a contrast to the silver strands along his receding hairline. A typical Willie outfit consisted of a short-sleeved polo shirt tucked neatly into a pair of creased Wrangler jeans, belted, of course. His favorite casual shoes seemed to be leather sneakers with a Velcro strap in beige, white, or black, whichever accented his polo that day. He kept a pair of reading glasses nearby and a subtle word of wisdom.

He started overseeing the group after one of the assistant pastors left Believers Ministries to form a new branch. The bishop asked Willie to step in, which seemed a natural fit since Pinky was heavily involved in the women's group. He had never been much of a talker, but this role was more about facilitating discussions, or just being around to watch the game or to hear a man talk out his troubles.

Lately, though, he hadn't talked as much with Blackwell, who seemed to be distancing himself from the group, a sign that he might break away from the church altogether. When Christians know they aren't doing right, the first thing they do is cut ties with people who are. Willie hadn't seen Blackwell in at least a month. A few guys who hung around him spoke up at the meeting. Keith had tried to call Blackwell, only to get his voice mail and a brief return call, claiming to be swamped with work. Eric had stopped by his house to watch a Colts preseason game one night, but they kept the conversation focused on football. He looked fine, as far as Eric could tell.

Willie nodded, not wanting anyone to know the depth of his concern. He turned the group's focus to the evening's discussion topic: "Being in Control without Controlling."

Blackwell took another route to First Friday at Monet's. His old path would have had him driving past the church just as Brothers Keepers started. Not that he cared whether anyone at church saw him cruise past—they all could spot his ragtop Chrysler Sebring and vanity plates yards away. He just had such distaste for the church that he barely wanted to pass by at all anymore. The way he saw it: Christians were hypocrites who had one set of rules for their own lives and a different set for everybody else.

Post-Camille he decided to hang out occasionally with Keith, Eric, and a few others who could hold a decent conversation without saying Jesus' name, but refused to get caught up in the Christian guilt trips. Like if you listen to rap or sleep with a woman or refuse to give a special sacrificial offering to the guest minister, you are not going to heaven. He didn't buy all that. A grown man could make his own decisions. God did grant free will, right?

As a matter of fact, Blackwell would exercise that free will tonight. He slid on his beige slacks and cream Tommy Bahama linen shirt. He'd just gotten his short Afro trimmed and put on a splash of scented aftershave. Camille may be living for the Lord, as she said, but Blackwell had a life to live, too.

Giselle had wanted a date with Blackwell for months, ever since she saw him at Believers Ministries. She hadn't wasted her time with religion in years, but saw no harm in signing up her five-year-old son, Nathaniel, for the church-run Tiny Tot basketball league. She noticed Blackwell helping out the first day. But opportunity didn't present itself until she coincidentally got a job at the accounting firm where he worked. A managerial assistant in the payroll department, she looked for ways to improve communication with the staff and often asked the accountants for feedback or help balancing her department's budget.

Actually, she didn't really need that much help, but it was a good excuse to get to know Blackwell—with his fine self. Clean-cut with a wonderful, bright smile. Tall and slim, but sculpted not bony. Just how she liked a man. You could tell he either went to the gym or lifted weights or jogged or something to be in such good shape. Popular, with a sense of humor, too.

A coworker told Giselle that Blackwell and his girlfriend broke up, and she figured her time had come. He needed to come out of that shell he'd built around himself, Giselle stopped to tell him one day. He should get out and loosen up a bit, let the world know who is Blackwell.

"How about it? Meet me at Monet's at eight on Friday. That's spoken word night, and I know several poets, so I really want to go. I may even flow on the mic a little myself."

Blackwell agreed to be there, and she twisted on her heels and sashayed away without looking back. She figured it was best to end the conversation abruptly, with him a little taken aback by her boldness. Most women are too afraid or too traditional to go after what they want. Not Giselle.

Giselle had come on much too strong for Blackwell's taste, leaning low over his desk so her cleavage could smile at him. He couldn't deny she looked good, though. Really good. Toffee skin, petite with curves in the right places. He didn't much care for the Rapunzel-like weave with tendrils flowing down her back, but the Beyoncés of the world did it, too, so maybe he could get used to it.

At Monet's a few days later, however, you would think they were engaged or something by the way she caressed his back. Every time he rested a hand on the table, she found a way to run her fingertips gently across his forearm. He feared what a slow dance might bring, and played it off like he wasn't into the music to avoid finding out. He ordered his classic ginger ale—he never was much of a drinker—and nursed it for at least an hour. At some point the music gave way to spoken word poetry performances, which he hoped would turn her attention from him and on to the stage. Not quite. The spoken word only heightened the sparks when Giselle herself stood and walked to the mic with an index card cuffed in her palm.

"This is titled 'Tonight,'" she told the crowd.

Your voice is a gentle howling wind, calling me from deep inside.

Your touch is electrifying, magnifying emotions I can't hide.

We were made to be connected long before I even knew your scent.

Here I am, take control tonight; tomorrow you can repent . . .

It went on like this for several minutes, mind you, as she stared across the room at Blackwell with eyes half opened for that dreamy look. Blackwell stared right back, head tilted upward with a half-cocked smile on his face. Every eye in the place followed Giselle back to her seat and watched as she giggled and pinched his cheek.

"Did you like my poem?"

"It was very interesting, very interesting," was all Blackwell could say.

So much aggression ordinarily would have killed Giselle's chances, but after Camille's rejection Blackwell questioned his taste for the supposed nice girls. He didn't want things to go too far too soon, though. Giselle had a son, a cute little kid, and Blackwell remembered how she would drop the boy off to play in the Tiny Tot league. Getting involved with her meant getting involved with him, too. Not that Blackwell was put off. Growing up without his parents, he saw something honorable in helping a single mother, picking up where others fell short. The relationship would have to develop gradually, although Giselle seemed ready to fast-track it. Shortly after the poetry ended, he told her that he needed to head home.

"It's budget season, and I've been staring at numbers at least ten hours a day all week. I'm afraid I'll go to sleep on this table if we stay much longer."

He saw Giselle's initial surprise before she managed to hide it. "Oh, I understand. I'm a bit worn out myself."

They agreed to talk later and went to their separate cars.

Back at his condo, Blackwell could hardly sleep from thinking about all that happened. For one thing, he couldn't understand himself. Was he becoming a punk or what? Not long ago, he would have taken Giselle up on the invitation to her bed. Now he almost did feel that he should repent, like the poem said, and he hadn't even done anything.

He must have dozed off for a few hours because the door knock jolted him awake. Who could it be at ten on a Saturday morning? Through the peephole, he saw a familiar face.

“Brother Willie, hey, how’re you doing?”

“Not too bad, man, not too bad.”

“Come on in, but you’ll have to excuse the place. It’s been busy at work, and I haven’t had time to straighten up.”

Willie scanned the room. “Looks like a typical bachelor’s pad to me. I wouldn’t expect anything less.” He noticed Blackwell’s tired eyes. “Long night?”

“Somewhat, somewhat,” Blackwell said, not wanting to go into details. He gestured toward the sofa for Willie to take a seat. “So what brings you by?”

“Just checking to see how you were doing since I hadn’t seen you in a while. How’s it going, son?”

“Well, I can’t complain.”

“You said things were busy at work. How’s that coming along?”

“It’s budget season, so I’ve got to make sure all the numbers line up and that everybody’s happy. You know how it is.”

“How’s your family doing, your aunt and your cousins?”

“They’re fine. I’m planning to fly up there, to Chicago, in a few weeks to surprise Auntie for her birthday.”

“Really? That’ll be nice. I’m sure she’ll like that.”

“Yep.”

Awkward silence stretched between the men.

“I see that you’re alive and apparently well, so I suppose I’ll leave now. My wife wants me to finish a few more things on her honey-do list this weekend,” Willie said, rising from his seat. “You’ll know what I’m talking about one of these days.”

“Hopefully not too soon,” Blackwell said, adding a forced sigh of relief.

It was the open door Willie had hoped for, and he turned to Blackwell with a serious expression. “You and that nice girl Camille broke up, right? I know you really liked her. How are you holding up?”

"Oh, her?" Blackwell shrugged. "I'm fine. Great, actually. I've started seeing someone else."

"Is that right?" Willie said, surprised.

"Hey, if Camille says I'm not the guy for her because I'm not religious enough, that's fine. It's all good. We've started down two different paths, I guess. I'm the kind of man who prefers to move on rather than change my course. You know?"

Blackwell's bottled emotions felt uncorked. Willie was a good listener.

"The way I see it," he continued, "I may not quote Scriptures every hour, but I believe in God, and I'm a good man with a good career. I'm dependable. I pay my bills and care about my family. I try to help people. I even volunteered for several years with Big Brothers Big Sisters, you know, trying to give a young boy the male role model that I never had. You see what I'm saying? But since that's not enough for her, fine. I have nothing to be ashamed of. Not to boast or anything, but a lot of women would be glad to have a man like me."

"Well, son, you're right about that."

"When Camille and I were together, I treated her well. I took her to nice places, bought her gifts. I never cheated on her with any other girls or anything like that. I thought we had a good thing going, but if it wasn't meant to be, it just wasn't meant to be. I'm man enough to accept that."

Blackwell shook his head. "Tell you the truth, I'm not sure if it was Camille's idea for us to break up or if it was the church that got in the way."

He pondered the thought for a moment then glanced at Willie. "Either way, it's cool, though. I'm all right with it."

"You're all right with it, huh?" Willie asked, unconvinced. He put his hand on Blackwell's shoulder. "Any man in your position would be hurt, would be asking himself the same questions you're asking. It's okay, son. It's okay to have feelings. It's okay to have questions and not know all the answers. It's even okay to make some changes to try to get what you want, especially if it's something, or someone, God wants you to have. None of that makes you any less of a man.

"One thing you are right about, though. It *was* the church that got in the way, those 'saints'—including my wife—who like to dabble in everybody's relationships. That's been going on a long, long time. Sometimes, meddling church folks are the worst thing that can happen to a relationship between a man and a woman. I've seen women leave good, strong husbands just because he didn't live up to church folks' expectations."

"I know, man, and that's crazy," Blackwell interjected. "God must want a church full of bitter, old, single women—"

"But, sometimes," Willie interrupted so he could continue, "the church is the best thing that can happen, too. I want to challenge you, Black, to forget about who may have influenced Camille's decision and ask yourself: Regardless of how it came about, was the breakup for the right reason? You said yourself that you and she were on different paths. I know that Camille is growing in her relationship with God. So I'm asking you, son, is the path you're on the right one?"

Blackwell didn't know what to say. He thought he had analyzed the situation with Camille from every possible angle, but these were questions he hadn't posed.

Mustering a response, he said, "I guess we'll see."

Willie extended his hand for a firm shake. "I guess we will."

Blackwell took Willie's hand and instead gave him a manly hug with a couple of pats on the back, then opened the door. "Thanks again for stopping by. I appreciate it."

"No problem, son. Hope to see you again soon."

Blackwell closed the door and looked up at his wall clock: 10:20 a.m. He was about to go lie down again, take some time to process his conversation with Willie, when the phone rang and he recognized Giselle's number on the caller ID.

He listened as she told him what a great time she had the night before.

"I'm hoping for a repeat," she said. "How about something a bit more intimate, tonight, at my place? My son is spending the entire weekend with my sister and her kids."

For a second, and only a second, Blackwell heard Willie asking: "Is the path you're on the right one?" Then it dawned on him that, maybe, he had drunk more of the religious juice than he'd thought. He had survived the setbacks of his upbringing to become the man he was today, and he couldn't start living by other people's rules and expectations now. Not Camille's, not Pinky's, not even Brother Willie's.

His attention returned to the sultry voice at the other end of the line. Giselle continued enticing him with talk of candlelight and smooth jazz. Perhaps Giselle wasn't moving too fast, but he was moving too slow.

"Tonight," he said into the receiver, "sounds good to me."

Rebellion feels good in the beginning, especially for a grown man who finds the muscle to do his own thing, and Blackwell's break from the church brought a freedom he didn't realize he missed. Not that life changed much, the only real exceptions being that he had Sunday mornings free and was with Giselle rather than Camille. But he stood his ground in the face of all those religious hypocrites who didn't have the guts to live their lives without the rule book. To himself, he laughed, *Ha*!

With that attitude, he accepted the invitation to Willie's birthday party. The invite came in the mail a few days after Willie's visit, and Blackwell would bet it was an attempt to bring him into the same bondage in which Willie's wife had shackled Camille. He had the perfect idea to let them know it wouldn't work.

By the time Blackwell walked through the gate to the Pinkstons' backyard, Willie had already blown out the sixty-five candles on his birthday cake and cut several slices. Heads turned to see the late arrival, then did the proverbial double take to see the woman holding his hand and trailing along behind. Not a regular at Believers Ministries, that was for sure. And judging by the skimpiness of her backless halter top, the skin-tightness of her jean Capri pants, and the height of her stiletto sandals, she didn't frequent church gatherings anywhere much.

Blackwell walked straight toward Willie and offered a half hug with a pat on the back before handing over a gift-wrapped package of cologne. "Happy birthday, Brother Willie. Sorry we're late," he said then winked in Giselle's direction. "We had a little something we couldn't help but finish up before coming over."

He chuckled and raised his fist for a man-to-man fist bump, which Willie uncomfortably obliged. Pinky, standing nearby, witnessed the exchange and turned first to give Willie the look before facing Blackwell with an expression cold enough to wipe the disrespectful smirk off his face.

"And what was that?" she asked.

But Blackwell was confused. "Excuse me, ma'am?"

"I heard you say that you and your lady friend here had something you couldn't help but finish before coming over, so since you saw fit to mention your business, I thought I'd go on and ask what it was."

Blackwell cleared his throat and fumbled for a response, while Willie and Giselle looked away embarrassed for him. Pinky broke through the awkwardness by extending her hand to introduce herself to Giselle and ask for her name.

"Giselle. I like that," Pinky said. "Now, I don't think I've seen you around our church, have I?"

"No ma'am, I'm not a member."

"I see, so where is your church home?"

Blackwell wrapped his arm around Giselle and attempted to cut through Pinky's attempt at evangelism. "She's still looking for a church right now, although I may bring her to Believers Ministries one day soon."

About that time Pinky looked up and saw Camille coming outside from the kitchen where she had been helping out by preparing another fruit tray for the guests. Blackwell's eyes followed Pinky's and caught sight of her, too. She looked even more beautiful than he last remembered in a casual summer dress with spaghetti straps that revealed only the delicate curve of her shoulders. It was fitted at the top and flowed loosely at the hips to the stylish flip-flops on her feet. His eyes followed her as she walked unknowingly from the back porch to the buffet on the deck. Knowing Camille's relationship with Pinky, Blackwell figured she would be here, but misjudged his own reaction to seeing her again.

Then, something else he hadn't counted on. A man, a white guy, who'd been sitting and talking to some church brothers in the corner, rose and walked up behind Camille. He placed his hand on the small of her back and whispered in her ear. She smiled bashfully and did a cute little giggle before whispering something back into his ear. Blackwell just stood there, staring. He felt his jaw clench.

Giselle noticed the change in his demeanor and looked in the direction of his glare, but couldn't pinpoint who he was looking at. "Honey, is something wrong?"

"No, not at all," he said, coming out of his spell. "Everything's great. I just noticed that it's getting late and we need to get you back home to pick up Nathaniel."

"He's at the movies with his cousins, so we still have plenty of time if you want to stay."

"No, I think we'd better go. Traffic is always bad on this side of town, so I don't want to take the chance on being late."

Blackwell found Willie, who by this time had been pulled away by other well-wishers, and said his good-byes. He walked toward the gate, tilting his head in acknowledgment at familiar faces from Brothers Keepers. Giselle, whose feet hurt from trying to keep up with him in her stilettos, pasted on a smile for people she passed on the way out.

On the way home, Blackwell didn't say much, and Giselle grew more unnerved with the extended silence.

"So who is she?"

"Who is who?"

"Whoever it is that made you so upset you had to leave the party."

"Oh, can we not start with the drama, please? I told you I didn't want to be late picking up Nate, your son, remember?"

Giselle was no fool. Blackwell had turned too defensive to be telling the truth. But she had no intentions of letting another woman come between them. Not now. Maybe, she should change her tactic.

"I'm sorry, sweetie. You just seemed so upset all of a sudden, and I didn't understand why. Let me make it up to you," she said, running a single finger up and down Blackwell's right bicep as he drove. "Like I said, we actually have plenty of time to pick up Nathaniel, at least another hour. How about we stop by your place and I give you a little more of that dessert you had this afternoon just before the party?"

Blackwell kept his eyes on the road. "Sorry, but I'm just kinda worn out."

Giselle twisted in her seat, turning away from him. Blackwell turned up the jazz station, and the music soothed the flow of his thoughts. He remembered Camille and how lovely she looked, how carefree she and her new boyfriend seemed together. Why had he run away? And why had Giselle's sexual advances started to feel more like a trap than a fantasy?

Meanwhile, back at the party, Pinky could be seen sucking the last nibbles of meat off a rib bone while perched against a maple tree, the best view in the yard. Incidentally, the entire scene with

Blackwell had played out exactly as she predicted. She couldn't help but laugh out loud, and Sister Corrine looked at her confused. "What in the world has gotten into you?"

"Corrine, all I can say is one day these youngsters gonna learn that you can try to fight God all you want to, and sometimes it'll even look like you're about to win. But just when you rise up to claim the victory, my Father in heaven will show up. He'll let you know that all the real winners are on His team. Ha, ha!"

THINK ABOUT IT

1. Blackwell is obviously living in the pink. Can you relate to his struggle—why or why not?
2. Second Corinthians 3:17 (NIV) says: *Now the Lord is the Spirit, and where the Spirit of the Lord is, there is freedom.* Discuss what is meant here by "freedom," which is translated as "liberty" in some versions. What kind of freedom did Blackwell seek, after rebelling against the church? Which kind of freedom would you prefer and why?
3. Is there any truth in Blackwell's theory that women lose themselves as they become more involved in church?
4. Have you been or do you know someone who has been turned off by what they deem to be a "hypocritical" church? Do you believe that Christians, in general, are any more hypocritical or more honest than the rest of society?
5. Plenty of non-Christian couples have beautiful love stories. Taking that into account, do you agree or disagree with Camille when she tells Blackwell that he can't truly love her if he's not a strong follower of Christ?
6. Why do you think women outnumber men in most churches? What might be some reasons for the disparity?

7. Should there be boundaries when giving advice or spiritual counsel to fellow sisters in relationships and marriages? If so, what are those boundaries?

STEPS TO VICTORY

"IS IT TRUE, Senator Holt? Did you do it?"

Courtney pushed through the crush of cameras without answering. She kept her head down to avoid a shot of her face in tomorrow's paper or on the six o'clock news. There had been too many of those already, posting sunken eyes and sagging cheeks below front-page headlines.

In the *Miami Sentinel*: "Probe Finds Sen. Holt Diverted Funds"

From the *Orlando Herald*: "Holt's Cruise, Clothes on Taxpayer Dime"

On the editorial page of the *St. Petersburg Register*: "Senator 'for the People' Fooled Us All"

And that was only a dollop of the scrutiny to come. Courtney realized as much as she headed from the state capitol building to the designated space where her Mercedes awaited. Reporters and photographers formed a canopy along her path.

"What's your side of the story, Senator?"

"Don't the people of Florida deserve an answer?"

Jewel Gibbons, one of the most powerful attorneys in the state, hurried alongside Courtney, holding up her hand to block camera flashes. "No comment," she said every few moments to ward off questions.

The chaotic journey ended when Courtney clicked the key fob to open her door. "I'll drive," Jewel announced, grabbing the keys and almost jogging around to the other side. Gradually, the reporters backed off, now seeing the futility of their attempts. The senator, who had become a powerful voice in Florida politics and destined, some said, for a U.S. Congressional seat, had no plans to explain results of the audit released several hours before. At least not now.

"Where are we going?" Jewel asked. "With all this attention at the state building, the media is bound to be waiting outside your house, too."

Courtney looked at the time on her BlackBerry and contemplated for a moment. "Take me to the airport."

"The airport? You can't leave Tallahassee at a time like this. It'll look like you're running away."

"I don't care what it looks like at this point. Just get me to the airport. A regular flight from Tally to Tampa takes off at a quarter past six o'clock. If we hurry, I can get there in time to fly standby."

"Courtney, I don't advise this. We've got things to do. I'm thinking a press conference tomorrow on the capitol steps, refuting all allegations."

"But how will I explain everything?"

"You won't have to explain anything. I'll draft a prepared statement, and you'll read directly from that. We won't take any questions afterward, just say what we have to say and leave. I can't believe they're hounding you like this," Jewel said, her fingers gripping the wheel. "But we'll fix them. We can have representatives from some organizations that you've helped stand behind you at the press conference. I'll make sure they call this the witch hunt that it is—that'll sound better coming from them than you. At least one of them can say a few words about how your initiatives created new programs in inner-city neighborhoods all over this state."

"Fine," Courtney answered. "I'll fly back early tomorrow morning, but I have to go. There's somebody I have to see before I take another step."

Pinky sat on the edge of the couch. She had flipped from one news channel to the next since getting out of bed this morning. Today the results of the audit would be released and, perhaps more than anyone else, she wanted to know the findings. Not that she didn't believe Courtney when she said the accusations were just lies. It's just that, if it's one thing Pinky had learned over the years, it's to put her complete trust and confidence in God, not a man or a woman—not even her baby sister. Only God knows what a person will do under enough pressure.

The whole mess started when a reporter for the *Register* started calling a couple months back. Pinky avoided the calls at first, seeing the newspaper's name flash across her caller ID. She assumed it was a solicitor and didn't feel like being persuaded to renew her subscription. It'd be nice to keep up with the latest news so she could pray for the problems of this world, but lately the unread papers had stacked up so high she gave up trying. The reporter never left a message, but lucked up one morning when Willie saw fit to answer the phone for a change. He never paid attention to caller ID. After talking a moment, he handed the phone to Pinky. A reporter wanted to talk with her, had something to do with Courtney.

"Mrs. Pinkston?"

"Indeed."

"My name is Sheryl Thomason, and I'm a reporter for the *St. Petersburg Register*. I'm sorry to bother you, but I'm calling to ask some questions for a story we're writing about your sister, Senator Courtney Holt."

"Yes, I know who my sister is," Pinky said, playfully. "How

can I help you? Is it one of those feature stories about her upbringing and her family life?"

"Not this time. Actually, the story is about recent allegations that Senator Holt has, well, been using public money for personal expenses."

"Excuse me? What are you talking about?"

"Mrs. Pinkston, I'm afraid that documents obtained by our paper a few days ago reveal what look like personal items paid for with taxpayer money filtered through budgets that Senator Holt controls. One of the expenses, for instance, is a flat-screen television that the senator had delivered to your home here in the Tampa Bay area, according to our records."

Pinky's eyes darted across the room to the sleek big-screen set that Courtney bought the family for Christmas last year.

"Ma'am?" she heard the reporter saying. "Do you have such a television in your house?"

"It's none of your business what I have in my house," Pinky said, as angry as she was confused.

"I know this call comes as a shock, Mrs. Pinkston, but believe me I'm just doing my job, trying to get to the truth of the matter."

"Look, I don't know what is going on and I need to talk to my sister before I say anything more to you. So I'm sorry, but I'm going to hang up—"

"What about your daughter Jasmine's wedding reception two years ago?"

At the sound of Jasmine's name, Pinky's thumb froze just shy of clicking the button to end the call.

The reporter continued hurriedly. "Ma'am, we've also obtained receipts from a catering company that supplied barbecue shrimp skewers, grilled vegetables, chocolate-covered strawberries—all paid for from a government account. Do you know anything about that?"

Pinky's hand trembled and she opened her mouth to speak but could think of nothing to say.

"Mrs. Pinkston?"

Unsure of what else to do, Pinky ended the call just as Willie walked back into the room, drinking a glass of lemon iced tea.

Pinky got up and paced the living room while explaining what had transpired between her and the reporter. Willie picked up the cordless, dialed Courtney's number, and gave the handset to his wife.

Courtney seemed equally shocked that the reporter had called Pinky. The newspaper's inquiries had been ongoing for days. Courtney initially told the reporter there had been a misunderstanding in the accounting department. The calls continued with more questions, so much so that she started ignoring them.

"The reporter said my TV set showed up on state expense reports," Pinky explained. "She even knew about the money you spent on Jasmine's wedding reception. How did that happen? How do they have receipts from Jasmine's caterer if you paid for it from your own account?"

Pinky could hear Courtney's breathing grow heavy with every detail. "I cannot believe these people! With all the corruption in Tallahassee, they're worried about a $5,000 catering bill from two years ago? They have been out to get me since Day One. They can't stand to see a woman in a position of power and making a difference for poor people. They would rather pave streets in wealthy neighborhoods and create tax breaks for big businesses. They want to play hardball with this one, well, they'll just have to bring it on 'cause I won't lie down without a fight."

"But what about—"

"Don't you worry, Pinky. If that reporter calls again, do the same thing you did this time. Don't answer any of her questions and just hang up the phone. I'll take care of this."

That was three or so months ago. In the time since, the story spread statewide and even earned a few spots on the national news channels. Major newspapers picked it up, reporters stumbling over one another to find fresh angles on the scandal every other week.

They printed detailed charts of credit card charges listed on state expense reports with dubious descriptions. A $2,300 shopping spree of St. John suits filed as "public speaking preparation." A cruise to the Bahamas labeled as "networking." Pinky's TV came under "miscellaneous" expenses, while Jasmine's reception had been dubbed "community outreach."

Courtney spoke sparingly to the press, explaining that she didn't want to battle something this important in the media. "My constituents know me," she'd been quoted as saying in one political journal. "They know this is nothing but partisan maneuvering meant to discredit me before the next election."

The uproar fueled a state investigation, the results of which were released today. Pinky made sure she watched every TV report. She'd already asked Willie to buy copies of both major newspapers in the area.

By the end of the day, just before dusk gave way to night, the doorbell rang and she wasn't at all surprised to see Courtney's face.

When it came to the three Holt siblings, Pinky's older brother, Julius, had always been somewhat disconnected from the rest, off doing his own thing. He turned out to be a good hardworking man, a mechanic. He and his wife had been married for more than thirty-five years and had two grown sons and a daughter in medical school. Pinky took on the mothering role in the family. She hosted the gatherings and counseled her nieces and nephews through teenage problems they didn't feel comfortable talking about with their parents.

Courtney—still called CeCe by those who knew her when—filled the successful slot and made the family proud. From her hometown high school outside of Jacksonville, she got a scholarship to the University of Virginia where she graduated with a degree in political science, then got her master's in government affairs. By the time she turned thirty, she had worked on political campaigns for everybody from small-town city council members to state legislators and even played a marginal role in the presidential campaign's push for a majority in Central Florida. Yet, political parties didn't faze her. She registered as an independent, saying politics should be about doing what's right not about joining a club. Come election time, she would knock on doors for a Republican candidate she favored in one race and mail brochures for a Democrat in another.

Eventually her experience and connections led to her appointment as head of the newly formed Department of Community Revitalization, created under the tenure of Gov. Andrew Childress. From him, Courtney learned all she could about the political game. Never mind her petite five-foot-four frame, she mingled in rooms full of power brokers and left with enough contacts to spin a deal for a new children's program, a library, or state-of-the-art recreation center and pool in an underserved neighborhood. Her path seemed inevitable. Fans encouraged her to take that next step into public office. Finally, just shy of her forty-fifth birthday, Courtney announced her first bid for a state Senate seat.

During the campaign, Pinky rallied her many friends at Believers Ministries to help stuff envelopes, pass out fliers, and hold up posters with Courtney's picture on election day. Of course, the church didn't jeopardize its tax-exempt status by formally endorsing her or any other candidate, and the bishop never mentioned her name from the pulpit. But in the privacy of his home, after putting his preaching robes aside, he also stuffed envelopes and slipped her slogan into conversations: "Courtney Holt, the People's Politician."

Earl and Myrlie Holt, still alive at the time, grinned wide while watching their baby daughter take the oath of office after being elected to the Florida legislature. Of course, Pinky and her family stood there, too, proud as could be. The only thing that might have made any of them happier would be Courtney in a wedding gown, but a husband never seemed to be in her plans. Romances had been short-lived, apparently trumped by an ongoing love affair with public service.

The first story of the scandal ran in the *Register* on a Wednesday, prayer and Bible study night at Believers Ministries. Willie asked Pinky if she planned to stay home. Of course not, she told him. No newspaper story could stop her from praising the Lord. That night the bishop led the congregation in a special prayer for Senator Holt, a faithful visitor to the church whenever she came to town. During the meet-and-greet portion of service, no less than ten people approached Pinky, offering their prayers and support. Some of them had helped in the campaign and were emotionally invested in the ordeal.

"I don't even listen to the news anymore and I've cancelled my subscription to the *Register* since this seems to be the only thing they want to write about these days," one member said about a month into the scandal.

Pinky got a call from the Tampa Bay chapter of the activist organization Equality for Women. Leaders planned to question whether the state discriminated against Courtney by singling her out for an investigation. Members would question other legislators' accounts, prompting an audit of their expenses, as well. One neighborhood association that had worked closely with Courtney to replace an outdated playground with safer equipment staged a protest outside the *Register*, claiming biased reporting. "Find the real CROOKS," one sign read. "Look in the MIRROR!" The next week, they held their signs outside one of the major TV network affiliates also aggressively reporting the story.

Pinky declined all offers to participate, from the protesters, from the women's group, even from her brother, Julius, who had organized some friends to ride up to Tallahassee and march outside the capitol building.

"I'll do my fighting in my prayer closet," she told him.

"But CeCe needs to see that she has our support more than anything. She needs to see that we stand behind her 100 percent."

"I love my sister, but my presence at another march is not what she needs most right now. I'm afraid that all the marches and signs and cancelled newspaper subscriptions can't do much good now. Everybody thinks this is between Senator Courtney Holt and the media, but it's not."

"Since you know so much, who is this between?"

"CeCe and God," Pinky responded, not at all bothered by her brother's attitude. "Whatever's going on, He's allowing it to happen. The question is why. Could be one of two reasons from what I can tell. Either He's battling her enemies so He can build her faith and let her know that He'll conquer any adversary, be it the media or her political rivals, or whomever. Or—and I'm praying this isn't it—He's wrestling with CeCe, herself, in which case I have no idea what the end will be."

Pinky opened the door and watched the cab drive off. She stepped aside to let her sister in. Courtney walked over to the middle of the room and placed her briefcase on the floor. There, just before she plopped onto the couch, Pinky grabbed her in an embrace that pumped free the well of tears she had held inside all day.

Willie heard the commotion from his den and got up to peek into the living room. He had just watched another report on the evening news showing a clip of Courtney with her head down, walking stridently from the capitol and into her car with a lawyer. The anchor made a point of saying that reporters waiting outside the senator's home had not seen her since she left the downtown office. People wondered where she had gone, whether she left the area to avoid facing the flurry of questions sure to come her way now that the audit confirmed the allegations against her.

On TV, she looked strong and unruffled, the opposite of the woman crumbling now in his wife's arms. He stepped forward, wanting to lend his support to Courtney, as well, but thought better of interrupting the moment and retreated to his den to study his lesson for the Brothers Keepers group meeting.

Pinky ushered her sister onto the couch. Courtney declined her offer to heat up the meat loaf and mashed potatoes she had cooked for dinner, so Pinky excused herself to the kitchen to put on a pot of Courtney's favorite gourmet coffee. By the time she returned, Courtney had turned the TV set completely off, tired of seeing the same news clip of herself with more speculative commentary about what would happen next and who might replace her if criminal charges were filed or she were forced to resign.

"Something told me I would see you soon," Pinky said, initiating the discussion Courtney obviously came here to have but didn't know how to begin. "Times like these often bring us closer to the family we can lean on and trust."

Courtney sipped on a large mug of caramel macchiato brew and looked straight ahead. "I know that better than anyone. These past few months have been the lowest point in my life. I feel like the Devil has just been after me, persecuting me, trying to hang me," she said, choking up and leaning her head back to stop another flow of tears.

"I know, baby. I know."

"No, Pinky, I don't think you do. I don't think anybody can know how something like this feels unless they've been put on the butcher block and sliced every which way."

Courtney paused, waiting for Pinky to respond. But she didn't, preferring to listen for now.

"Pinky, I've been praying and begging God to please make this go away. After all, I am a believer," Courtney said—now talking more to herself than to Pinky. "I go to church when I can. And I give into the offering bucket, too, a lot more than most. Yet, I'm still going through this.

"You know what I'm doing tomorrow?" she continued, and gave a sarcastic chuckle. "I'm going to give a press conference on the steps of the capitol. Jewel is drawing up the text right now, so I can defend myself to all those big shots who want to pretend that they're better than me. Every last one of them knows that this stuff is nothing compared to what's going on elsewhere in state government. You want to see corruption? Go over to the governor's mansion. Find out how his biggest campaign contributors file their donations under phony business names so he'll give them any and every thing they want without raising red flags with the press. Corruption? Audit the attorney general and see how he got the money for the secret beach chateau he shares with his mistress every other weekend. Catch up with the former head of the Department of Education and find out how his son just happened to get a job with the largest public university in the state, despite having no experience in that field whatsoever.

"See, they better not push me too far. I know how to play this game . . ."

Courtney kept talking, but Pinky began to daydream. She saw CeCe as the little girl their parents forced Pinky to drag along to the corner store. The girl whose thick hair Pinky would separate and braid into cornrows during the summertime. She remembered the young woman graduating from college, so eager to help the people in inner-city neighborhoods like the one where she grew up. The way Courtney sounded now, Pinky wondered whether that innocence had long slipped away.

"They want corruption?" she heard Courtney saying now, "I can show them some corruption."

Pinky sat up on the couch, as if to steady herself for what would come next. She needed to cut through Courtney's rant and ask the question her sister had avoided since the matter began.

Courtney quieted, seeing that her big sister was about to speak. Pinky not only played the mothering role in the family, but the older she got, the more she actually looked like their mother. Same caramel skin tone and full frame. Same mole, just above the left eyebrow. Same loving, yet firm tone in her voice. Myrlie Holt had gone on to be with the Lord, but Courtney knew her presence would never leave this earth as long as Pinky lived.

"CeCe, you know that nobody cares for you more than me.

Nobody wants to see you succeed more than I do. But right now, baby sister, I need you to tell me something and I need you to tell it straight."

Courtney nodded.

"Did you do it? Did you use public money to buy this here TV or to pay for any of the other things they talk about on those reports?"

Courtney said nothing at first, instead diverting her gaze to the darkness outside the living room bay window. Until, that is, the little spunk she had left rose inside of her.

"So you're starting to believe the newspapers, too, huh? I thought the one person I could turn to would be you. I guess I was wrong—way wrong." She got up from the couch.

Pinky tried to interrupt, but Courtney raised her palm, letting her know that it would be no use, and kept talking.

"You know why I had to get down here tonight?" she asked rhetorically. "I needed somebody who had the Lord's ear to pray with me, to help me figure out the next step. I had no idea I'd be put on trial by my own family."

She walked into the den. "Willie, can you help me find the nearest hotel so I can get out of here? My sister thinks I'm a thief and I know you don't want any criminals in the house."

Pinky didn't move. She was still sitting there with her coffee mug in hand when Willie led Courtney back to the living room. Pinky and Willie had already discussed their concerns about Courtney's evasiveness when it came to addressing the allegations head-on. But wherever the truth lay, he didn't want it to affect the relationship between sisters.

"Pinky, please, let CeCe know she's more than welcome to stay with us."

"She already knows that, Willie. It ain't us she's running away from."

Courtney stopped just short of the door and looked back. "And just who do you think I'm running from?"

"God."

Courtney's eyes squinted and her lips squeezed together so tightly it's a wonder the sound of her next words eked through. "You think you know it all, don't you, Pinky? You got me and everybody else in this world figured out? Well, you don't know what it's like to be me, to be a woman who had to fight for every foothold on her way up the mountain to Capitol Hill. There were people who had a third of my qualifications and skill that flew right on past because of their family ties, the people they knew, or the color of their skin."

Pinky took another sip of her coffee then looked at Willie. "Honey, would you please let me know when the pity party is over?"

"Pinky!" Willie said, frowning.

"That's okay, Willie," Courtney said. "I'd forgotten what a self-righteous, arrogant heifer my sister is."

Pinky stood up now and strode over to Courtney, standing inches away from her face. "You can try to avoid the issue all you want. You can talk about other politicians who steal money. You can talk about how hard it was for you to make it. You can even try to put the spotlight on me and call me names. But none of that will change the bottom line on that state investigation. It won't change the fact that you, CeCe Holt, took those people's money."

Courtney began to tremble and Pinky steadied her with a firm hand on her shoulder.

"Don't be deceived. This is between you and the Lord now, baby sister. He allowed this mess to come to light because the Bible says He chastens those He loves. You got off track somewhere, got caught up with those people behind big desks who want to get ahead and don't care how they go about doing it. But God has had enough of your foolishness now. He wants you back doing the work He called you to do. You'll have to pay the consequences, and we can pray that they aren't too severe, but He won't pay our prayers no mind till you stop running, stop lying, and ask for forgiveness."

The steps of the capitol building seemed steeper than they ever had. Maybe because Courtney hadn't even closed her eyes the night before. Maybe because she knew she may never climb those steps again.

Early that morning, she thanked God for the people who meant most to her, which included Willie. He ran to catch up with her last night after she stomped out the door and insisted on driving her to the airport hotel. The whole way there, he told her how much Pinky had cried and prayed over the situation in the previous months.

"She's a strong-willed woman," he told Courtney. "She's only doing what she believes is right."

Once settled at the Marriott, Courtney thought about her mistakes. She had been careless in accounting and mingling use of the state's credit card with her own. She had paid for Pinky's TV, although she couldn't be sure if she actually reimbursed the state for the total cost of Jasmine's reception at some point. As for her St. John suits and networking cruise, some state officials considered those to be routine perks that came with the job. A fellow legislator once advised Courtney to upgrade her wardrobe and put it on the state's time. Courtney knew deep down that the expenses were questionable, but figured no one would ever ask since they were the norm. And that state representative hadn't spoken a word to Courtney since the scandal broke. In fact, one article quoted her as saying that the senator used poor judgment.

The clock tower downtown struck two, and the scene extended to the edge of the capitol lawn with TV camera crews and regular people wanting to hear Courtney explain herself. Members of Equality for Women stood together with matching EFW T-shirts. Jewel had arranged for the pastor of a local church that Courtney often visited to stand among a group of supporters behind her at the top of the steps.

The night before, Jewel had e-mailed the prepared statement, which basically said the allegations against Courtney were false and would be proven so. Jewel planned to release scattered bank records that showed at least partial payments for some of the expenses in question. Once officials saw discrepancies in the allegations, they might drop the matter rather than spend more time and money to go through records with a fine-toothed comb.

"Are you ready?" Jewel said into Courtney's ear.

Courtney nodded, and Jewel turned on the podium microphone and adjusted it to the appropriate height. Courtney held onto the statement and leaned forward to speak. The crowd hushed.

Shakily, Courtney said, "I have called you all here today because I . . . because I . . ." She looked around as if she didn't know what to say next.

Jewel rested a hand on her shoulder for comfort, hoping Courtney could quickly pull herself together. The more she wavered, the more she would appear guilty, defeating the whole purpose of the press conference. Moments passed and the crowd murmured. Cameras continued to flash, capturing a bewildered looking Courtney standing at her own press conference in complete silence. Jewel reached for the microphone in an effort to take over, but Courtney moved her lawyer's hand away and finally began talking again. This time, her voice sounded confident and direct.

"Let me start over again. I called you here today because I want to tell you the truth. You, the people of the great 'Sunshine State,' deserve that much from someone you've elected to office."

Jewel noticed Courtney turning over the statement as if she had no more use for it. She clutched Courtney's shoulder again, as a warning this time, and whispered in her ear, "Senator, what are you doing?"

Courtney smoothly brushed Jewel's hand away and kept talking. "The truth is I have not been as judicious as I should have been in my oversight of the accounts that you entrusted to me. For this, I am deeply sorry."

She heard a collective gasp from the supporters standing behind her on the steps and turned toward them with a conciliatory nod and mouthed the words "I'm sorry" again. She again faced those in front of her, ignoring Jewel's whispers to stop the speech.

"Please understand that I am not saying that the report released yesterday is totally accurate. It is not. On some occasions, I used state funding sources out of convenience, a credit card, for instance, but in fact reimbursed our coffers for personal expenses. For those instances, I have records. From this day forward, I will cooperate fully with officials to rectify any monies that were not reimbursed that should have been. And I will pay whatever is owed."

People in the crowd looked at each other in shock. Many figured that the senator had been wrong, but couldn't believe her public admission. Courtney paused, trying to find a way to conclude what could possibly be the end of her dream political career.

"I want all of you, my constituents, to know that I have enjoyed my time as your senator perhaps more than anything else I have ever done. I love meeting you at your neighborhood association meetings and helping you to better your communities by securing the funding that you so desperately need. I even enjoy reading your letters and taking your phone calls, all of which give me the confidence that when people invest their time and their hearts in where they live, they can make a difference. My first prayer is that my mistakes will not weaken your faith in what you, as ordinary people with a goal, can do. My next prayer is that you will forgive me of my poor judgment and continue to lend me your patience and your understanding."

In Tampa, Pinky and Willie watched the conference live on TV. "Thank You, Lord," Pinky said, as if the Savior was sitting in her living room. "She's coming back to You."

Back in Tallahassee, Courtney stepped back from the podium. She picked up her briefcase, turned and shook hands with supporters behind her, and hugged those who held their arms open in support. She ignored Jewel who stood back in disbelief, and began her descent down all those steps.

Reporters blurted out questions, hoping she might choose one randomly and respond.

"Senator, what's next, what will happen if there's a criminal investigation?"

"Is this the end of your political career, Senator? Will you resign?"

"Exactly how much of the public's money did you spend?"

Courtney looked straight ahead, the camera flashes highlighting what looked more like relief than fear in her eyes. Midway through the crowd, she stopped and held up a hand to demand silence. "I wish I could answer your questions, but the truth is that I don't have the facts right now. As you can imagine, there are many decisions to be made in the days to come. Now, if you'll excuse me."

The reporters wrote down her quote and scattered to get reaction from other taxpayers and politicians in the crowd.

THINK ABOUT IT

1. How was Senator Courtney Holt living in the pink?
2. Think of a time when you did something dishonest and you were found out. How did you handle the consequences—did you blame someone else, point the finger at others who did the same thing, or take responsibility for your actions?
3. What role did Courtney's supporters play in her continuing to avoid the truth?
4. As a woman, have you had to struggle more than men in your profession to achieve success? If so, to what extents do you think women should be willing to go to in order to reach their career goals?
5. Unisex names, such as Courtney, Taylor, or Cameron, have become popular, partly because mothers believe such names could give their daughters an edge in a male-dominated workforce. What are your thoughts on this?

6. Dishonest people are not limited to certain professions, but why do you think politicians, lawyers, car salesmen, etc., are stereotyped as such?
7. Give personal examples of the battles that Pinky described: one where God fought your enemies and another where God wrestled with you.

THE TRUTH ABOUT DINA

YOU CAN'T SIZE UP a woman by the clothes she wears, how she styles her hair, or whether or not she does the makeup and polished nail thing—not the whole of a woman anyway, not who she is inside, how she feels, and where she's been. If you could, somebody at Believers Ministries might have figured out that Dina had been through some things in life. But all that they knew of her played out in the choir stand or onstage, like tonight at the annual Southeast Regional Choir Sing-off in Orlando where the Sounds of Glory would be the third choir to perform.

Singers filed onto the stage in synchronized fashion wearing black slacks or skirts with satin shirts in hot shades of purple, lime green, red, pink, and gold. As choir director, Dina McClatchen led the way modeling a traditional march into their respective positions. They stepped side-to-side in time with the music, while bouncing their shoulders to add modern spice to their entrance. Members from the ten churches with choirs involved packed the auditorium. Those from Believers Ministries had come for the first time. They never heard anything about a "sing-off" till Dina came on as the worship leader. The church's traditional choir had been shrinking for years, comprised of mostly elderly women who loved to sing old-school favorites, such as *Down at the Cross* or *Precious Lord*. Then Dina emerged with ideas for contemporary medleys and a praise team that harmonized signature voices in the church.

She felt comfortable at Believers Ministries where the size of the congregation could swallow you up, if you wanted it to. And Dina did. She turned down Madeline Everett's invitations to Sunday dinner, as well as Sister Pinky's attempts to engage in conversation. Dina had no desire to make nice with the church leadership, or even the choir members for that matter. Not yet—it was too soon. All she wanted to do was direct. Here, in the choir pit, she shined as she always had. And that was good enough.

Dina grew up in church, her father the pastor of a medium-size ministry in Los Angeles. She started singing in the children's choir at age three. Even then, her voice had the strength of a child four times her age. The choir director had always intrigued her most, forcing octaves to rise or fall with a single arm motion, hushing the organist with a wave of the hand, and commanding the choir's naked voices to carry a verse a cappella. Most of all, the director set the tone of the church service by ushering the congregation into quiet worship or exuberant praise.

At age fourteen, Dina directed the church's youth choir for the first time. The piano sounded an Andrae Crouch tune, and she lifted her arms cueing the first note to "Soon and Very Soon." The beat gradually picked up, and she rocked back and forth, enticing the singers to follow. Her arm motions grew quicker with the music's faster pace before slowing again to the initial beat and a fancifully dramatic end. For their second song, she guided members in a series of spontaneous riffs then ended by holding the final note, her fingers moving rapidly and beckoning them and the organist to give her more, more. By the time they finished, everyone in the pews stood clapping.

Pastor K. C. McClatchen had dreamed of his daughter someday becoming a doctor, an instrument for God's healing hands. But after that performance, even he couldn't deny his only child's talent in the choir stand.

"You're at an age now when you're growing into the woman that God created you to become," he told her after church that day.

"Yes, Daddy," she'd said, grinning. She could tell he was proud of her.

"Crucial seeds are being planted in your life, so you have to stay focused on the talents that God has given you so that you'll grow and mature spiritually. I'm sure you don't understand everything that's going on in your life right now, but in time you will."

Later in her room that night, Dina meditated on her father's words. He had underestimated her in one sense—she understood her calling. She would be a church worship leader someday, of that much she was sure. But plenty of other things were starting to happen that she did feel too young to understand and too confused to try. Like why she didn't share her friends' interest in the boys at her school or at church. That's all they talked about, Jeffrey this or Damian that. Not Dina. She couldn't remember ever feeling attracted to a boy. Once in middle school she got one of those would-you-be-my-girlfriend notes taped to her locker. Dina quickly checked the "no" box and politely handed it back to little slew-footed Christopher James during English class.

Lately, though, she'd felt a tingle in her heart for a certain someone slightly older, an alto in the young adult choir. Every time they saw each other, they smiled, and on the few occasions when they got a chance to talk about music or whatever else came to mind, Dina wished their time would never end. When it did, she replayed their dialogue while alone in her bedroom, analyzing whether she had said the wrong thing. Was this love? That's what she didn't know. And if it was love, how could it be so wrong? That's what she didn't understand, because as far as Dina was concerned, Belinda Colby was perfect.

Most choirs tried to dazzle crowds with fast-paced selections to get them clapping, but for this sing-off Dina arranged a medley that began upbeat then segued into contemporary worship songs to put the focus on God. She participated in many gospel choir concerts in her forty-two years, but this one particularly excited her because she'd come to Believers Ministries less than a year before the event. Although people called it a "sing-off," no one would win, at least not technically. To rank choirs would border on the sacrilegious since they were supposed to sing for God, not a panel of judges. Nonetheless, everyone knew the crowd response designated the "people's choice." At Dina's last sing-off five years ago on the West Coast, the applause put her choir second, after an energetic younger group that incorporated elements of the electric slide into their choreography. Dina tended to avoid such blatant showmanship.

Tonight, the melody started out smooth, and the choir swayed side-to-side, humming in perfect harmony, mimicking Dina as she faced them. She had created the intro to give Hezekiah Walker's "God Favored Me" her own twist. When the organist and drummer lowered their beat, she signaled the choir to sing softly: *And I know You favored me because my enemies did try but couldn't triumph over me.* From there, the medley flowed smoothly to lyrics in the next tune: *He saw the best in me when everyone else around could only see the worst in me,* with Brother Jenkins's baritone voice leading a remix of the Marvin Sapp song.

By the time Sounds of Glory sang their final note, the crowd stood on their feet. Many had their hands raised, as if surrendering to God. Some shed joyful tears. The singers were visibly caught up in emotion as they exited the stage, shouting "hallelujahs." Dina, too, felt the Spirit of God moving in the auditorium. She'd chosen the songs because they had special meaning for her. It hadn't been long ago when only whispers followed as she walked into her father's church in Los Angeles, when it seemed that everyone around her focused on her mistakes—everyone, except God.

During that time, her brief marriage was ending in divorce, and Dina blamed no one but herself. Much of her life she had at least tried to look the part of a pastor's princess, having gained a reputation for always being put-together. With the exception of her parents, no one had seen her with a hair out of place since high school. She transitioned over the years from a chemically relaxed bob to an easily managed natural cut that she often styled with short twists or by occasionally applying a texturizer to create more of a wavy look. She shopped for bargains, but didn't mind splurging on a must-have suit that slimmed her shapely hips or a pair of heels that matched perfectly and added four inches to her five-foot-two-inch frame. A compact of rich cocoa foundation and bronze lip gloss rested in the bottom of whichever clutch she carried that day.

Her sense of style intimidated some men who thought her too high-maintenance, but it attracted those like her ex-husband who nursed a certain flair all his own and sought a woman to complement his image. By the time he came along in Dina's late thirties, she had tired of her aunts and uncles asking why such a nice looking woman like her never married.

Was she to tell them that her first sexual experience, at age fifteen, involved an eighteen-year-old girl in the church choir? That she'd gone to Belinda Colby's house one day while Belinda's mother worked and that they were talking and sitting on her bed when she moved in closer and awakened a sensuality that Dina didn't know existed? Their first actual kiss had come weeks before, in the church basement after choir practice as Belinda waited on her mother to pick her up and Dina waited on her father to finish some work in his office. Ever so briefly, their lips touched and Dina's heart thumped when her father's voice at the top of the basement steps interrupted the moment.

"Dina? You down there?"

"Yes, sir. We're just, um, talking about some stuff."

"Well, come on up, it's time to go," he said, then alerted Belinda that her mother's car had just pulled up outside.

Was Dina to tell the relatives who questioned her singleness that she'd felt more in tune, emotionally and physically, with Belinda than she did with any of the boyfriends who followed? No, that's not something you tell a family full of churchgoing saints—at least not if you want to be invited to Thanksgiving dinner or the next reunion.

She did try dating men after high school. It just never worked out. Inevitably, either she lost interest or they did and soon Dina figured she couldn't do any worse with a woman. That's when the secret life started: same-sex nightclubs, gay-friendly bars, restaurants, and novelty shops in West Hollywood. She stopped going to church, so she wouldn't have to pretend she was somebody she wasn't, especially when her father went on one of his tirades about homosexuality being an abomination to God. Each time she visited her parents, the pastor offered a dining room sermon about how God still loves sinners. Her mother assumed Dina had gotten caught up with a good-for-nothing man. Her father speculated she might be doing drugs, for no other reason than that everybody else they knew had at least one family member addicted to something.

But her parents weren't the reason Dina woke up one Sunday, put on her chocolate-colored two-piece suit with matching heels, and marched into the church where she grew up. It was an overcast sky with a slight spring breeze and she had stumbled lazily out of bed, her only intention being to make a pot of coffee. She looked at the clock and remembered that, back in the day, she would have happily been getting ready for church at that hour. She missed that. She missed the sense that she belonged to God and that she could kneel and pray and somehow hear Him speak to her. She missed the chill she felt during worship or the sense that someone larger than anything she could describe wrapped His arms around her, held her, and kept her strong.

Heads turned to catch sight of the pastor's "prodigal" daughter walking down the aisle that morning, including that of someone new, Roderick Upshaw, who had swaggered into the Sanctuary at Bethesda just a few months before. From then on, he watched her every Sunday to the point where it's a wonder if he ever heard the pastor at all. Dina welcomed the attention. She had prayed that God would take away her desire for women. Soon, Roderick regularly visited her home, sure to keep his hands to himself and to leave at a respectable hour. They referred to their relationship as a "courtship," the proper spiritual terminology for a preacher's daughter.

He began taking ministry training classes to become a church elder. Dina reclaimed her old spot as head of the praise team. They seemed the perfect couple, and Pastor McClatchen had a man-to-man with Roderick and explained how lust could destroy all that he had worked for. Roderick gave his word that he would not touch Dina unless, or until, they married. He also took the opportunity to ask the pastor for permission to join the McClatchen family, which he received. A few weeks later, he proposed, and she said yes.

Roderick sensed something wrong almost immediately after four hundred guests left the reception at a seaside ballroom they'd rented for the occasion. That night—the night he'd been waiting for—she lay in bed limp and unexcited. It all made sense four months later when Roderick returned home early because of a cancelled church meeting. Dina, relaxing in a bubble bath, had forgotten to log off the computer. Roderick revived the screen from sleep mode only to find an Internet chat room for lesbians. Dina's screen name: Unhappily Married.

Dina tried to save the marriage, although even she wondered if her motive was love or fear that her secret would get out. She told him snippets of her past and acknowledged that she still wrestled with her sexuality. But with his understanding, Dina promised, she would change for good. For two days, her pleas were met with his icy stares and silence. He didn't believe her. Even if she really wanted to change, Roderick questioned whether she could.

"So, where do we go from here?" Dina had asked, again trying to reopen dialogue. Roderick didn't bother to face her before picking up the remote to turn on the TV, but he did finally speak. "*You* are going to hell," he said matter-of-factly. "*I* am going to get myself a lawyer."

Dina packed her bags that night and moved in with a friend she had met years before in West Hollywood. Roderick went the next day to Pastor McClatchen, then to the church elders to rally support. He definitely had biblical grounds for divorce, they told him. Days passed before Dina got up the courage to answer her parents' calls and stop by the house to tell her side. When she did, she confessed the truth that she'd hidden for so long.

Sobbing, her mother covered her face with her hands and shook her head.

Dina reached out to comfort her. "Mama, I haven't done any of those things you're thinking in years."

"But you were looking at them, talking to them on the Internet, Dina!" she screamed. "That sin is still in your heart, and that's what counts with God.

"Lord, I don't know what would've been worse," she mumbled, "a daughter on drugs or a daughter who's like that."

Dina flinched. "You would prefer a crack addict over me?"

Her mother didn't respond, and Pastor McClatchen didn't look Dina in the eye. He got up and walked across the living room to look out of the bay window.

"Homosexuality is an abomination before God," he said, straining to keep his voice even-toned.

He rattled off the biblical story of Sodom and Gomorrah and reminded her of God's plan when He created Adam and Eve. He offered to pay for counseling and to send Dina to a monthlong camp intended to convert homosexuals. In the meantime, she could no longer sing in his choir. No way would he let her lead others when she had lost the way to God herself.

Dina didn't know what to believe, what to do.

"Mom, Dad, I love you," she said on the way out the door. "And, from the bottom of my heart, I'm so sorry."

A little more than a year had passed since that scene. Now sitting in the auditorium for the sing-off, Dina distinctly remembered the sound of her parents' door latch catching as it closed behind her that day. Such a small thing resonated so loudly, she figured, because it symbolized the closed door that continued to separate her from her family.

She had left Los Angeles to keep the peace and minimize her parents' embarrassment. It would've been worse for them had she stayed around while people grasped for whatever nugget of gossip they could get. She researched cities on the other side of the country and a headhunter found a few job possibilities in consulting, Dina's college major. Two conference-call interviews and a plane trip later, she landed 2,500 miles away at Tampa International Airport. She settled into an apartment then opened the yellow pages one day to find a church.

She deleted her profile from the chat rooms and cut off communication with gay friends in LA. She joined a Christian support group for homosexuals that focused on studying the Bible and memorizing "power Scriptures" to recite whenever same-sex thoughts came to mind.

Dina reflected on the events of the last few years of her life from her auditorium seat, paying little attention to the efforts of other choirs in the sing-off. That is, until the very last group. The members, donning purple and white and drawing mass applause, readied to end their set with a BeBe and CeCe Winans duet. A woman, tall and lanky, stepped forward with a distinctive sinewy alto voice. Dina squinted and focused her gaze so that she could be sure. The woman had put on a few pounds since their high school days and her hair stretched longer and straighter than before. Still, Dina knew. There, on the stage thousands of miles and more than twenty years from when she saw her last, stood Belinda Colby.

"Belinda?" Dina said, hesitantly approaching. After the program ended, she'd debated whether to make her presence known at all. Judging from the crowd response, the choirs from Believers Ministries and Belinda's church had tied for top honors. A whisper in the back of Dina's mind told her to simply congratulate her own choir members and head straight home. A stronger voice urged her to at least say hello, even if only out of curiosity. She followed the second, all the way up to the front of the auditorium where Belinda mingled with singers from her group.

At the sound of her name, Belinda looked up to see Dina standing directly beside her. Her shocked expression led those around her to look at Dina with raised eyebrows.

"Dina? Wow. I haven't seen you in years," she said, trying to sound cordial. From the outfit, she realized that Dina had directed the other "winning" choir. "I had no idea that was you up there with your new hairdo and everything. You look good."

"Thanks, so do you," Dina said simply. She felt uneasy as the crowd of purple and white singers grew around them.

"Everyone," Belinda said, her eyes sweeping around the circle, "this is Dina, an old friend of mine from my hometown in California. We used to sing in the youth choir together, a long, long time ago."

About that time a man walked up behind Belinda and slipped his arm around her waist.

"Hi, Pastor," someone in the crowd said. He nodded to acknowledge the person then looked at Belinda.

She cleared her throat to hide her nervousness. "Honey," she said, "meet Dina, an old friend from LA."

"It's my pleasure," he said, reaching out for a strong handshake. "I always like to meet people who knew my wife way back when." With a wink, he added, "They might be able to give me some good dirt on her that I can use when she starts getting on me about mowing the yard."

At that, Belinda dropped the clutch purse she'd been holding. A compact, lipstick, and other knickknacks scattered across the floor. "You okay?" her husband asked, puzzled. "You seem jittery."

People moved away to clear the area and a boy of about ten or eleven years emerged from behind Belinda's husband and started picking everything up.

"You women and your purses," the pastor said, turning back to Dina and shaking his head. "Now, what was your name again?"

"Dina. Dina McClatchen."

"I can't say I remember Belinda mentioning that name," he said, looking off to jog his memory before giving up. "I'm Pastor Cedric Monroe. I have a small church a couple of hours from here in Fort Meyers where I was born and raised. But I must say that LA knows how to turn out some lovely Christian women," he said, tightening his arm around Belinda's waist.

The little boy stood up with Belinda's clutch intact, and Pastor Monroe continued his introductions. "This is our son, Cedric Jr., and over there," he said, pointing a few yards away to a teenager giggling among a group of girls, "is our daughter, Celeste."

The most Dina could think of to say: "What a nice family."

She couldn't identify the emotions churning inside her. Here was Belinda, standing at the center of what appeared to be a happy, wholesome family, the picture of what Dina's parents wished she had. How could the very person who introduced Dina to an "alternative lifestyle" have switched sides and left her to struggle alone?

"My goodness, look at the time," Belinda said, pointing to the wall clock in a transparent effort to end the encounter. "I had no idea it was so late. Cedric, we've got to drive all the way home, so we'd better leave now." She paused before facing Dina. "Nice to see you again," she said. "I wish you all the best."

Belinda grabbed her son by the arm and walked hurriedly over to her daughter. Pastor Monroe started to follow right on her heels, but first looked at Dina once more. "I just want to say that I truly enjoyed your choir today. I can tell that you love the Lord and you have a gift to usher people into worship."

"Thank you so much, Pastor."

Then, almost impulsively, Dina reached out for a hug, and he obliged. He felt her body tremble slightly and heard her sniffle. The emotional reaction made something click in his mind, and, still holding Dina in his arms, he raised his head and looked across the auditorium where his wife stood. Belinda met his stare for a moment before turning away.

Dina got a hold of herself and stepped back. Embarrassed, she tried to turn and walk away, but the pastor gently grabbed her elbow.

"No matter what you're feeling right now," he told her, "remember that you are beautiful and you are blessed. God has given you a special gift to use for His glory. Your job is to recognize who you are in His eyes, so that you can keep on glorifying Him."

Dina arrived home from work to find her mother's number on the caller ID. Right on schedule for Mom's quarterly call. About three months had passed since they last spoke.

Mrs. McClatchen never mentioned the turmoil that drove Dina away from LA, steering conversations to everybody else's business—except Roderick's. She didn't tell Dina that he had already proposed to one of the lead singers in the choir. Pastor McClatchen, who avoided speaking to his daughter directly, could be heard in the background telling Dina's mother to tell Dina that he said hello.

After seeing Belinda at the sing-off, Dina felt more isolated than ever. They hadn't even talked to one another in twenty years, but Dina assumed that Belinda endured the same pain she had. Now she realized Belinda lived a "normal" life.

She grabbed the cordless phone to dial her mother's number, but stopped when she heard breathing on the other end of the line.

Someone must've been calling her, but Dina picked up the phone before it could ring.

"Hello, who's there?"

"Dina?"

"Yes, this is Dina. Who's this?"

"Dina, it's me . . . It's Belinda."

Something—her heart, her soul?—sank. She tightened her fingers around the phone and pressed it to her ear.

"I know you're surprised to hear from me," Belinda continued, "but please don't hang up. I called your church and told the secretary who I am and convinced her to give me your phone number. Dina, I've wanted to reach out to you for so long, but I was so shocked to see you here, in Florida, the other night that I didn't know how to handle it. We really need to talk."

"About what?"

"About the past. I want you to know how sorry I am. The things that happened between us never should have taken place. What we did—what I did—was so wrong."

It hurt to hear Belinda denounce their history. Her words jabbed at Dina's heart where she still held a fondness for what they once shared.

Dina searched for words to sting back.

"Oh, I get it. Now that you're pretending you aren't gay, you want to try to brush off the past as a so-called mistake?"

"I'm not pretending," Belinda said, her voice stern. "I'm not. Dina, I could tell as soon as I saw you that you were still lost," Belinda went on calmly. "But I no longer am. Today, I'm a child of God who has been delivered more than twenty years, and you can be delivered, too. That's what I called to tell you."

"Delivered from what?" Dina said, almost spitting out each word. "Look, if you want to continue your charade of a life, go right ahead, but I refuse to lie to myself. Not anymore. I'm tired of the depression."

Dina paused to catch her breath then continued, no longer trying to stay composed.

"Do you know how many times I've wanted to kill myself to end the pain? Do you know how many times I've cried out to God, asking Him to give me a new heart, a new mind? Sometimes it seems like He hears me, and I go on for days or weeks or months, hoping that I've been 'cured,' as they say. Then something will happen—like seeing you—and those same old emotions come right back again. So, that's who I am.

"Now, would you mind telling me who you really are?" Dina said, on a roll now. "Unless you think I'm dumb enough to believe that you got married and, voilà, you never wanted to be with a woman ever again. Get real. Who do you think you're talking to—some old church mother who believes reciting some Scriptures and saying a couple prayers will take the gay away?"

Belinda allowed the silence to linger while she chose the right words to say.

"Dina," she said, "my heart is breaking for you right now because I've been where you are. I know how you feel. But listen to what I'm saying. As believers, we can use God's strength to overcome sin. And that's what I've done. Can I tell you that once I got married I never wanted to be with another woman again? No, I can't tell you that—there were times when that's exactly what I wanted. But I turned my focus to God because I knew I had a choice to make. I could either follow God and be blessed or sever my relationship with Him and lose everything. And I'm as real as real can be when I tell you today that I made the right choice."

Dina shook her head and looked up at the ceiling. "I wish it were that simple for me," she said, as much to herself as to Belinda. "This is about the way I view life and love from the deepest part of me. How can it be sin when the expert psychologists say it's not something I have a choice in? Why does the church force me to choose? I've studied the verses that people say denounce homosexuality, but plenty of believers debate those Scriptures. I've even thought about going to one of the gay-friendly churches. But something keeps drawing me back to a church with the same flavor and style of worship as where I grew up."

"I know, I know," Belinda said, "and you're not the only one. I know how you feel—I felt that way before. But, what is God saying to *you*?"

Both women paused, not quite knowing where to take the conversation from there.

Dina spoke up. "So, I suppose your husband doesn't know about us?"

"Actually, he does," Belinda said. "In fact, he encouraged me to call you. He didn't know your name before the other night, but I had told him about my past before we married. When he met you, he connected the dots."

"Oh?" Dina replied, not quite knowing how to express her surprise.

"God has blessed me with a wonderful, understanding husband, Dina. We've been married for fifteen years."

Dina thought back to her shaky marriage with Roderick: "But you're living a lie, just like I was. How can you do that to yourself? How can you do that to him?"

"It's not a lie," Belinda said. "This is genuine. I love my husband and my children. The past that you and I shared, Dina, that was the lie."

Dina got just a few hours of sleep the night of Belinda's call, their conversation dominating her thoughts. She lay in bed weighing both sides against her own reality. Would she ever be at peace, as Belinda seemed to be?

As usual, Dina found rest in a song. Right there in bed, she began humming, and the words to an old-school Walter Hawkins tune flowed from deep within: *He changed my life complete, and now I sit at His feet. To do what must be done, I'll work and work until He comes.*

The more she sang, the more she sensed God's presence.

"Lord, I need You," she said. "I need You to strengthen me."

THINK ABOUT IT

1. Was Dina living in the pink? How so?
2. Read Romans 1:18–32 and the story of Sodom and Gomorrah in Genesis 19:1–29—two passages that many Christians refer to in discussions about homosexuality. There are various interpretations of these Scriptures; what do you think God is saying in these passages?
3. Have you learned that someone close to you is gay? Compare how you dealt with that revelation with how Dina's parents handled it concerning their only child.
4. Dina initially hid her past from her ex-husband, her family, and the people at Believers Ministries. What might have been the advantages and disadvantages of being up front with them?
5. How can knowing that God is faithful and that His love is unconditional help you to accept your past and to move forward?

EVERYTHING SHE WANTS

A SLING-BACK SANDAL made of crushed Italian leather with a three-and-a-half-inch platform heel, in wine red, and available in a size 9? Fifty percent off never looked so good to Kendra.

She stuffed the black flats she'd worn to Dominique's Boutique inside her oversized bag and walked barefoot to the checkout counter, ready to slip on her latest find as soon as her credit card cleared for eighty-five dollars. Under normal circumstances, she wouldn't have spent the water bill money on a pair of shoes she didn't need, but you'd have to see these shoes to understand.

"You can keep the box," she told the clerk.

On a TV shopping channel, Kendra had heard that high-quality shoes maintained their sheen longer if the leather were allowed to breathe. She bought two sets of ForeverWear shoe containers created from a durable cloth interwoven with linen. For both sets, she paid only $49.95. No more cardboard boxes clogging her closet.

A mirror at the boutique's exit showcased what she already knew: the red shoes perfectly set off her navy slacks and camisole, and red and white checkered blazer with navy specks. An added bonus: they mimicked the shade of her favorite crinkled leather Sak purse.

Kendra clicked a button on her key fob, unlocking the driver-side door of her silver Nissan Murano SUV. With two kids going back and forth to day care and Pee Wee football practices, she had put nearly 60,000 miles on it in just a few years and the fob was so worn, she had to click it at least twice to make anything happen. In a few months, she figured, she would have worn down Darnell enough to trade the car for a newer model. That is, if she could tolerate him for that much longer.

They argued constantly, almost since the day they got married. They fought over which bills to catch up on and the kids' extracurricular sports. She wanted them involved. He said the family couldn't afford it. They even fought over gas money. And anytime she bought a little something extra for herself, he threw a fit. A few weeks ago he got so mad he balled his fist like he was about to hit her, until their four-year-old son and two-year-old daughter started screaming. Kendra ran into the bedroom raging and cursing.

She couldn't take it anymore. A man should want his wife to look good. Right? Bottom line: Darnell couldn't provide for their needs, not still working for the pest control company. He needed to get a better job and, with the economy the way it was, who knew when that would happen.

Kendra rounded the corner into Fawnview Apartments, officially ending her getaway trip to the boutique. She and Darnell rented their two-bedroom for the past two years since moving out of his parents' house. She swerved around a group of girls playing hopscotch in the middle of the cramped parking lot and pulled into an open space, right next to her neighbor's rusted Ford Tempo with duct tape for a rear window. One day, she would live in a real neighborhood where kids played in sprawling parks and swam in backyard pools.

For now she made a mental note to complain, for the third

time, about the wobbly railing on her way up the concrete steps to her front door. As she drew closer, the scent of boiled hot dogs attacked her nose, and she heard the TV blaring as usual. Likely a college football game. Lately Darnell did little else than sit in front of the television set with a plate of junk food. What a man.

The kids screamed at each other across the kitchen table where they played with the few remaining pieces of a puzzle Kendra bought for Christmas.

"Mommy!" Janay and little Darnell screeched when Kendra entered.

Darnell looked up briefly then took another bite of his hot dog and resumed watching the Florida Gators take on the Arizona Razorbacks. Kendra kissed the kids' cheeks then ordered them back to the table to play.

That didn't satisfy little Darnell. "Can I go outside?"

"Not unless your daddy takes you," Kendra said, knowing good and well Darnell wasn't moving until that football game ended.

Her son scurried nonetheless to his father, with little sister stumbling close behind. While they distracted Darnell, Kendra walked right on by and into the bedroom without him noticing the shoes on her feet. Once inside, she held the sandals up to the sunshine yellow wrap dress she'd bought the month before. She envisioned pulling the outfit together with a bold multicolored necklace and matching earrings.

Commotion in the living room interrupted the thought. Maybe the Gators got a touchdown, which seemed to be the only thing that roused Darnell and brought any excitement to the house these days. That wasn't it, though. Soon Kendra heard the only two words worse than Darnell finding out about her new shoes.

"Grandma! PaPa!" her children screamed.

Since Kendra's mother lived nearly four hours away in Miami, and her father in New York, this could only mean that her in-laws stopped by unannounced. She pursed her lips shut to stop the flow of curse words weighing on her tongue, all of them special names for her meddling, uppity, judgmental mother-in-law. None of them came close to "First Lady," which people at Believers Ministries called Madeline Everett. Kendra laughed the first time she heard that. The woman had married a bishop, not the president of the United States. Kendra simply called her Madeline, although it irked Darnell.

"You'll get over it," she told him whenever he brought it up. "When your mother gets a room at 1600 Pennsylvania Avenue, I'll call her First Lady, or if she ever treats me like a daughter, I'll call her Mom. Until then, she'll be Madeline to me."

The year Kendra and Darnell lived with the Everetts had been unbearable. Madeline micromanaged everything; from what food Kendra fed the children, to how she dressed, to how she spent her own money. She and Darnell had lost their home to foreclosure at the start of the national housing crisis. It was Kendra's dream house, newly built in the suburbs with a community play area nearby and a recreation hall for adults. The mortgage and high interest rate left little for their other bills or for the kids. They fell behind after only a few months and never recovered. The sheriff stapled a bright blue notice to the front door.

Having no other option, Darnell moved his wife and one son at the time to his parents' house—a move that surprised no one in the Everett family. The middle child of three, he always struggled to get his life together. His older brother, an architect, designed landmark structures throughout the Southeast, from his own eccentric home in Alexandria, Virginia, to a mirrorlike high-rise in Miami, and the library and shopping mall complex in Biloxi. The bishop initially wanted Glenn Jr. to follow him to the pulpit, but accepted his eldest son's career. Darnell's little sister, Deniece, or "Neesi," developed a love for all things natural and studied the environment, so she got on everybody's nerves whenever she came home from college and insisted that they recycle even the smallest piece of scratch paper.

As for Darnell, he'd never been a good student in school, not that he ever actually tried to be. Thank God he earned enough credits for a high school diploma and could walk across the stage for graduation. On a Super Bowl Sunday at Sporty's bar, he met Kendra, the beginning of a years-long on-again off-again relationship. When she got pregnant, he did the honorable thing and proposed.

He figured on something quick, maybe a small ceremony in his father's office on a Saturday afternoon. Kendra wasn't having that. She wanted a destination wedding and honeymoon, in Jamaica. Her mother took out a $10,000 loan to help pay for everything. Kendra made up the difference on her charge cards. She had secured a new job in the admissions office of a community college and figured she could pay off the debt over the next year or so.

Even then, before they were actually married, Madeline couldn't resist chiming in with unsolicited advice. One day when Kendra and Darnell stopped by to visit his parents, Kendra overheard Madeline tell Darnell to teach his fiancée the value of a dollar.

"How in the world can y'all afford a wedding in Jamaica when her health care benefits don't even kick in till after the due date and you will have to pay those hospital bills? Do you know how much it costs to have a baby these days?"

Madeline thought Kendra was still in the bathroom, as opposed to standing in the hallway on the other side of the wall. After a while, she emerged as if she hadn't heard a thing.

Until she and Darnell got into the car on their way home.

"I can't believe you let your mother talk about me that way!"

"Kendra, calm down. She knows we don't make that much money and she was just trying to help. This wedding is getting expensive. I mean, your mom is taking out a loan and—"

"Excuse me, but your mother doesn't know anything about my paycheck, so she has no idea what I can or cannot afford. My salary is not her business, and neither is my mother's loan for that matter,"

Kendra said without taking a breath. "Nobody's asking her to pay for anything except the wedding rehearsal dinner, and she's too cheap to even have that catered!"

"And why should she have it catered?" Darnell asked, growing irritated. "I hate to bust your bubble, but my last name is Everett, not Gates or Hilton or whatever other millionaire you've been watching on *Entertainment Tonight*. We are simple down-home people. And my mother, my Auntie Dee, and Sister Pinky from church can cook food just as good as any caterer. My parents already have to pay to get to Jamaica and for their clothes to be in the wedding. Why waste money on a caterer, too?"

"See, that's what I'm talking about!" Kendra erupted. "I'm so sick of the mentality that you have to be rich to have class. We are getting married in an island ceremony, off the sands of the Atlantic Ocean. My dress alone will cost more than a thousand dollars, once they finish all those alterations. My mother and my cousins are flying in from Miami to see me in this wedding, and their dresses cost almost three hundred dollars apiece. They're buying plane tickets and paying for their hotel rooms, on top of the dresses. You want them to do all that then have to eat your mama's homemade jerk chicken and brown rice after rehearsal? I can't believe I'm marrying someone so tacky!"

By now, Darnell had arrived in front of Kendra's apartment and parked the car. He tightened his lips to control his anger.

"Look, I'm not the one who wanted this destination wedding. I'm not the one asking everybody to pay hundreds of dollars for dresses and plane tickets. So I definitely won't be the one to tell my parents to spend a few thousand more on catering when there's a kitchen in the hotel where we're staying and they can cook it themselves. They want to cook it themselves. It makes my mom feel like she's really a part of this," he said, his voice softening. "Come on, babe, don't make an issue out of this."

He added jokingly, "Besides, you never tasted my Auntie Dee's plantains. Your family would fly down for those alone."

Kendra rolled her eyes. "You are not funny, Mr. Everett," she said, looking away. She opened the door and was about to get out when Darnell gently grabbed her arm.

"Are you mad?"

"Not at you," she said, calming down. "I just want our wedding to be all that I ever wanted since I was a little girl."

Darnell stroked her cheek. "Look, I want you to be happy, too. If we can just make it through this ceremony, I promise, I'll be the husband, the man, you always dreamed about."

That promise lodged deep in Kendra's heart. Back then, she believed him. She believed he would be the first man who could fulfill her heart's desires. In the years since, they had lost their home, moved in with his parents then into a low-budget apartment complex, and could barely afford private gymnastics classes for their daughter, Janay. Not to mention, the mailman continually delivered hospital bills and past due notices for debts from their wedding.

Thinking of it all, Kendra stayed in the bedroom a little while longer, leaving her in-laws to entertain themselves with Darnell and the kids in the cramped living room. Darnell had started dragging the family to church every week since the wedding, so waving to his parents on Sundays was enough contact for Kendra. She would have to remind him yet again about his promise to be the man of her dreams. She took her time wrapping the microbraids in her hair into a bun, then finally opened the door and walked the short hallway before putting on a big smile.

With arms opened wide for a hug, she saw the bishop first. "Dad!" she said, giving him a tight embrace. Then, "Madeline."

Darnell figured his parents' visit could only be a sign from God. The night before, he lied to Kendra. Told her he was going to Walmart to look around. For real, he drove out to the beach where the Everetts spent holidays grilling under the pavilion when he was a kid. The beach at nighttime, with the sky clear and the sound of gentle waves, offered a perfect setting for prayer. It would take God to help him now.

Three weeks had passed since he got laid off from his job at the pest control company. With all the cutbacks in recent months, Darnell and the four other workers shouldn't have been surprised when their manager pulled them into his office one by one.

"Darnell, you're a good, hard worker," Mr. Tillis told him. "But the number of contracts in your district have decreased 60 percent in two years."

That had nothing to do with Darnell, who knew most home owners by name and even did odd jobs for those in need, like mowing Mrs. Jackson's yard once a month since her husband died or bringing in the mail for Old Man Bowles who couldn't walk the distance to his mailbox because of his weak knees. When money gets tight, home owners look for areas to trim the budget, and pest control made for a logical cutback.

Darnell went to his locker and turned in his uniform polo-style shirts and the black company-issued boots, then drove home, trying to think of some way to tell Kendra. Their marriage already teetered between unhappy and miserable. She didn't appreciate how hard he worked. To tell her that he lost his job could mean the end.

He needed time, so he pretended to go to work each morning but actually went looking for another job that would soften the blow of losing the first one. Too bad so many other people were in the same situation. Darnell's cell phone never rang for a second interview. Sometimes he grabbed temporary work with a construction crew or call center. That paid the electric bill and bought gas, but not much else. Truth be told, he struggled to keep up the payments on everything when he did have a job; now he didn't know what to do. No way could they move back in with his parents.

He applied for unemployment, but that wouldn't be enough. Kendra would have to step up and pay for more than the water bill and cell phone service—and new clothes and shoes. They would have to get rid of cable for a while and see if the car dealership would let them trade in the Murano for something with lower payments. But every time he tried to tell Kendra the truth, something happened. Like the day she came home with a new dress.

"Woman, what is wrong with you?" he'd asked, snatching it off the hanger. "Don't you see we're barely making it?"

"No, what I see is *you're* barely making it," she'd said. "*I'm* making it just fine!"

No ambition, Kendra told him. "I don't know why I have to say it again and again, but you need to get another job so you can support your family like a man is supposed to. If you did, maybe you could afford to get yourself something new, too. Besides, this dress was on sale."

"On sale? We still can't afford it. We can't afford the dress. We can't afford the SUV. We can't afford five hundred dollars for you to get braids and highlights in your hair every three months."

"Well, then, what can we afford, huh? Because before I married you, I could afford whatever I wanted."

"That was before we had two kids to take care of, to send to day care, to feed—"

"You don't want the finer things in life, do you? You're content twiddling your toes in this dump. Well, not me. I have dreams and goals. I want my kids to have a better life than I did."

"So do I, Kendra, but we can't get there throwing away money like this."

"My God says He wants me to live an abundant life," Kendra said, piecing together words from one of her father-in-law's recent sermons.

"But, baby, it's not the time for us, not yet. You're trying to live like the *Jeffersons* when all we have is a *Good Times* budget."

"Maybe we could live a decent life if you were half the man you pretended to be when we got married."

Darnell just stood there, his stocky body stiff with tension. All his life, he had felt like a disappointment, to his parents, his brother and sister, the teachers at school. Then Kendra came along. She believed in him, believed he could be something in life. But now nothing he did satisfied her either.

Yes, he balled his fist that day. He wanted to hit her, knock her out so she could feel just how strong of a man he actually was. Thinking back, he doubted he would have done it. He had never hit a woman and didn't intend to start. But who knows for sure what might've happened if his kids hadn't been there screaming loud enough to shake him out of his angry daze? After all that, he couldn't tell her about losing his job. The next day, then the next week, didn't seem like better timing either. Recently, the landlord started calling and leaving voice mail messages about the rent, which had almost doubled because of the daily late fees. He erased them before Kendra got home.

At the beach that night, Darnell walked along the shoreline, oblivious to the grains of sand that crept into his sandals. He stuffed his hands deep into the pockets of his shorts and put his head down, searching for words to pray. Since being laid off, he spent a lot more time studying the Bible after filling out job applications. That night on the beach, he asked the Holy Spirit to give him direction.

"Lord, You know what's inside of me. You know I want to take care of my wife and my kids. I want to be the kind of man who makes them proud to say, 'That's my husband' or 'That's my daddy.'"

Darnell felt his throat tighten. He couldn't remember crying since his grandmother died ten years earlier. He buried his head in his hands and wiped away the tears, then ran his palm over his bald head. He looked up to a clear sky.

"God, I just need You to show me," he said. "Show me what to do so we don't get evicted from another home. The Bible says You'll provide all my needs. We need a home, God. My kids need food. I need another job. Make a way, Lord, 'cause I don't know what else to do. Just show me what to do."

On the drive home, Darnell talked to himself. Since praying, a flurry of possible solutions came to mind. The strongest involved his parents. He dreaded the idea, but maybe they could help out with a loan. Then his mother and father showed up the next day. Darnell stalled, distracting himself with hot dogs and the game. Soon, he knew, he would have to tell his father what happened and ask to borrow enough money to make it through the next few months.

Darnell coaxed his father to take a walk outside and check out the sound of his old Nissan Sentra. It'd been acting up lately. The bishop had a knack for diagnosing car problems, although he couldn't fix them himself.

"You hear that, right?" Darnell said from behind the wheel after starting the ignition. "What you thinking?"

"It's definitely the exhaust system. But it's not the muffler. Sounds like something jogged loose at the front end."

Darnell got out of the car and walked around to the front where his father propped up the hood. His favorite times with his father had always taken place around the hood of a car. Darnell's siblings didn't share their father's interest, so those were the only times when he really felt special.

The bishop cut into his thoughts. "You'll probably need to get down under the car and take a look, son."

"Yeah, you're right. I'll take a look in the morning," Darnell said, unhooking the latch and shutting the hood. He positioned himself on top of it and turned to his father.

"While we're out here, I, uh, I wonder if you have time for me to talk to you about something else."

"Of course, son. Actually, I had something I wanted to talk to you about, too. That's why your mother and I came over."

Darnell grabbed the chance to delay his request. "Since you came all the way over here, why don't you go first?"

"I don't quite know how to say this," the bishop started. He backed up a few steps from the car. "I've seen a lot of spiritual growth in you in the last year or so. I know things are still a little rocky financially with you and Kendra," he said, glancing at the outdated Sentra before turning to face his son again. "But if there's one thing I know for sure, it's that God uses rough times to strengthen our faith, to get us to turn to Him and realize that He is all we need.

"So, first of all, I want to say that I'm proud of you, Darnell. I'm proud of the man you've become, proud of how you're leaving your past behind and trying to be a good husband, a good father."

Darnell sat nearly paralyzed on the hood. He couldn't remember ever hearing his father express pride in him. His father looked at Darnell and paused for a response, but there was none. Darnell was busy wondering whether his father would change his mind after finding out that Darnell had been laid off.

The bishop's words interrupted the thought. "The second thing I want to say is that I believe the Lord is revealing a calling on your life to serve in the church. Now, I'm not sure what that calling is yet, but I know that if the Lord is speaking to me about this, that means He's likely already spoken to you about it or at least tried to anyway."

Darnell thought about his intense desire to study the Bible, but he'd been so worried about his job situation that if God were calling him, he had too much else going on to hear.

"Dad, there's something I have to tell you," Darnell said, hoping he hadn't let the conversation go too far already. "I lost my job a few weeks ago."

"Oh?"

Darnell told him how the contracts had dwindled and how his boss called him into the office. He explained that he had looked for employment every day and worked odd jobs, but still couldn't even pay the bills. And, no, Kendra didn't know yet.

"Dad, I'm sorry. You probably wish you hadn't said all those things about me. Guess there's not much to be proud of after all."

The bishop squeezed Darnell's shoulder. "No, son, actually I'm just as proud of you now as I was when I walked through your front door today and you were home with your family. You've come a long way, son.

"As a matter of fact, you might not believe this now, but I think God was behind your layoff. Have you considered that He has something better lined up for you? Maybe He released you from that position there, so you could work for Him."

"What?"

"That's right, Darnell. I want you to come and work for the church."

"Doing what?" Darnell asked, almost incredulous.

"That, I don't know. It just came to me as you were speaking. You can start out with something small, getting to know more about the workings of a church and giving you time to study the Word."

Then he stopped short. He had another idea. "We lost our building maintenance guy a few months back and we've been looking for someone through one of these contract companies ever since. I can't promise you a big salary, maybe not even as much as you made in your last job. I can guarantee that when you follow God's path, money isn't important because you're not working for money, you're working for purpose."

Darnell reached up to shake his father's hand. "One last thing, Dad," he said with a nervous laugh. "You think you could give your son an advance on that first paycheck?"

While father and son talked outside, Madeline hoped to repair her relationship with Kendra. It took Madeline awhile to get to this point; one reason being that Kendra had made such a bad impression from the very beginning. The first time they met, Kendra pranced around the Everett house with her stomach six months' full, like she didn't know Darnell's father was a bishop or that fornication was a sin. To top it off, she wore a hot pink halter dress with sandals, acrylic nails, and lip gloss, all the exact same shade as the dress. She'd gone to the salon and had her hair styled into a bouquet of puffy Shirley Temple-like curls that extended to her shoulders. One curl dangling in front was also hot pink, thanks to a can of temporary hair-dye spray. It obviously took a lot of attention and money to maintain this flashy, slightly tacky, appearance. Money that Madeline knew her son didn't have.

Still, Kendra was part of the family now. Madeline had to ask herself: How could she reach out to all the other women at church and remain so distant from her own daughter-in-law?

"While the men are outside, Kendra, I'm hoping we can talk a bit," she said, taking *The Princess and the Frog* DVD from her purse and sliding it into the player to keep her grandkids occupied.

Kendra wished she'd never left the bedroom. "What did you want to talk about?"

Madeline decided it best to be totally honest. She admitted that she had been too judgmental from the beginning of their relationship, and Kendra listened in disbelief.

"But now," Madeline continued, "God has shown me that I was wrong, and I want to apologize for not being a better mother-in-law to you."

She could tell that Kendra didn't know how to respond, so she continued.

"I love my son and I know that my son loves you. That's why I not only want to be a good mother-in-law but also a friend. I want us to laugh together over my two beautiful grandchildren. I want us to cry together when something is hurting you. And I want to be here to give you the guidance you need as a young woman learning what it means to be a wife and a mother."

"I wasn't expecting this," Kendra said, her voice cracking. "I thought you hated me. I thought you didn't think I was good enough to be part of your family." She buried her face in her hands to compose herself.

Madeline realized for the first time that the prejudices she thought were hushed actually spoke loudly to Kendra.

"I'm so sorry, sweetheart."

"Thank you," Kendra said. "Thank you so much for everything you've said today."

Kendra paused, trying to figure out how to voice her feelings. "I know that Darnell and I have our problems. And I may not be the best wife in the world, but I'm trying. My mother never married, so she's always saying, 'When it comes to playing the submissive wife, you're on your own,'" Kendra said, mimicking her mother's sassiness.

Then she looked into Madeline's eyes, the first time she could ever remember doing so. "Maybe I do need a little advice sometimes when it comes to being that 'helpmeet' the Bible talks about."

Kendra could tell something had changed as soon as Darnell and his father came back inside the house. His eyes held a certain life that hadn't been there in a while. She wondered if he could tell that something in her had changed, too.

Over lemonade, the two couples talked a little while longer about whatever: the recent joint service with House of Faith, the choir's performance at the regional sing-off, a new ministry for adulterous women that Sister Pinky had organized. The bishop didn't mention his talk with Darnell since Kendra didn't know about the layoff. When the kids' movie ended, the Everetts got up to leave.

Before their car drove away, Kendra started telling Darnell about the conversation she'd had with his mother. He was as shocked as she had been.

"I can't even imagine you and my mom having a decent conversation, let alone becoming friends."

They both laughed together, for the first time in months. Kendra gathered the kids to prepare for their baths and then put on their nightclothes. As she tucked them into bed, she overheard Darnell pacing and mumbling to himself in the living room. She figured he wanted to tell her something. She wanted to press him and get the conversation over with, but resisted. Maybe she should give him a little space this time.

She went into their bedroom and lay across the bed, thinking about some things she and Madeline discussed. Darnell wasn't perfect, but he's a good man who loves me, she thought. How could she be a better wife? How could they have more peaceful days like today? She remembered their most explosive argument, when he saw that yellow dress. She walked over to the closet and took it off the hanger, the price tag still attached. Admiring it one last time, Kendra folded it and put it inside an extra shopping bag in back of the closet. She got the receipt from her purse and put it in the bag. After church tomorrow, she would stop by the mall to return it.

Just then, Darnell walked through the doorway: "Uh, baby," he said, his hands shaking. "I have something to tell you."

THINK ABOUT IT

1. How was Kendra living in the pink? What about Madeline?
2. Kendra wanted to live above her financial means. Do you or someone you know have the same problem? Discuss reasons why some women struggle in this area, spending more than they can afford on their appearance and material things.
3. Discuss your views on a wife's financial role in a marriage. Should the greatest responsibility be on the husband to provide when it comes to paying the bills? What about marriages where the wife makes more money than the husband—can he still be considered the head of the household? If so, in what ways?

4. What is your definition of a helpmeet?
5. Madeline realized that she had been more critical than compassionate in her approach toward Kendra. What relationships in your life would benefit from more love and less judgment?
6. What could Kendra have done to improve the relationship with her mother-in-law?
7. So often we look to our spouse to fulfill our every need. According to the Bible, whom should we really depend on? (Read Philippians 4:19: *But my God shall supply all your need according to his riches in glory by Christ Jesus.*)

FAITH UNDER FIRE

CORRINE STEPPED cautiously into the hospital room. She hadn't heard other voices seeping into the hallway and didn't want to disturb a tender moment or, perhaps, a quiet time of prayer. Once on the other side of the doorway, she realized there was no need to worry. The family must've taken a break and gone out for lunch or something to get their minds off this. The patient was asleep and alone, lying there beneath a thin white sheet. Corrine couldn't see her body entirely, but an arm resting above the sheet looked pale and her cheeks had caved like somebody drained out all the laughter.

No tears, Corrine promised herself. She had asked the Lord to help her be strong for her friend and the family. She positioned a get-well card from the gift shop on the windowsill and sat down in an empty chair. She'd sit awhile until somebody else showed up. She was looking around the room, decorated with at least five flower bouquets and a slew of greeting cards, when Willie walked in.

"Corrine?" he whispered to avoid waking his wife. He spread his arms for an embrace. "I'm so glad you could stop by."

"Of course I came," she said, returning the hug. "How did the surgery go?"

Willie shook his head. The mastectomy itself went fine, he explained, but doctors also had to take out the lymph nodes. From the looks of it, the cancer had already spread.

He paused to take a deep breath. "They'll do more tests, but they say it's Stage III."

"Oh, Lord," Corrine said, slumping back into the chair.

Just then, slight movements on the bed diverted their attention. Pinky slowly came to herself, and they moved to stand on either side of the bed rails. Her eyes opened halfway, and she drearily called out to Willie.

"I'm here." He cupped her left hand in both of his. "I sent the girls home to rest, but Sister Corrine from the church is here now."

Pinky turned her head and smiled. "How you doing, sweetie?" she asked lazily. "How's that son of yours?"

"Now ain't the time to be worried about me or Melvin. We just want to make sure you get better."

"I'm hoping and praying my God will heal me, give me a few more years on this earth," she said before turning back to Willie.

"They didn't find anything else, did they?" she asked him. "Tell me they didn't find any more cancer."

A select few knew about Pinky's condition at that point. She'd asked the bishop and Madeline to spare her any announcements from the pulpit. Only after much persuading from Willie did she tell Brianna and Jasmine.

Corrine found out by accident. Some time after kicking Melvin out of her house, he found his way to a drug treatment facility that happened to be in the same medical complex as the lab where Pinky's oncologist worked. No one knew for sure whether Melvin had the heart to leave the drugs for good this time, but Corrine dropped off homemade banana pudding and told him that she would support him as long as he did right. On the other hand, if he went back to the streets, he shouldn't bother knocking on her door. She had left his room and was jiggling her car keys in the parking lot when she noticed Pinky leaving the radiologist's office. Once Corrine spotted her, Pinky knew there was no use in lying. Corrine tried to pray with Pinky right then and there, but Pinky refused and made Corrine promise not to tell anyone else.

The disease had come as much of a surprise to Pinky as it had anyone else. She felt fine when she scheduled the appointment for a routine checkup. Sister Towery, a doctor's assistant, had given a talk at a community health forum that inspired Pinky to give her doctor a call. She hadn't had a checkup the year before. Too much else to settle: her daughter's abusive marriage and pregnancy, plans for the annual Women's Day Breakfast, her sister's political scandal, and, of course, seeing after all the little odds and ends at home with Willie. Plus, around the same time that she got a postcard reminder from the doctor's office, Pinky was reeling in a new member—a young woman who had moved back to Tampa after the Lord spared her jail time for a horrible DUI accident in Philadelphia.

Finally getting around to her checkup, Dr. Steele noticed a lime-sized lump as soon as she pressed her fingertips into the upper regions of Pinky's right breast.

"Have you noticed this?"

"No, I hadn't paid it any attention," Pinky said, lifting her hand to feel the mass. "Honey, when you get my age and your boobs are this flabby, all you want to do is hurry up and put 'em in a heavy-duty bra that'll get these melons off your stomach," Pinky added, cracking herself up.

"Please be still," Dr. Steele said, continuing to move her fingertips in tiny circles all over her chest. "I'm not liking the way this feels, not liking it at all."

She called a specialist and set up an appointment for the next day. "This might be nothing," she told Pinky. "But we need to check it out as soon as possible to be sure."

Pinky wrote down the information for the radiologist who would administer her mammogram, but left Dr. Steele's office determined not to think about it anymore. God had delivered her from so many tough situations in life—single motherhood, an abusive relationship, loneliness—Pinky figured this would be another testimony.

"The Devil tried it again," she would tell the church one day soon. "This time, he showed up at the doctor's office with a lump that felt like cancer but, glory to God, it turned out to be nothing at all!"

She didn't bother to tell Willie about it, not that first day. She walked into the house humming an old gospel tune like she had just come from a good garage sale and lucked up on a priceless find. She stopped to give him a quick shoulder massage, as he sat at the kitchen table reading the day's paper, and asked if he would mind having his favorite meat loaf and mashed potatoes for dinner.

"You're mighty spry this afternoon," he said, turning to watch her prance by. "What's gotten into you?"

"Just the glory of the Lord," she told him.

The next day, the radiologist looked even more concerned than Dr. Steele. He pointed out the odd shape of Pinky's right breast when compared with her left, especially in the area surrounding the lump. Analyzing the X-rays, he determined that the mass definitely appeared to be a tumor. Still, only after a biopsy confirmed cancer cells did Pinky tell Willie, and even then she asked that he keep it quiet. She didn't want the bishop and folks at church finding out. Their sympathy, mingled with the typical church gossip, would only make her uncomfortable. She imagined them calling each other up:

"Have you heard about Sister Pinky? I hear she's got breast cancer."

"Whaaaat?"

"Girl, that's what they say."

"I could tell something was wrong with her the other week. She didn't quite look like herself."

And the conversation would go on and on from there with people saying they could see this or they could tell that to prove they had some keen skills of discernment when God knows they didn't notice a thing. No, Pinky didn't want to be the subject of any of it.

"We can tell the people at church when this is all over," she told Willie.

The doctor suggested a relative accompany her to her next appointment, so Pinky didn't make too much of a fuss about Willie going along. He, meanwhile, strained to suppress his frustration with her for waiting to tell him about the lump in the first place. He didn't want to upset her more.

Few people knew Pinky better than he did, and even Willie had never seen her like this. She kept saying she didn't want people to worry, but he sensed more to it than that. His wife had always been the strong one who prayed for everybody else and now she couldn't stand the thought of being prayed for. All the prayers and well wishes would only prove what she apparently was trying to deny: Pinky, too, could be vulnerable.

Doctors had studied the results of Pinky's exam and determined it best to remove her breast. They told her and Willie this during their initial visit. Willie saw Pinky flinch in her seat but she remained silent as the doctors continued talking calmly, as if reciting a routine statement. They explained the procedures for surgery and said it should be scheduled as soon as possible. After that, they could determine the extent of the cancer more precisely.

"So removing her breast wouldn't be the end of it?" Willie asked, interrupting their flow.

"I'm afraid not, sir," one of them said. "The cancer may have spread to other areas of your wife's body."

After the mastectomy, they might try a number of treatments, including chemotherapy, radiation, and various powerful medications.

They kept talking, but Pinky had tuned out by this time. She was glad Willie insisted on coming. Seemed like she was floating through a thick cloud with a bunch of smart-looking people standing all around her. None of them could answer how she got there in the first place or if she would ever get out.

How could God let this happen to me?

The question lodged itself in her mind. She had told people through the years that God was a healer. She told them that He would deliver them from whatever sickness, even if that deliverance took them into His loving arms in heaven. But she didn't deserve to go through this. No, no woman is perfect, but she had spent so much of her life doing what He told her.

For that, her reward would be to lose a part of her womanhood and perhaps her life?

By the time her thoughts returned to the doctors, they were talking about reconstructive surgery that would restore the removed breast and reduce and shape the left one to match.

Willie didn't know what to say. Maybe some humor would help.

"You've been complaining about your breasts ever since I can remember," he said jokingly. "Now, you'll get two new ones."

Pinky didn't even look at him. Uncomfortable with Willie's untimely humor, the doctors stiffly assured her that everything would be all right and offered some pamphlets with more information.

Once in the car, Willie faced her before pulling off. "You know I'll always love you no matter what, right?"

She nodded and kept looking out the passenger side window.

Pinky insisted on putting off the surgery for two weeks, so she could get her house in order first. She busied herself scrubbing every crevice of the house and cooking and freezing meals for Willie to reheat during her hospital stay. She refused to talk with anyone besides God and Willie, who struggled to keep the truth secret from extended friends and family, as his wife requested.

Hiding the news from CeCe proved especially difficult. Pinky insisted that her sister had too much else on her mind to be burdened with this. She had been forced to resign from her post as a state senator, and after being convicted of embezzlement, a judge sentenced her to jail time, which was drastically reduced to sixty days. Pinky had flown to Tallahassee to be with her the day of the sentencing. During his ruling, the judge said that Courtney's story should serve as a cautionary tale to other legislators tempted to dip into the state's coffers. In letters from jail since then, Courtney talked about reading the Bible and rededicating her life to God. She mentioned other inmates who looked up to her and followed her to chapel services. A publishing company already had contacted her for a possible book deal.

She used several of her allotted calls from jail to try and tell Pinky all about it, but each time Willie explained that she hadn't been feeling like herself lately. He told the same thing to people at church, several of whom speculated something amiss as soon as Pinky missed her first Bible study session.

"Sister Pinky's still not feeling well, huh?" Sister Sho'nuff asked Willie the following Sunday.

Willie nodded in affirmation, but said nothing else before walking away.

Of course, Sho'nuff wasn't as concerned with Pinky's health as she was with the story behind her absence. The woman hadn't changed, sitting in the same seat after all these decades, singing the same songs, and mired in the same old tired traditions. She still held a grudge because Willie married Pinky instead of her. Nothing he could do about that now. He didn't tell Pinky about Sho'nuff, certain that any mention of her snooping would set Pinky on a tirade about nosy church folk.

While some pressed Willie for details, he was surprised that Bishop and Madeline didn't, at least not at first. He put off Madeline's attempt to bring a pot of her special chicken noodle stew over by saying Pinky didn't feel up to company, and to his surprise she accepted that.

Pinky pointed out how the Everetts had their hands full weaving their son Darnell and his wife into the church leadership after so many years away from the faith. Darnell started out as the church maintenance man but had proved faithful by helping beyond his job duties. He quickly moved up to an assistant pastor position, working with the teenagers, and started taking seminary classes in the evenings. Kendra, meanwhile, joined the choir and, against Madeline's advice, organized a church shopping trip to the outlet mall in Orlando, swearing on a stack of mini Bibles not to spend the money intended to get her and her husband out of debt.

"I can look at that Kendra and tell she's a handful," Pinky said, with a laugh that made Willie glad to see her smile, if only for a moment.

Pinky did agree to tell her daughters, as well as the Everetts the night before surgery, though. She called and told them all quickly and without emotion.

"I just want to let you know that I have breast cancer and will be having a mastectomy in the morning," she repeated with each phone call, before handing the phone over to Willie to avoid hearing their pity. Willie then filled in the details, answered questions, and offered as much comfort as he could.

While in bed later that night, he tried to prepare his wife for the possibility she had refused to consider. "Pinky," he said, "how do you think you'll feel if the doctors find out the cancer has spread?"

Pinky turned a sharp stare on him. "Willie Pinkston, please leave my room!" she snapped. "I'm going through the toughest battle of my life and I need to be surrounded with people who have at least a mustard seed of faith, not somebody determined to think the worst."

"Honey, I know this is hard, but we need to talk about it."

"Leave. My. Room!"

He got up from the edge of the bed and walked out. He looked back before shutting the bedroom door only to see that she had already turned her face away.

Pinky stared at the beam from a streetlight shining through the bedroom curtains. She had tried to answer that same question so many times. How would she feel, what would she do, if even after having her breast removed, the nightmare still wasn't over?

After rousing awake from the surgery and seeing Corrine there, Pinky had hoped for good news, but the look on Willie's face told the story. She gripped his hand so tight he felt the rush of fear piercing through her. For the first time since her diagnosis, tears trickled down Pinky's face. Corrine started rubbing her shoulder.

"God is still with you, Pinky," she said, swallowing to stop from crying herself. "You're still His child and He hasn't left you. He's gonna come through, Pinky. I know He will."

Pinky lay with her eyes closed, still holding on to Willie's hand. Corrine moved slightly to grab a tissue and gently wipe her face. Neither she nor Willie knew what to expect when suddenly Pinky opened her eyes and stared straight ahead as if looking at something greater than either of them. She had thought about what she would tell another sister if she lay in the bed and Pinky were the one standing beside it, holding her hand.

"Willie," Pinky said, trembling, "I want you to tell my sister and brother what's going on, every detail. Tell them that I would like to see them—sometime soon if they can spare the time. Then I want you to tell Bishop and Madeline that I'd like everybody at Believers Ministries, as well as all the branch churches to know, if it's not too much trouble."

Willie looked at Corrine, who stared back at him.

"You sure about this, Pinky?" Corrine eventually asked. "You want us to tell everybody?"

"Yes, I'm sure," Pinky answered, her voice gaining strength. "It's praying time."

Bishop Everett held off on his announcement about Pinky until the end of service. Doctors had prescribed medications and put together a schedule of radiation and chemotherapy in hopes of killing the cancer cells. Yet they couldn't be sure how effective the treatments would be.

Bishop knew that once the word filtered into the sanctuary, people wouldn't be up for singing praise songs to God or for listening to his sermon. He had sent a statement to the Believers Ministries' branch churches, asking that their pastor read it aloud at the end of their services, too.

"Before I give the benediction," he said, looking into the mass of faces before him, "I need to ask for your prayers for a dear friend and beloved church member who has touched many lives."

He took a deep breath and the sanctuary hushed. "Sister Laura Pinkston was diagnosed with breast cancer recently and has been weathering this battle with a small circle of family and friends. But now the doctors say the cancer has spread to other parts of her body. She will be undergoing further treatment," he explained, "but doctors say the chance of long-term survival is less than 50 percent."

The bishop heard a collective gasp and paused as church members looked around at each other, some putting their hands over gaping mouths. Camille placed her hand to her chest in shock. She had called Pinky several times over the past few weeks only to be put off by Willie. He had hinted at a health issue, but Camille didn't think it could be serious. Pinky was indestructible, incapable of being broken. Paul, now Camille's fiancé, wrapped his arm around her shoulder and she buried her face into his chest.

"No matter what the doctors say, we have the ultimate physician in Jesus Christ," Bishop told the congregation, some taking the statement as a call to pump up the atmosphere.

"Hallelujaaaaaah!" someone shouted from the balcony.

"The Devil is a liar!" a singer yelled from the choir loft.

"Sho'nuff, Bishop, sho'nuff!" came, of course, from near the front of the pews. Sho'nuff then tapped Sister Towery on the thigh. "I told you something was going on, didn't I?" she whispered. "I knew it all along. I knew it."

The church stayed full for at least an hour after dismissal with people milling around in disbelief and trying to find out more information. Willie and Brianna chose not to attend service that morning, although Brianna's husband, Roland, did. The couple still lived apart, but had taken steps to save their marriage. Weekly counseling sessions helped him pinpoint the real reasons behind his anger and abuse. They decided to start all over and had gone out on several "dates." He also confessed his sin to members of the church's Brothers Keepers group. They suggested he call one of them if ever he got the urge to turn violent with Brianna or anyone else.

One Sunday, as the congregation prayed, Roland strode to the front of the church, knelt at the altar, and began praying and crying out to God for so long that Blackwell eventually walked up to tap him on the shoulder so the bishop could proceed with the rest of the service. At this point, he told Blackwell, he would do almost anything to get his wife back by the time their baby son was born so they could be a family. Of course, Blackwell knew the feeling, having gone through his own period of brokenness in the past year. In recent months, he had split from his girlfriend Giselle and decided to remain single for a while. When he found out about Camille's engagement, he became depressed and started studying the Bible at night, searching for peace and comfort in its pages.

Now, with all the Scriptures he had read about God's mercy, Blackwell didn't know what to think about Pinky's situation. Roland, meanwhile, was feeling privileged that Pinky gave Brianna the okay to include him in the details of her illness, along with Jasmine and her husband, who attended the branch church Believers Promised Land. Members bombarded Roland that night with questions: When did Pinky find out? Why didn't she tell anyone? How was she feeling? Was she still in the hospital or back at home? Could they stop by for a visit? He answered what he could and told others they should call Willie for specifics.

By the end of the morning, Madeline, Corrine, and a few other ladies on the culinary team organized a twenty-four-hour fast and prayer chain to begin Friday morning and conclude Saturday with a service in the fellowship hall. People from all of the Believers churches would be invited, as well as anyone in the community who wanted to participate. Sister Towery had walked away from Sho'nuff, tired of her gibbering about how she'd already figured out what was going on, and joined Sister Madeline's circle to see what she could bring for the Saturday meal that would break the daylong fast.

Back at Pinky's house, the phone didn't stop ringing. Every time Willie or Brianna answered, someone else beeped in on the two-way calling feature, and as soon as they hung up, the phone rang again. Pinky lay in bed, having gone through her first round of chemotherapy treatments in the past few days and facing many more in the months to come. Willie and Brianna thanked callers for their prayers and told them to hold off for another week or so, giving her a chance to adjust to the treatments before stopping by.

Pastor and Destiny Hopewell at Believers Promised Land set up a rotation of members to take meals to Pinky and her family five days a week for a month, relieving Willie and pregnant Brianna from the added stress of preparing something to eat. Jasmine expressed her thanks and announced to everyone how thankful she knew her mother would be when she found out.

The next day, when the family gathered in Pinky's bedroom to tell her of the outpouring, she behaved predictably, complaining that people shouldn't make a fuss over her. She only went on for a minute or so, however, and Willie heard beyond her words to the gratefulness in her heart.

By the time Joy called from North Carolina, Pinky had adjusted to the chemo. Her hair had thinned, but did not fall out completely as was true with some women. Since she was used to wearing a short Afro, it just looked like she'd gotten a trim. The nausea and drowsiness crept up on her occasionally, although not every time she had a treatment. She thanked God for the little things.

"Of course, you can come down," Pinky said, comfortable enough to start answering the phone and talking to friends again. "I would love to see you."

That weekend, Pinky was sitting on the couch with her Bible open and a pencil and notepad when Joy's rental car pulled into the driveway. "Ma'am, do I know you?" Pinky joked as Joy walked through the door. Joy had lost thirty pounds since her last visit to Tampa for her cousin Rebekah's wedding. Pinky could see that she looked happier and more confident than before.

They went outside to sit on the porch swing, which Willie had recently installed. Pinky always wanted a porch swing to remind her of the days she sat on one with her mother and father as a child in the country. One day when Brianna picked her up from a treatment, Willie surprised her by sitting on the porch with a big slice of watermelon, just like she used to do back in the day.

With Joy, Pinky rocked back and forth.

"Doctors say the chemo has stopped the cancer from spreading and, Lord willing, they'll kill those cells altogether pretty soon," she said, before spooning a bite of the homemade peach cobbler and butter pecan ice cream Joy brought over.

Every ounce of faith in her confirmed that she would be healed. "But if I'm wrong and for whatever reason He chooses not to deliver me on earth, I still know that my God is well able to cure me no matter what the doctors say," she told Joy, recounting the story of the three Hebrew boys thrown into the fiery furnace. "If He takes me on to glory, it'll be because my work in this world is done. If He sees fit to leave me here," she said with a chuckle, "watch out, Devil!"

Just then, another car pulled into the driveway, one that Pinky didn't immediately recognize. She and Joy could only see a woman's silhouette through the tinted windows, and it seemed like the woman hesitated to get out of the car. Pinky waved a hand, urging whomever it was to come out. The car door finally opened, and Pinky understood the delay as soon as she saw those light-skinned, manicured toes peeking from a golden high-heeled sandal that could only belong to Maxine Short.

"Hi, Miss Pinky," Maxine said, sheepishly, while balancing a flower arrangement in one hand and a covered dish in the other. She stood by her car door for a moment, like a squire waiting on permission to approach the queen.

"Whatcha got there?" Pinky asked. "Get on up here so I can see."

Joy's muscles tensed, as her eyes scanned every inch of the woman who'd carried on an affair with her husband a few years before.

Maxine slowly walked toward the porch with her head down. Determined to avoid eye contact with Joy, she focused on Pinky and explained that she and Jayshell had picked out the flowers and brought a container of chicken Caesar pasta salad. They didn't want to bring anything too heavy until Pinky regained her full appetite, but figured she and the family could snack on the pasta salad.

"Jayshell had to get back to work, but sends her love," she said.

"I see you two have become good friends since our little 'intervention,' huh?"

"Yes, ma'am," Maxine said. "Jayshell and I definitely hit it off. We're opposites in some respects, but we tend to balance each other out."

"Well, you tell Jayshell that I missed seeing her, but I understand."

Maxine couldn't wait to put the flowers and the bag down on a table beside Pinky, so she could turn and walk away from Joy's merciless stare. Pinky wouldn't have it, though.

"Maxine, stay right there," she said then looked at Joy and back again at Maxine. "Ladies, we might as well go on and get this over with. Since the Lord has seen fit to bring y'all this close together, I suppose it's time."

Joy looked at Pinky like she had lost her mind. Undeterred, Pinky got up and gently grabbed Maxine by the elbow and led her to sit down on one of the cushioned porch chairs near the swing.

"I tried to apologize years ago; what do you want me to say now?"

"Just say what you said in that letter she never read, say what's on your heart."

"There's nothing to say," Joy butt in. "What can you tell a woman after you slept with her husband and destroyed her life?"

"Destroyed your life?" Pinky said, regaining her old fire. "Look at you, sitting here today stronger and wiser than you ever were. The truth is Maxine wasn't in that affair by herself and if it hadn't been her, Brent would've found somebody else. No woman or man can destroy the life God gave you—not unless you let 'em."

Joy sat back on the swing, and Pinky added her final contribution. "Nobody's expecting you two to become best girlfriends. All God requires is true repentance from you," she said to Maxine, "and forgiveness from you," she said turning to face Joy.

"All I can say now, all that I wrote in that letter, is that I'm truly sorry," Maxine said, opening the dialogue. Her voice shook, but she'd found the courage to look Joy in the eyes. "I was wrong for getting involved with Brent. I knew he had a wife and I chose to believe the lies he told me. My prayer is that one day you'll forgive me just as God has."

The whistle of an afternoon breeze rustling leaves in Pinky's big maple tree created the only sound after that. Joy had turned away and looked out on the empty street, while Pinky and Maxine waited for a response. After what seemed like thirty seconds or more, Joy, with tears welled in her eyes, turned back to face Maxine. Very simply, she said, "Thank you."

After months of treatments and taking medications, Willie and Pinky got the report that even the doctors were surprised to see when viewing her test results. They found no more trace of the cancer in her body. She would have to follow their prescribed regimen for a while longer, they said, warning her that the cancer wouldn't be considered in remission until it had been gone for several years.

Pinky started praising God right in the office, forcing the doctor to pause until she mouthed her final "God is good." Willie's thoughts immediately turned to planning one of his big backyard barbecues to thank everyone for their prayers.

When the day came, just about everybody Pinky loved attended the barbecue, including her brother and his family who flew in for the occasion, and her sister CeCe.

Even those she wasn't fond of made their way there, but Pinky had gone through too much to hold grudges. She gave Sho'nuff a big hug as she walked through the gate.

Halfway through the afternoon, Willie stood on the patio and held his hand up to get everyone's attention. Pinky, he said, wanted to say a few words.

She began by thanking everyone for their support, especially those who took the time to bring food to her family and those who fasted and prayed around the clock. "The Bible says that the prayers offered in faith can heal the sick," she said, "and I have no doubt that all of your prayers are the reason I'm standing here today."

The backyard quieted even more as Pinky's expression turned serious. "I also need to share my testimony," she said. "You see, before this happened, I thought I was this strong, unbreakable

Christian woman. But I've since realized that, when it came to humility and complete trust in God, I was 'in the pink,' as you all have heard me say many times. I kept asking the Lord, 'Why me?'

"I hid it from most everybody. I was too proud to let anyone see that Sister Pinky, too, could be attacked by the same illnesses, hurts, and heartbreaks as everybody else. Now, I know God didn't bring this disease on me—that was nothing but the Devil trying to tear me down. But the Lord could've stopped it and He didn't. He allowed me to go through this and He brought something good out of it. He brought me to a place where I know how it feels to lose all control and have to lean totally on God for my very survival. And despite all that I've gone through," she said, looking up now, "I thank You, Lord."

Women in the yard struggled to hold in their emotions.

"I say this to encourage all of you," she continued, scanning the crowd. "Everybody lives in the pink sometimes, but if your heart is right, if you truly want to move away from sin and into God's will, He'll reveal your weaknesses. He might use a family member, maybe an old friend or even a stranger. He might even allow you to go through the fire like I've been, but it's all to show you that your mouth is saying one thing, but your actions, your life is saying something else."

"Yes, Lord!" someone said from the rear of the yard, jump-starting a chorus of random "amens."

Pinky waved her hand to regain their attention. "The last thing I want to say is that I'm so thankful I'm still here with all of you, which must mean that God has something left for me to do and as long as I'm able, I'm going to do it."

She stepped off the patio to a line of people waiting for hugs, the last of them being Blackwell, whom she pecked on the cheek. "The Lord is going to use you mightily," she told him. "You wait and see."

"Thank you, ma'am," he said.

As he stepped away, Pinky's gaze caught sight of Courtney

standing under a tree with Dina, the church worship leader. They must've just met, Pinky figured, as she watched them talking and trading smiles. After a few seconds, though, she got a strange feeling in her spirit. Something about their exchange, the way they looked at each other, seemed different than most. Pinky couldn't quite pin it down, at least not in the moment. She decided to walk the other way—for now. In time, God would reveal it, whatever it was. He always did.

THINK ABOUT IT

1. Pinky acknowledged that she was living in the pink. Why does a loving God allow people, even strong believers like Pinky, to suffer? (For a deeper study on God and suffering, read the book of Job then discuss this issue with a group.)
2. Do you believe that there's power in prayer? Read James 5:14–15 (NIV) below then discuss a time when you prayed for something and God answered the way you wanted Him to and a time when His answer was not what you'd asked for. In retrospect, do you have any idea why He answered the way that He did in either case?

   Is any one of you sick? He should call the elders of the church to pray over him and anoint him with oil in the name of the Lord. And the prayer offered in faith will make the sick person well; the Lord will raise him up.

3. Have you ever put all your trust in God because you saw no other option than to wait for Him to come through? How did you feel during the process and what was the end result?
4. Pinky kept her illness a secret because of pride. Proverbs 11:2 (NIV) says: *When pride comes, then comes disgrace, but with humility comes wisdom.* Think of a time when your pride

stopped you from asking for help or support from others. What were the consequences?

5. If you were in Maxine's shoes, would you apologize to your former lover's wife? If you were in Joy's shoes, would you be able to forgive your ex-husband's mistress? Why should you? Read Matthew 6:14–15 (NIV): *For if you forgive men when they sin against you, your heavenly Father will also forgive you. But if you do not forgive men their sins, your Father will not forgive your sins.*
6. Do you find yourself so busy with work and caring for your family that you neglect your own health or doing something nice for yourself? Talk about ways you can strike a balance in your life.
7. When was the last time you had an annual checkup? Have you learned to give yourself a breast exam? If not, take some time today to research methods of self-examination and to set an appointment for your annual physical.

ACKNOWLEDGMENTS

FIRST OF ALL, thank You to my heavenly Father, whose faithfulness and mercy have sustained me.

Thank you to all of my loved ones who endured, as I constantly bounced ideas off of them for this project. Also, thanks to the women nationwide who took the time to read the first online version of *Living in the Pink* stories each month and who offered feedback. Your interest was my motivation and I will be forever grateful. I know exactly who you are!

I have been blessed by my family, particularly my parents, John and Julia Tubbs, for their support and Deborah York and Shellie Carter for their encouragement and ideas, and for spreading the word about *Living in the Pink.*

I can't forget the "Beautiful Believers" study group who gave me a boost when I needed it and who kept me accountable to the Word of God or author Sallie Bricker whose feedback guided me in taking my ideas to the next level. And, finally, thank you to Sonja Moffett, whose creativity, design skills, and marketing know-how helped bring my initial vision for this project to life.

STEPPIN' INTO THE GOOD LIFE

Sheila Rushmore thought she'd be the last woman standing when it was time to fight for her man. Instead Ace, her boyfriend of two years, chose to reunite with his ex-wife, leaving Sheila emotionally devastated. It's a year later when Sheila is convinced that sneaking into their wedding ceremony will put closure on the gaping hole in her heart. But it's on the back pew of the church where a new relationship begins for Sheila. She can't explain the touch she received from God on that day, but she's determined to be a better woman—a woman of faith.

lifteveryvoicebooks.com

The Last Woman Standing

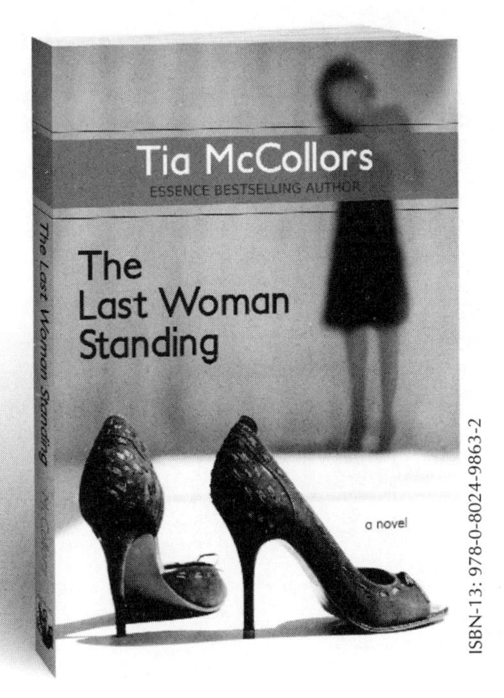

After being married to their careers instead of each other for ten years, "Ace" and Lynette Bowers ended their marriage. Four years later however, it seems as though their love never ended—to both their surprise and denial. Sheila Rushmore is Ace's current girlfriend and a woman who is used to getting what she wants—all except Ace's commitment to marriage. When Sheila realizes Lynette may be the cause, she launches a plan to play the hand of God, instead of allowing God to bring the love they all desire in His way.

lifteveryvoicebooks.com

Lift Every Voice Books

Lift every voice and sing
Till earth and heaven ring,
Ring with the harmonies of Liberty;
Let our rejoicing rise
High as the listening skies,
Let it resound loud as the rolling sea.
Sing a song full of the faith that the dark past has taught us,
Sing a song full of the hope that the present has brought us,
Facing the rising sun of our new day begun
Let us march on till victory is won.

The Black National Anthem, written by James Weldon Johnson in 1900, captures the essence of Lift Every Voice Books. Lift Every Voice Books is an imprint of Moody Publishers that celebrates a rich culture and great heritage of faith, based on the foundation of eternal truth—God's Word. We endeavor to restore the fabric of the African-American soul and reclaim the indomitable spirit that kept our forefathers true to God in spite of insurmountable odds.

We are Lift Every Voice Books—Christ-centered books and resources for restoring the African-American soul.

For more information on other books and products
written and produced from a biblical perspective, go to
www.lifteveryvoicebooks.com or write to:

Lift Every Voice Books
820 N. LaSalle Boulevard
Chicago, IL 60610
www.lifteveryvoicebooks.com